BETTER
OCCASIONS

Better Occasions

ELIOT WAGNER

THOMAS Y. CROWELL COMPANY
NEW YORK   ESTABLISHED 1834

Designed by Ingrid Beckman

Manufactured in the United States of America

ISBN 0-690-00439-7

Library of Congress Cataloging in Publication Data

Wagner, Eliot.
    Better occasions.

I. Title.
PZ4.W132Be   [PS3573.A3834]   813'.5'4   73-22463
ISBN 0-690-00439-7

1   2   3   4   5   6   7   8   9   10

To Miriam

BETTER
OCCASIONS

WHAT? THREE FLIGHTS UP with the ladder and dropcloth, and nobody home? Heyyy, what's this one trying to pull with Moe Gross?

I glued my thumb to the doorbell—"Painter!"—and hammered the door at one and the same time. So what did I get? The neighbors. In his bathrobe and knock-knees Morning Mouth Krupnick, and Lady Krupnick plus two other pots with curlers and angry faces.

"What goes on here," from Morning Mouth, "at seven thirty A.M.?"

I gave him a look.

"You want peace and quiet? Go stick your head in the gas stove."

Morning Mouth made a move and quick as a flash I pulled the plaster knife, shiny and sharp, out of the overalls.

"Shall we dance?"

The bathing beauties began clicking their tongues while the good wife Krupnick restrained her beloved spouse.

Hey Krupnick, you should have been home the winter before last when Gross did your apartment, and did your wife on the side. That was just after Christmas, just after my daughter Liz made her glorious marriage, the time I began wondering why live, and sat down with that bottle of pills in my hand, and came close to using them too. So that was when I was up on my ladder following negotiations with La Krupnick over what shade pink her sensitive heart desired besides which the Commies are the spirit of happy compromise; and from far off, through my happy thoughts about Liz, came a mooing from the hostess.

"That's pink?"

Down I went off the ladder and looked her in the eye then, Madam Krupnick. Forty she'll never see again, this dish, and built like a wrestler only short and with a bosom Mt. Plenty. In her negligée, not her bathrobe like now, Lady Nudnick.

Without further discussion then, up my hand shot between the fat thighs, right on the spot. She didn't know what to do first, slug me one or yell murder. Ever see feeding time at the zoo? The eyes popped, the jaw hung, I still grin remembering. So, "Mrs. Krupnick, you're beautiful," I gave 'er, and a soul-kiss like Marlon Pecker and Audrey Heartburn. Next I was flipping 'er right there on the bed, hardly cool from where Morning Mouth slept. And when I'd jumped up and zipped up and quick started painting where I left off, she laughed I was a fast worker.

"Yankee efficiency," I told 'er.

Time is money. I'm my own contractor, a one-man team. So drop around early some evening and we'll count up my fortune: enough for a cheap funeral.

She stopped me in the street later on that winter, lugging the plaster sack out of the station wagon. And what a wagon, an old man, huffing and puffing just like the boss. La Krupnick, she wanted to know where did I keep myself, why didn't I drop around?

"Look darling, don't I want to drop? Only right now is the busy season."

Or to translate from the Talmud, a Jew never has to look far for pig.

And now in the hallway half-past seven in the morning, she shot me hate-daggers, this one-round love of my life. And to Mr. Mouth that better half of his said, "Don't go near him, Herman, you can see he's got a screw loose."

Thank your wife, lucky Krupnick that a breath would blow over, who keeps you from committing violent deeds you don't have the guts for anyway. And Gross, that understands rage, that one wrong word and his eyes fill with blood, you thank God Who's preserved you fifty long years and more when your fist goes folding around that knife handle.

Commit murder, for Folks?

"It's true darling," I cracked, "with Moe Gross loose screws are never at a premium."

I headed downstairs for the super and the passkey. The passkey I got, the super's missus handed it over with scared eyes. Don't worry, missus, I won't squeal to the landlord that your husband's dead drunk again at eight in the morning. A man has to handle a lot of booze to drink one son through New Guinea in the infantry, and the middle son through Korea in the infantry, and now his youngest boy target practice for the Reds on the Berlin border. Can you imagine? We're defending the liberty-loving Fatherland! Well, so thank God for daughters, Gross, at least they ain't in the draft.

And back upstairs don't think that Morning Mouth Krupnick and his bride, and the two cows from Apartments 4D and 4E, didn't have the gall to follow me into 4H. In the kitchen the curtains were off and the sun was like heaven in the little room. It caught at my chest, that sweet sunshine. A day to be in the country, and I hardly could wait. Because at one sharp there's my date in the cemetery, with the trees and the grass and Lou Berenson, my cousin Bella's husband that they're burying today, God rest that poor soul.

The livingroom also was ready, with the dishes stacked on the couch with edges shining like halos. I looked at the adventurers behind me, and they looked at me. Dead silence, and the house stripped for the painter. And—would you believe it, in the bedroom—likewise the tenant!

Yeh, there she was, 4H, sprawled out on the bed in her nightgown, ready for action, and not a bad piece as pieces go: slim, with a nice pair of bubbies and that nice light fluffy hair, even if the good Lord didn't shortchange her on the schnozzola. Only, Mrs. Hungry, after you finish nosing around with that thin curving beak into Moe Gross's business—monkey business I mean—with your neighbors I mean fellow denizens of the treetops, you don't pull these stunts. You open the door, you woman of our time, you let in the painter. Gross'll take it from there.

Or else Gross does have a screw loose, a persecution complex perhaps? Then how about the other night with the present recumbent, how she brazened me in the eye when I asked 'er the simple question, "The same color paint?"

"I want white, pure white, to begin a new life."

"A new bride?" I cracked.

She'd laughed, "An old widow with new furniture."

"Old, a young woman like you?" How old could she be: thirty-eight, thirty-nine. "When you get to be Moe Gross's age, your age thirty-five is the cradle."

"Thirty-five?" Not too happy, but there was that smile— come hither, what else?—"I'm forty-eight this coming Friday."

"Now"—and this part hadn't been a line—"you're kidding poor Gross."

Still she'd kept smiling. "If a person's never lived, why should they age?"

Like an engraved invitation: So Gross bring new life. If I hadn't had a pinochle game on I could have, as my elder

BETTER OCCASIONS / 5

daughter the psychologist Susan would put it, lowered 4H and her tensions then and there on the couch. But for the likes of these ladies, there's always tomorrow. And you know how long she's a widow? I got it from the super. New Year's Eve her husband dropped dead and there it was already the first of May! Loyal four whole months to his memory, not counting whoever she went after before she went after Gross.

So I cracked, that night, "with your livingroom blue and your bedroom yellow, pure white'll cost you for one coat extra, and don't cry on my shoulder if it comes out gray."

"Well thank you," she told me without the smile, "thanks very much," and we'd finished our business fast.

They don't like it when you show you see through 'em, these respectable cunts. But between then and this morning she must have decided all out for Gross. The bell rings, she'll play the deep sleeper and grab Gross for breakfast. And still to keep at it, with this crowd watching over my shoulder?

"Hey rise and shine lady, company's here!"

But up close those eyes weren't shut: glazed narrow slits. And there it was on the night table, my God, the sleeping-pill bottle half-empty. Quick I pulled her half-sitting and shoved two fingers right down her throat.

"Herman stop him"—now La Krupnick was inciting the master—"that maniac's strangling her!"

"We better get the police, that nut and his knives."

So the neighbors took off and left 4H to her doom. Meanwhile thank God she started gagging, and fighting off Gross her worst enemy, weak as she was.

As she threw up she lurched up. And where did it land? Better than vaudeville: on Gross.

"Come on darling, come on—"

I wiped her face with my handkerchief, I walked her around. She kept gagging, she sobbed.

"Leave me alone," again she was pushing me, poor creature, "let me die."

And to tell you the truth, I had sudden respect for this widow, I'd had her all wrong. When Gross croaks, Lady Gross will reach for the suicide jar? My insurance, that's what she'll reach for!

"Let worse die first though they never do, why should you say such a thing?"

"Let me lie down, I'm too tired—"

I kept her moving in spite of the sobs, and I kept reasoning into her ear. "Dead is a sucker. Say you swallowed them pills at bedtime last night instead of this morning. Then the painter shows up. See this diamond ring on your finger? I happen to be looking for legacies, to buy a house in the country. Off she goes, into his pocket, before the cops come and grab it and naturally ransack the closets and all the drawers going after the hidden assailant that slipped the pills down your throat. That's when the midget radio also vanishes, silverware, loose change, whatever fits in the pocket. Money pinned to the underwear goes to the prospectors for gold in the funeral catering outfit, also any dental inlays of value. Hyenas. Soon your bare bones are ready for the Last Trumpet shuffle through the ground to Jerusalem . . . Hey, I see you must like the country, with all those plants in your front room there. Just a second, let me look at your thumb—green, just as I thought!" There, that got a laugh out of her, well more a snort than a laugh and it led to more sobs. But gee, so many plants, all colors green stretching into the sunshine. Ah, and this picture on the front room dresser here, the little bride daughter. "Yeh, it's tough," I said, "on top of losing a husband, then the daughter gets married and you're all by yourself. Still it looks like a nice boy, that tall skinny groom there, not like the bum my daughter hitched onto."

She glared at me. "You're crazy. The boy is my son and he

married that bitch. Oh God, I just want to die!" And on went the waterworks, full force.

"So I guessed wrong. Would they have horse-racing otherwise? Come on." I walked her into the bathroom and she walked better already, not such a deadweight, and I sat her down there, and washed her face with a cool cloth, and her wrists, and her chest where she'd thrown up. First she gave in and let me, then she struggled again.

She moaned, "What do you want from me?"

"I want you to live, so I can paint your apartment pure white."

So, ahh!—"I'm sorry," she said.

"That's more like it. Here"—where blood was crusted, in the corner of her mouth—"make like this Becky, you know that old joke?"

And another laugh, "From my bridal shower," sick, but a laugh, and she twisted her mouth so I could clean it off easier.

"You laugh good, 4H."

"And cry even better—"

But she laughed, she laughed.

Then the doorbell went off, we almost jumped out of our skin.

"Police—"

"4H," I said, "You want cops in your life?"

"I don't even want life."

"Just a minute," I let out a bellow. And to her, "Then stand up . . . Very good, you're a very good girl. Now take a deep breath, get a grip on yourself . . . You're okay, kid. Now I'll get you into your bathrobe?"

So I found the robe and helped her on with it.

"Okay, here, lean on Gross"—besides my paunch, my map of Jerusalem and the hairy-ape arms, I'm at least equipped with this big pair of shoulders—"we'll go to the door."

And at the door stood civilization before us: the cop and the

Folks. Me, I picked up my dropcloth in the hall outside, begged the cop's pardon and went back in while he was asking Mrs. 4H if there was anything wrong. I was heading back out for the paint pails as she was answering, "No. Why do you ask?" And the look that that officer gave to Mr. and Mrs. Mouth, and 4D and 4E, and some new recruits from upstairs and downstairs, let me tell you, it did Gross's heart good.

Then my lady 4H closed the door and again fell apart, with the twisting, the moaning, the gasps while I held her. She gave a retch, and I swung around, tactfully, we should both be facing the same direction this round. After all.

The spasm passed, but the sickness didn't. To tell the truth she had me real scared.

"Listen darling, the closest I ever got to medical school was two years of accounting back in nineteen twenty-seven at night. So what do you say, let's give your doctor a ring."

"No, I'm ashamed." Again she moaned. "Oh, I'm sorry, to be such a bother. I wanted to die," she could laugh yet, "not be sick."

And oy, was she sick. I had to half-carry her, half-drag her back into the bedroom, and I let her sit down.

So I phoned my own doctor, Ginzburg, and naturally who'd answer but the answering service?

"Girlie," I pleaded, "tell the doctor, it's life and death."

And what do you know, I must have hit the rare bird that works for her pay. I only had to hold the patient's hand a few minutes and stroke her forehead while she leaned on my shoulder and gasped—like with my daughter Liz, when Liz was my baby—before Ginzburg phoned back.

"What's on your mind Moe?"

"For what's on my mind Doc, they ain't got doctors. But listen—"

He laughed. "Go on, Gross the ox."

"Sure, Gross the ox, Gross in a box. Listen—"

I told him what I had here, what color pills, yeh, that she was partly awake when I broke in and she broke out, that no, she wasn't still sleepy, just sick.

"Yeah yeah yeah, you've done fine. The sick sounds like nerves. So just check her pulse and blood pressure and pick up your medical diploma this afternoon."

"Hey Doc, I'm not joking."

"And do you hear me laughing? I'll be over, to prescribe her some sugar water."

Then how about this? The suicide sat straight up under her own power, and that scared pair of blue eyes, they looked in my eyes with their question. So I transmitted Ginzie's side of the conversation verbatim.

She said, "Doctors don't talk like that. You're trying to cheer me up."

"Why shouldn't I cheer you up, 4H? I bet you look nice when you're cheerful," like to my baby, my Liz, in the olden days, "in fact you don't look so bad right now."

And hey—a slow change of weather: Gross got a smile! "Stop calling me 4H," she said, "my name is Ruth."

"I know your name is Ruth. And if you keep smiling like that, I might even go so far as to call you Mrs. Amin."

So the tears started again, but in a happier way, and she could wipe them herself. She said, "You've wasted a whole morning on me. I've heard of rough outside, with a heart of gold, but I'm forty-eight years old today and you're the first one I've ever met." And look—still more tears, but a waterfall now, tears for a lifetime.

Or else staged for Gross, for some scheme of sympathy?

Maniac, look at the poor creature wrought up from her morning! I sat down, "Sha, sha now," and I kept patting her hand.

"Better Occasions."

"Better Occasions."

"We should meet on better occasions."

So I worked my way through whichever of Lou's mourners I knew in the sunshine outside the funeral parlor, then inside in the eclipse of the sun with the gloomy plush carpets. Our side of the family stood out by their absence. All right, so Bella's a joke. But you don't treat her husband's funeral like one, poor Lou with all of his hopes: easy money, love, a job, to walk again after his stroke—forever reaching for the moon.

She's skinny, my cousin Bella, with a nose and a chin and the wild hair and a black sack of a dress—everything but the broomstick. Inside the chapel she stood next to the coffin, with her hand on that arm dead now that swung many a punch at her through their long years together. She saw Gross, she pushed the handkerchief at the eyes and she started right in.

"What am I gonna do now, what am I gonna do?"

"You could go shopping and buy yourself some nice shoes to go with that dress."

"Ha ha, very funny, a fine time for jokes—"

I nodded toward the coffin.

"Is Lou complaining?"

He wasn't, the losing horseplayer Lou, two-packs-of-butts-a-day Lou with the burnt tongue, Lou that fell in love for the first time at forty-five years of age, only the girl already was married. The girl loved Lou too. Except then, when Lou left Bella, this girl instead of leaving her husband that she was only part of the furniture to, went and killed herself. Why? Because she knew she couldn't say no to Lou, and she was all worked up that that kind of shenanigans was bad for her child! Where do you find a woman like that? And if you do find her, how can you tell, until it's too late? So Lou wasn't complaining, but if the dead could complain he was entitled to. Yeh, without luck, brother, go peddle your papers in some other world, not this one.

But oy, Bella gave a sob from the heart. "Look at my Lou, in a cheap pine box. I couldn't afford to get him no better."

I was touched. I took Bella's arm.

"So what?" I said. "He looks peaceful, young." And I wasn't kidding her either. He had the cut-rate job from the caterers: lipstick and rouge slapdash. Yet through no fault of theirs, with that bald bean wrapped in the winding sheet, and the high cheekbones with pink on them, and the red lips, and that thin jutting nose— "Like an adolescent," I said to Bella, "a choirboy, he reminds me of, innocent, without troubles, thank God anyway for that."

She snorted, my cousin.

"Some choirboy, with his woman-chasing. But God punished him."

"That He did and how, Bella. From start to finish, tough luck Lou."

"He called me his Jonah, but it wasn't my fault, even if I did give 'im the fingers once or twice, when he two-timed me with that false friend of mine Nettie."

"When you gave him that ring finger Bella, that was what finished him off."

"Is that so! And how about my two thousand dollars inheritance that he blew on the horses?"

Yeh, Lou went to some dance hall, and met Bella. Others, when they saw Bella coming, ran. Not tough-luck Lou. He danced, with his pointy shoes. While dancing, Bella disclosed that she was an heiress. And just then Lou had to have figured out a new system for beating the horses. All he lacked was the cash. So one bright morning a long time ago Lou and Bella took themselves down to City Hall. And by one black afternoon not many months later all Lou had to show for it was Bella and his shirt.

"If you ask me," Bella said, "he made his own bad luck."

Sure, like his stroke, and the wheelchair five years, Lou never-say-die, with the buckles, the clamps, the appliances that he was sure were going to put him on his feet again: always the next day.

Meanwhile, people came into the chapel, the empty benches filled up, and the rabbi praised Lou in the sermon: pious Lou from the strokes, nonsmoking nongambling Lou that stopped turning on a horse race on TV even to just watch. In other words, dead Lou.

The funeral lined up in back of the hearse, and Lou's chauffeur—that was one of his early dreams, to be rich, with a chauffeur—the chauffeur stepped on the gas. We drove around the corner, half the procession—and we all had to pull up. And we sat in the sunshine, and sat.

What's going on? I got out of the car to see.

A cop—God strike me dead if I lie—was writing a ticket for the hearse. The funeral'd gone through a red light, and the caterer hadn't paid the cops graft this week.

From there on, smooth sailing for Lou. No accidents on the highway, and us pallbearers didn't even drop the box carrying it over to the hole.

Then—Lou forgive Moe that loved you—came my moment of pleasure, to look around away from the gravediggers, away from the folks, at the fresh grass sprouting and the buds clustering in sunlight.

Look, what I like is the country.

At that moment, two pots behind me, lady neighbors of Lou's out on a funeral jag with the sighs whispers and eye-rolling, discoursed as follows.

"What I can't figure out," said Lady 1 to Lady 2, "is how a nice intelligent man like Mr. Berenson ever married a woman like Mrs. Berenson."

Said Lady 2 to Lady 1, "Love is blind."

On top of that, when pauper Lou was let down and the last prayer said, and no one to sit mourning for Lou, no one to care, what do you do? You let the caterers drive home the widow the folks run from like leprosy, and let her sit in her apartment alone? When they threw in the dirt, Bella cried, and those tears were as real as my previous weeper's today.

And what about that one, Ruth Amin, laying there drained out when I left her, all but a corpse? I'd asked her, "You'll be okay?"

She said, "I'm so blue." Then out came that sad little laugh of hers. "You helped a stray dog and now it won't let you alone."

"You have put your finger on Gross's weakness, haven't you," I tested her out, "that he's an all-day sucker for losers and grief?"

"As far as I'm concerned there's more to your weakness than to most people's strength."

Well, that showed a warm heart if true, and what did I have to do later on anyway? So I'd stuck her pills in my pocket and promised I'd drop by after the funeral.

Only after the funeral I sent the caterer's limousine away and I drove Bella home in my station wagon. "And where's your rich brother my cousin Sid from New Jersey?" I asked her.

"Pneumonia, his wife said."

"From the mild May weather we're having?"

"That's it, my own brother. Nobody gives a damn about me."

"Except—" I gave her a prompt.

"Hey, ha ha, except you Moe, I forgot about you."

So up in Bella's gorgeous two rooms with the dustballs under the sink and the gray dishtowels over the sink, I went into the bedroom to phone Mrs. Amin the later would be later. "Unless," I gave 'er an out, "you can dispense with the visit altogether, you're sounding much better."

"Thanks to you," she said, "I'm sounding much better."

So far a surprise on all counts.

Bella said, "I seen your hand hiding the phone piece. That was your girlfriend I bet, while your wife's away in the country."

"Who needs a girlfriend when I got you, Bella?"

So Lou's widow giggled.

As long as I was there, I gathered together Lou's things and brought 'em down to the car in case I can scrape up a few cents for 'em for Bella. Then to keep Bella cheered up I took her around the corner for chow mein, which she assured me was poison for your system while she gobbled it down. Toward the end of the meal she passed me her fortune to read from her fortune cookie because she couldn't read good with her glasses upstairs.

I sang out, "Virtue is its own reward," and Bella took back the fortune slip and ripped it right up.

"Anybody knows that!"

So could you blame me if I was even looking forward to visiting Mrs. Amin again?

First, for a gag, around the corner from her house I stopped in the bakery and bought her a nice chocolate layer cake: black outside with a heart of gold, just like Moe Gross. The penny birthday candle the bakery folks threw in only five cents extra.

But upstairs, what's this? When Madam Despair said she felt blue this morning, that meant a blue dress to put on, slim, chic, with white trimmings? Now let's see, what's dumb Gross being set up for? Big Mouth, in the course of the day did you give 'er a hint about Charlotte my Madam Iceberg? Did I mention my glorious married life?

But always keep the opposition off-balance. "Say, a miraculous recovery," I gave 'er.

And boy did she bite! "Thanks," she said, like to a compliment. Only, "But I'm still pretty shaky," she kept Gross off-balance too. And that nice laugh. "Suicide takes a lot out of you."

So I had to laugh in spite of myself.

"Shut your eyes a second," I told her. She looked surprised, but she shut. I went into the kitchen, I opened the box, I put the cake on the table, I lit the candle, and I sang. "Happy birthday to you!"

She came in, she shook her head, and—would you believe it?—once more the waterworks! So I brought out handkerchief number two of the day.

"One sight of Gross," I grinned, "and you burst into tears. Is that good?"

She told me, still blotting those tears, "You're good, Gross. You're almost too good to be true."

So now she really had Gross on his heels. "Yeh?" And my grin was an idiot's grin. "What's the gag?"

"The gag?" She looked honestly surprised. "Haven't you heard that before, with your life-saving and your birthday layer-cakes? Don't you have a family, or friends? How about the cousin whose husband's funeral you went to today?"

"Friends? They're for pinochle. And family? You should meet mine God forbid, what a collection. Except for my daughter Liz, my younger—and she dug herself up a husband out of a father's worst nightmare. You're thirty-eight, did you ever run into a shell-game professor, with a sad twisted smile to make the heart bleed?"

All of a sudden Ruth Amin shut her eyes and blew out the birthday candle. So too good to be true Gross must have moved in too fast with his troubles. But I forced the old smile.

"Make a good wish?" I said.

"That I did." She drew out a chair for me. "Sit down, while I put up the coffee . . . Tell me about your daughter."

AH, THAT AIR RUSHING and the shadows the few blocks' drive home from Ruth Amin's. A nice lady, that listens.

Then the midnight news on the car radio: Whites beat up colored in Dear Old Southland; Cuba signs up with Red thugs; Khrushchev's gonna blast us out of Berlin. Plus one disaster: air crash in Sahara, only seventy-nine dead.

So what in the world could have made my rich in-laws the Hotel Henry gang pop up in my head?—Bulldog Henry Schwarzman my brother-in-law, his mad consort Tillie, their forty-year-old pups Sneering Sheldon and the Royal Fatness Howie, etcetera etcetera.

But also present at Schwarzman's Hotel Henry in the mountains up there are the outlaws: my wife Madam Arsenic and my daughter the widow Siren Sue, out hunting new game.

"So wise me up, Susan," Shmo Moe put his two cents in a few months ago, "how much do you care for that blind boy?"

"Charles Davis is not blind, and I care for him a great deal."

"As much as for your deceased husband Meier even, he should rest in peace?"

"And what is the latent content of that statement?"

See, she's forever giving me the satisfaction, my psychologist, that the college education I gave her was not thrown away.

"Latent content Pop, or Dad, or Father, you forgot to add. But let's just suppose poor Charlie Davis stays poor. Suppose his rich grandpa God forbid outlives us all, and suppose Charlie never gets anything better from grandpa's clothing chain than his cheap suits and his cheap job? Then you'll still care a great deal for Charlie? Or maybe your feelings will change, the way they did about George Meier—remember him, that husband of yours?—before he finished himself off with a plastic bag?"

So she looked me straight in the eye with those dark burning eyes. Women, what can you tell about 'em? Intelligence, good looks, sincerity: all plain on her face—and all fake.

"For sensitivity and perception, Father," Susan touched off both barrels at me, "you're unparalleled of course. But since you raise the question, let me inform you that I did care and cared deeply for my husband, and when he committed suicide I could have died."

Poor Charlie, you're marked for the slaughter, boy.

And like most of the killing nowadays, so senseless, so needless. What? Those bloodsuckers, those soaring vultures my wife's rich relatives would stand by and let Charlotte the medical aide—for taking care of her crazy sister Tillie free of charge she's okay—let humble Charlotte snatch off rich live meat for her daughter? Yeh, up at Hotel Henry when sister Tillie is napping, Charlotte is casing the guests. Then Susan comes up weekends. So Charlotte cased Charlie, and Susan came up and got him. But got what? Not money, like she thinks. Just sweet Charlie, that's all.

So, much as Gross loves the country, the meadows and those blue mountains that always make me reach out my arms to them, why should I go up there tomorrow? To see Sweet Sue give sweet Charlie the finishing touches? Or for Charlotte's sake, to keep up appearances as the husband of my wife?

Not Gross! I lost today on the job, I'll catch up tomorrow. And why should Mrs. Amin have to be stuck a whole weekend with her place upside down and no work accomplished?

On my street the pair of trees that forgot to shrivel from the exhaust fumes were like bouquets in the lamplight and I whistled my way into the house to give Mrs. Amin a ring and let her know Gross'll be there in the A.M. sharp!

But upstairs I paused for my panting exercises, and—the heart almost fell out of the chest.

Under the door a light. And the door open a crack.

So Madam Poison was home, the esteemed Mrs. Gross? The heart climbed a little, not too high. I needed that for the weekend? Expense, no expense, she wants, she don't want, maybe the time is ripe for Gross to cut loose completely.

Meanwhile, the wealthy relations must have booted her out again? And—call God a bad name to the rabbi—that dig would always cut deep. "Nobody booted anybody out, you vulgar mouth you," she'd growl with blood in her eyes, "my room was required for paying guests!" The rich relatives are that lady's religion.

But with the door unlocked, so the world and his helper could stroll in? Would that be the Lady Tightass I've known and loved?

Are you kidding?

Then it had to be thugs, and you can't imagine the instant rage in my heart. Gross works and has nothing, and they come to rob Gross?

So hero Gross, I nudged the door a crack wider with my shoe and crouched to dodge bullets, Moe the Shmo, like TV.

From her, on the couch? Curled up, my Liz, my butterball, in her stocking feet, fast asleep, with the long black hair and the beautiful olive complexion, like an Italian girl, those gifts from her mother—the only ones that mother could spare. And with the door open to anyone, when they murder you quick as look at you, rape you, expunge you? But this is her failing—some failing, eh?—always trusting, always open, with the heart always on the sleeve.

The next thought that bobbed up in my mind was the wish I have always and never think. She left her husband, oh dear Lord in Heaven, she left Phony Georgie, she left him!

A father shouldn't have such a thought, eh, about a daughter happily married? Two winters ago you should have seen the love in Lizzie's eyes, looking up at Smirk-face George that gala evening when she brought home a brand-new husband to surprise Mother with. Yeh, the happy minstrel George Young, that even to think of gives me a sick feeling downstairs. But let me be fair to Gross also. It ain't his being Chinese, Georgie. A jolt, yes. After all, I'm the average Bronx citizen. Still that I could shake off. You bump your skull against a low rafter so you tear down the house? Also, I been educated. What difference is color? And who educated me? Liz. From the age ten she preached the old man justice and right. You shut your heart to a preacher like this?

Charlotte, my spouse, began with some shouts about annulling the marriage that were bound to sound silly even in her own ears. Then she addressed the groom: "I understood that you people were particular about family relationships."

"Oh we're particular," Georgie came back with his purse-lipped smile, "that's why I asked Lizzie to marry me."

"In that case," the mother told him, "it might interest you to know that you've picked yourself some very stale goods."

Gross, he was ready to let fly, at last in my life, the big fist in that kisser. But George, he put his arm around bewildered Liz with the tears.

He said, "I'm sorry to hear you say that, Mrs. Gross. In any case, our generation takes a different view of such matters than yours. Let's go, Lizzie."

They went, and I grabbed my coat and hat and went after

them. That was my girl—and my boy, let him be from China let him be from Mars!

Some boy.

Through the freezing cold we wound up in Zion Delicatessen on the corner for the wedding dinner. Christmas Eve, and there was us and the delicatessen man. To celebrate, I ordered turkey, and it came as usual tough as life. What Lizzie ordered I forget, but her turkey was sitting alongside her. And what Lizzie wore I also forget, except the shining eyes that were a little more so from the tears that the mother drew upstairs. But Georgie Young, with that outfit, had to be the Ambassador from Taiwan—or his nephew at least.

First he hung up, with the care it deserved, the tan cashmere overcoat with the belt over the stomach. A worsted like he had on—checked gray, conservative, slim shoulders—only my rich in-laws and the local bookmaker can afford. His shirt was a light-blue tab collar, with a tie dark-blue silk in a fat, careful knot. He also wore a light-blue monogrammed handkerchief over where his heart is supposed to be.

I might as well say here that when I first laid eyes on him I cried to myself, Liz, that you'd go so far to get even on your mother I can understand, but how about your Pop, how about me? Now—I reveal all my vices—a patriotic American respect for large bank accounts crept in. This young man just had to be loaded!

Some loaded.

He smiled at me, Mr. Flap-ears, with the white teeth and the twisted little mouth. "You like the outfit, Mr. Gross? It's all from Lizzie—her wedding present."

Liz cried out, "Doesn't he look nice, Pop?"

"Like a million dollars."

They both went hysterical, and Liz kissed me for the bright saying. Afterwards we went back and they waited in the lobby while I packed up for Liz. To my surprise, my elder, the brilliant the beautiful the cool Susan, put down her book and gave me a hand. And Charlotte watched us with iceberg eyes, and from the lips of that mother began falling the pearls.

"First-class service for whores."

Susan quietly remarked, without stopping the packing, "Oh shut up, Mother."

"You have some nerve, when you yourself told me!"

But Susan only smiled, while the other kept spewing sludge for Gross's ears. And oy, what Gross heard, that my Liz should have been anybody's Liz maybe, anyone's fool if I should believe them, Susan my daughter and Charlotte my wife. Oh Liz, did that make me sick . . . No, no . . .

Gross, he said nothing. Gross took it. Later, in bed in the dark, Gross dished it out, good and hard, right up Charlotte's middle, what she hated the most! She growled and she fought, but in whispers, with clenched teeth, because Susan slept on the daybed outside. "What are you doing, you maniac!" And what I did I woke 'er up and I did over again right after she fell asleep, and once more later, when she fell asleep again.

"You animal, you coarse animal."

"Rejoice, bride," Gross told 'er, "or else go out and sleep on the daybed, with your secret agent out there."

"So that's what it is. Some secret!"

"Sha, you want it again?"

And God blessed our household with quiet.

Except inside Gross, who had a long night to think everything over, especially their malice, those two bitches of mine, because wouldn't Liz be just the innocent, the fool, to be passed from one to another by wise guys, by the young men of our time. Feh, feh on our time, feh on existence. And feh on the brilliant Sue, that finds hating so easy even apart from fathers and sisters. You should see her, clever young lady, making fun of the crazy little kids it's her profession to help—mind you profession! But to slander Liz! Why Susan is the idol to this girl, the wonderful older sister. Susan took up the modern dance, Liz had to dance modern. Susan took up psychology, psychology for Liz. Susan took up a husband, Liz got married—even to the same name George!

Or maybe it's all a coincidence. And what did it matter?

The next night, with my ladies asleep, Charlotte in the bedroom and Susan in the livingroom, Gross shut himself in the kitchen with his bottle of bitter pills. I figured sure, why not, it's too boring. My Liz, she's taken care of, such as it is, without hope. You want a country plantation Gross? Swallow these and your dream will come true. And for precedent your late son-in-law George Meier: such turmoil, and now completely forgotten—even to the name. And why should so young a widow as Susan Gross call herself Mrs. Meier? What did she get out of her husband, except his life? And even that, what did it amount to? It wasn't as if she could have had his head stuffed to show off in a trophy room, like the moose in the joke that heard the hunter whistle and mistook it for love.

But just that thought of George Meier stopped me. To wind up their sucker, like him? Charlotte I could picture gloating over my insurance, and Susan the helpful daughter liquidating Gross's other effects, such as Papa's gold watch that he gave me for luck when I married—ah Papa, what luck—with the picture of my sainted Mama inside. Wake up Gross! They on top, you underneath? I stuck the pills back in the bottle. Let me see them dead first!

And even George Young: Be an optimist. Every day of the week Folks have fatal accidents.

But not Georgie. Georgie looks both directions before he steps off the sidewalk.

Barely a month after Lizzie got married, I got home a bitter cold night late from some friend—friend, a piece of ass that I know. But the vital juices require their flow for good health, and that was a fat horse of another off-color. On the

Depression-décor imitation marble slab in my lobby, what sat perched patiently, like the Angel of Death in a sporty tan cashmere?

Yeh, him, my son-in-law.

"Liz is well?"

"Oh sure," he could be nonchalant enough to tell me, "she has classes tonight."

Poor kid, that has to slave the whole day with the sick kids she loves in the mental clinic and then have classes at night so she can support Master Georgie at home while, as he says, he completes his Dissertation, his Doctorate. And what will you be a doctor of, George? Will you take Gross's pulse, and cure the old man's tired feeling? Who you kidding, old man? Georgie says he will be a Doctor of Educational Administration. Well, maybe he does go to some school like he says. Could he fool Lizzie about that too?

I asked him, "Why are you downstairs?"

And his little, pursed grin.

"I'm afraid I'm not too popular upstairs."

"Mrs. Gross is back at Hotel Henry with her sick sister, didn't Liz tell you?"

How could Liz tell him if nobody asked her, Sir Secrecy? But Georgie always had his good reasons. Upstairs he enjoyed a warm welcome, including kiss, from sister-in-law Susan. In Georgie's absence, one of Susan's knife-twists in her mother on the subject of sister's hubby I hate to admit expressed my opinion.

"She could have done better though," Susan had said, "even among Asians."

Although if Georgie is Asian, why then call me Polack. Georgie is 100 percent American, certified U.S.A. A young man of our time, right down to the guitar.

So help me, a folksinger. Smooth, forever with the apologetic smile, he takes Susan's guitar out of her hand that she was practicing when we came in, me and Georgie. Susan of course also is up-to-date: folksinging, The Twist, contraception pills. The latter she keeps in full sight on her shelf in the medicine chest, another dagger in Mother. It works, too. You should hear the tumult: one-sided, Susan never raises her voice.

Next thing I knew, through the nose but not bad though it hurts me to say so, Georgie is singing to us about some paleface cowboy in a linen suit. As a cowboy outfit, to me linen was news. But I suppose if Georgie was a cowboy, that's what he'd wear. Next Georgie went Deep South colored and let us know he wasn't agonna study war no mo'. And on top of that he turned up in an English accent under the yew tree with his heart broken from love—he should live so long.

Susan clapped, and I told him it was a wonder that one and the same man should have such wide talents: for this, and for Educational Administration. But sarcastic to Georgie is like spit in the ocean.

"That's how Liz and I met." He smiled me his little boy twisted up smile. "I don't have to now—Liz's spared me that—but I used to sing professionally, at The Tiger's Eye, and Lizzie dropped in one day."

Oy Liz, what a drop that was!

But down to business. He had to speak to me on the Q.T. Why the Q.T., Georgie without shame? He was ashamed on account of Susan? Yeh yeh. Georgie handled his prospects one at a time, confidential. You, only you, were the privileged one that he was allowing to help him out, for only a loan of course, always a loan. A couple of months later it became Susan's turn and she laughed in his face. Me, I shelled out, for a good cause, after all, a commendable purpose. He needed two hundred, to put together a hi-fi for Liz. How did he guess Sucker Gross could just go two hundred? Another talent, among his many. And suddenly, Liz's one lack was a hi-fi?

Georgie switched on the serious face: pained at gross Pop

Gross, but no complaints. Oh Georgie, what the stage lost when you quit show business!

"It's not a lack, Pop," he told me, "it simply would please her."

Please you you mean.

It must be that I could use a psychologist. He took my two hundred, and, just as promised, bought some kind of hi-fi, for Liz. And one day I drove out there to them, to their flat in hell-and-gone Brooklyn, but—you couldn't argue with Georgie's taste, in hi-fi's, in apartments, in (bitter day) a wife. The rooms were airy, solid, not the 1961 luxury cardboxes today where next door the bell rings and you rush to pick up the phone call that'll change your whole life, or at least break the monotony. Under Georgie's studio you saw the church garden, a regular little winter wonderland, with snow on the branches, nice. Furniture, it's true, they were short of, except for Georgie's magnificent solid oak desk. But for a coming Doctor-Professor that was basic equipment, easily worth the price Liz paid for it. In the livingroom they found me a chair, a backbreaker, from the kitchen. And could you argue with Georgie's motto better not buy than buy ugly?

Every minute such gems dropped from his lips, and Liz, she gathered them in with her eyes.

"Isn't he nice, Pop, my husband?"

She ran over to him—they were both standing, where was there to sit?—and she threw her arms around his neck. Then behold, from his collection of faces he produced an oriental item, the inscrutable Dr. Fu Manchu, while he patted her on the head, his favorite dog.

He switched on the hi-fi, and Liz settled down on the floor Indian style. She, that womanly young woman, slim then, with the fine features, the sensitive, the intelligent eyes, she beamed at me full of pride . . . in that.

"Georgie's one-month anniversary present to me, Pop.

Wait till you hear it, it'll convert you to music." She leaned her head back, she shut her eyes. "Play the Mozart, Georgie—"

"No," pronounced Master George, "the *1812 Overture*. I want to show off those cannons booming."

She jumped up laughing, poor Liz. "He's becoming a hi-fi nut," she explained to the old man. "I'll start supper."

She didn't start supper so fast either. Georgie touched off his cannons, and—God can be merciful sometimes—nothing. Mum.

"Liz—"

And Lizzie raced back, with her laugh, and—she played it safe this round—with a peck on the cheek for baby. Get a peck don't necessarily mean give a peck. He dodged with a Fu Manchu.

Then Liz the mechanic, she went to work: diagram, screwdriver, wires. Why not, top honors in mathematics, physics, even—oh innocence, forever striving toward her ideal: Sister Susan—even psychology. So wasn't it natural that for Georgie she should put on the brakes, transfer to evening sessions, stretch out terms to years, and put her talents to a practical use?

In no time the cannons were booming. Oy did they boom, I thought my skull would blow off. Lizzie laughed, "Make it lower, Georgie." Georgie made it. He might be deaf, but he ain't so dumb. Plausible Georgie—he's plausible.

I assured Georgie that when it came to cannons I never heard better, and I made my getaway into the kitchen, with the good smells, and Liz on top of everything else the little housewife in the apron, mixing her salad.

"I know, Pop," she smiled at whatever was written on my face: hard to keep secrets between me and Liz, "it's a toy. But he's had so little in life. And besides"—oy proud, proud on account of his lie—"it was his money."

And from those innocent lips I heard the whole courtship,

the conman's whole stale secondhand spiel. Raised in a slum, Chinatown yet, San Francisco, poor Georgie. Need more be said. A boy raised in a slum, nothing is too good for him. Georgie, he's the beneficiary of the Mission, of the Foundation, of—it sticks in my craw—yeh, Lizzie Gross. Then what should be too good for Boob Gross—I mean me—from the capital of Slumland, Hester Street on the Lower East Side? Sweat for a living, mister, exit quietly in the rear, and keep off the grass: wrong slum! And that ain't Georgie's only tune for the heartstrings. At two a punching bag—it would go without saying—for his old man. At twelve running with the tong, now known as juneviles, with accent on the viles. At fourteen—Lizzie's eyes moistened even repeating it—ulcers from inner turmoil, the (oy oy oy) good boy vs the bad environment. At fifteen in at a knifing, and just ducked the cops. Then he decided—maestro, "Hearts and Flowers" please—quit, or quit living maybe. To this day he still suffers from ulcers.

Maybe so. Mashed potatoes and steak, they fit into an ulcers diet. For herself and me Lizzie fried flounder; but was Gross there to balance up books? It was delicious. But the way Georgie gobbled everything down, wolfed it calling for seconds, what was that? Well, this young man, so his story went, slept many a night curled up on the stone in cold doorways, and many a day eating off handouts or even from garbage cans. So there are also reasons for gluttony. The dirty dishes—when his mother was pregnant with George she had to be scared by a sink—he left for the little woman. So I stayed behind and gave Liz a hand.

"Still," I had to say it or bust, "he's a bit on the helpless side."

Lizzie turned those dark smiling eyes on me.

"But that's one reason I married him Pop. He needs me so much."

So tonight, Lizzie dozed curled up on my couch and—fool's paradise—the father sat dreaming, happy that happy marriage had broken up, or else why would she be here? Sure. The black marks under the eyes. And filled out so in that long year-and-a-half and yet haggard always? And—go remember details—didn't the onesided affection stop altogether, in the course of my visits?

My visits!

Oy, dinner with them tonight, and I forgot, I forgot. That's why Lizzie traveled all the way up, to find out, to make sure the old man wasn't . . .

She woke, she smiled.

"Forgive, forgive . . ."

She squeezed my hand. "As long as you're well, Pop."

Did you ever see such a Liz?

Her eyes roamed around Chateau Shabbiness, that she ran from to marriage and who could blame her? She said, "I thought I was ten years old again." She sat up fast, she smoothed down her blouse, a young woman—why is it sad to me?—adult. Then she said, "It's easier to be a baby than grownup."

"Yeh? If grownup is good, why be a baby?"

She gave me a sad smile, my baby. "No illusions, no disillusions, just living."

"Like the kids in your clinic?"

"No, I mean— I don't know what I mean." So ain't something rotten in the borough of Brooklyn, and ain't his name George? Then quick, Lizzie said, "I'm going up to Hotel Henry with you tomorrow, Pop." And who said I was going up to Hotel Henry tomorrow? "Susan phoned," she said, "Mother's all broken up, Aunt Tillie died today," she looked at her watch, she yawned. "Yesterday, that is."

"So you want to go comfort your mother while she's all broken up, you think she'll be softer?"

"Yes, exactly."

I had to smile at this innocent. "Saint Lizzie," I asked her, "who do you take after, which grandparent?"

Those dark eyes went moist. "Don't say such things to me, I don't want to hear them." Because she knew I was disparaging that loving mother of hers.

So Gross was rebuked. On the other hand, if not for Elizabeth you wouldn't catch Gross within miles of the installation of that eminent Jewish clubwoman of years past, that former hobnobber with His Honor the Senator, the Real Estate boys and other assorted crooks, my late esteemed sister-in-law Tillie the Rock, six feet down Sunday. And for this pleasure Gross has to lose out on a full day's earnings painting that lady's apartment.

But a good father doesn't say this to a daughter, and I didn't say it to Liz.

To BRIGHTEN UP TILLIE'S FUNERAL George the Dude came along, with his blue suit and white pocket handkerchief courtesy Elizabeth Gross Young. Still what's right is right, and I led with an apology for missing my night-before's visit.

"I hope she was worth it," George aimed one at my balls.

Gross inhaled to give him a worth it, but Liz jumped in quick. "Pop said he was sorry. Shall we drop the subject?" Like married ten years, and no kisses asked or given.

Gross preferred this to kisses? You want heartache, have children.

But cheer up, Gross. With one eye on your fellow motorists so they shouldn't obliterate you in their mad haste to pleasure, enjoy the glints on the Hudson below the bridge to the Jersey side and remember your happy New Year's resolution from when you sat with your suicide pills two New Years ago.

Folks? Forget 'em! When you croak, they'll peel your hide. So outlast 'em—peel theirs!

Pinch, Folks, hoard, save for the rainy day. Then, before you got time to break out the umbrella: knock knock knock. Who's there? Parcel service, the pickup man. What parcel, I ain't got no parcel. You brother, or sister as case may be, you're the parcel! Then up comes Gross, after they plant you,

31

to clear the apartment. And behold: in every drawer bank-books—for Gross to cash in on! Now little Sadie—ha ha ha!—my first fiancée, if you had to wind up marrying a cousin of Gross's, why Holy Willie with so many brothers?

Nah, Willie never stole Sadie from Gross. Nobody steals nothing from Gross, and Will was no crook. Will was sweet, a religious man, that should have been a rabbi—the real, not the reformed. Or else his father my cousin Joe with the razbuck-niks in Concord should have laid off the bookkeeper that while he screwed her at home screwed him at the factory. So when the bookkeeper had hers and Joseph was broke, Willie wound up a house painter too. But before that, starry-eyed Moe engaged to Sadie, he loves the girl and he loves the country, he takes his Sadie for a weekend at friend Will's at the outskirts of Concord with the big trees and the lawns and the shadows along the road.

To me love meant respect first of all, and pride in the person, also trust. Jerk Moe.

Cousin Joseph, the father, he took us on a tour of the factory, the ice-cream plant. A short man, but with shoulders, arms, a chest: big as Gross's, with ease. And Sadie, Miss Goldenhair, what if she was twenty-six then, five years older than Gross? You walked down Delancey Street with her, the boys turned, the boys goggled. Joseph cracked jokes, he winked, he fed smiling Sadie a pink ice-cream cone and asked her was it good. She flicked her little pink tongue over that ball, and she smiled at him with her eyes and her tight, creamy cheeks. "Can't you tell?" Sadie said. She stretched out the cone to him. "Have a bite." Which meant have a different kind of a bite later, but innocent Moe.

At night there was Sadie's room, then my room, and then there was Joseph's room. That the father had a room of his own and the mother another, Gross never thought anything of.

Lights out and Gross sat by the window, in love with the leaves and the moonlight, dreaming, imagining me and Sadie together in our own house like this.

Suddenly a sound, a door closing? Then Sadie's laugh, soft, from outside. I leaned out of the window—happy!—to wave to her, to whisper I'd be right down, that me too, I felt that way too about the sweet night air and the country.

At the edge of the lawn, near the trees, a rabbit stood listening. Nothing else.

Was I losing my mind? But again sounds, that laugh again. I listened. Be frank, I plastered my ear up against Cousin Joe's wall. My rabbit was indoors, in Joe's room. After they had their fun, she came out and I opened my door. Sick as I was, sore as I was, I whispered to her, Idiot Moe, "Where were you?"

"Where do you think," she brazened it at me, "in the middle of the night," smiled even.

"But you weren't," I told her, "I heard you with him, from beginning to end."

Now if she'd shed a tear, said she was sorry—

She said, "You mean you heard the blood drumming in your ears." She yawned, and stretched. She flaunted those tits in the nightgown right in my face. And as if God unveiled Gross's eyes, I saw how hard those good looks really were. She said, "I don't know what you're doing, I'm going to sleep."

She went, and Gross took one step to follow, to squeeze the life out of that neck with this pair of hands. But thank God, I stopped.

Next day in the train going home, I said to her, "I proposed, you said Yes. You could have said No."

She smiled. "Such beauty can't be resisted."

I grabbed hold of her arm and ripped that wristwatch I'd given 'er right off and flung it out of the window at the rolling-by scenery that I hardly saw. Later, give Gross credit, I became more conservative with wristwatches. But flaming youth.

Sadie said, "Do you know that you're crazy?"

"And you're right in the head?"

But if Sadie was crazy then, who's crazy now? Now for the alleycats flaunt is the word and you're a fool if you don't. Self-fulfillment it's called, I know from my daughter Psycholo-logical Sue. So times change, and Sadie's only tough luck was to be ahead of her time. Then, even Sadie, you were an alleycat, you followed alley rules: quiet, in the dark, at night. So luck enters into it, and revenge is sweet—and did Gross live to see his revenge!

Cousin Joe lost the factory, the family broke up, and Will and his mother came to live in New York. And who does Will meet in the neighborhood and marry in spite of Cousin Moe's hints? Yeh.

Picture my wedded Miss Goldentough, with a mother-in-law part of the family unit. How could the alleycat go, with a built-in watchdog? Sadie couldn't, and Sadie didn't. Six months and Sadie was laid up, the doctors said heart trouble. So, you got to suffer the drawbacks of heart trouble, should you be stupid enough not to enjoy the fringe benefits? Sadie never lifted a finger from then on, her health was too delicate. That was her revenge, on the mother-in-law. Not that the mother-in-law minded running the house, she just hated Sadie. Will, he loved 'em both, honestly. He lived to pray in shul and cater to his beautiful wife and loving mother. And the pure are rewarded. In the twenty years with the mother-in-law, Sadie became sweet, resigned, a changed person. Oy was she sweet! She'd look at you: poor, afflicted, but smiling through. Even the sisters-in-law loved her, especially after Will's mother died, and Sadie put on glasses, and broadened. Who was there to aggravate with her good looks? What good were they? So she dug into Will's cooking, mostly spaghetti. A few years ago Sadie insisted to me, I had to stay for dinner. Will cooked and served, while Sadie sat there with her gentle moonface and told me what a wonderful man her husband was. Then I had my spaghetti. And a year and a half ago, the day before her fifty-ninth birthday, what do you think happened to Sadie? She had a heart attack maybe? Ha ha!

She went out to ride up to Fordham Road and buy herself a birthday treat in the stores, a new hat for the old Sadie, and downstairs, across the Grand Concourse, what does she see but the bus standing with open doors. So she made a dash—the poor neighbor that witnessed it couldn't believe a woman in such health could have ripped off such speed—and she dashed under a car. Then, poor Will, they called him to the morgue, and he dropped, right there in the hospital, with heart failure! Oh, hahaha, I shouldn't have laughed like that when my cousin Stan called up with the news, he thought I was crazy, oh hahahaha, they couldn't do—oxygen, massage, mouth-to-mouth—they couldn't do a thing for poor Will, hahahaha!

What a funeral—two in one blow. For Will the shul came and carried him out of the chapel in procession. He had a turnout, the street was full. So he lived his life, and he went out in style. But Sadie, that was an expensive night's fun you had thirty years ago back in Concord, that cost you your life. And would you believe it, there was a tug at my heartstrings, for Sadie.

After the mourning period Will's three brothers came up, Stan, Mickey, and Irving, to clear out the deceased pair's worn-out clothes and secondhand furniture. And what did they find? The bankbooks. A dozen. For their rainy day Sadie and Will didn't trust just one bank. Three, five, seven thousand dollars a book! Some reading for those boys, eh, the brothers? They split up a good fifty G's—from a lifetime of spaghetti.

So, since then . . .

What did I have in mind?

Oh yeh, Folks and resolutions. Now soon we'll be coming to the place, along the country road here, the little house on the hill, with the white porch and the shade trees, and the pond just off the road. All my life I've longed for a house like that. So Gross for the right funeral and a share of the loot. Fuck Folks! Grab a bundle out of the grave—and live!

Ah, there it is, where the road turns: the hill, and the house. So there Gross sits, in my longings, on that porch, with a smile, inhaling the green air. And look, look who comes out through the screen door to say, *It is nice, Moe, isn't it?*—Ruth Amin!

Sure shmuck, dream on. As long as you don't really know what her angle is.

For my passengers I pointed.

"That's my dream house up there."

And like a chorus, "Oh it's so sweet, Pop," from Liz; and from laughing George, "Tobacco Road, so it must be pipe dreams."

My third passenger, misery, kept quiet inside me.

But pessimist Gross, worrying over new insults for Liz from the mother. There I was wrong.

The old station wagon groaned up the mountainside, where the Hotel Henry sails near the top like a white steamer with pennants. We passed the golf course (with customers) and the outdoor pool (without customers). Then at the lower veranda of the establishment itself Gross drew the usual hard look from the doorman-in-chief with the epaulettes for driving right by (no tip) and through the pine woods, and parking outside the mansion instead of in the hotel garage.

And first of all there was Charlie Davis, that sweet young fella, on the lookout and coming out of the mansion to greet us.

"It's hardly the occasion," Charles said, with handshakes all around, "but I can't keep it in. Congratulate me. Sue's said Yes!"

Gross said, "What was the question?"

Charles laughed, with those dim eyes smiling behind the thick glasses. "Well, I'll be one son-in-law who'll always look forward to seeing his father-in-law."

So it was official, they were engaged, and what could be a more appropriate occasion for such a fatality than a funeral weekend? We went into the house, and outside of Tillie, the guest at the undertaker's, the whole gang was there. The bereaved husband, Barrel Henry Schwarzman, he was really bereaved, you could tell. We clasped hands, he shook his head, he sighed, almost human for once in his life. The two sons, gloomy Sheldon and fat Howie? Well, Sheldon was bright, he could feel for himself and his, if for nobody else. But a mother *non compos mentis* five long years, she'd already been dead to him, worse than dead.

Because those five years see, every Friday the bookkeeper Miss Hess had to enter Tillie's bedroom, curtsy before her Royal Mad Presence, give her an account of the business, and produce what was supposed to be the loot of the week. Her family tried small sums first, a few singles—but Tillie howled those away. Her husband's suggestion of stage money—she may have been crazy but she wasn't so dumb—that didn't work either. Fifty, sixty, seventy-five bills: that was the least that would quiet her. And where did she bury the paper? Under the pillow till no one was watching. Then—whssst!—it would vanish. If Barrel Henry, who gave the orders, had to swallow hard every Friday before he sent in Miss Hess, you must imagine that to Sheldon and Howie it was beyond human endurance.

"And what," Shelley Schwarzman yelped out one Friday, "if she's giving it away?"

"I could have the housekeeper search the maid," was Howie's proposal and they looked at him like crazy.

So finally the paterfamilias gave in. He ordered Miss Hess, "Tell Mrs. Schwarzman we were in the red this week."

Miss Hess delivered the message and came out all tears. And over her tears you could hear the wailing, the moaning upstairs.

"It's too pitiful," Miss Hess sniffled, "I can't do that again."

"I'll treat you to earplugs," said Sheldon.

But he couldn't treat his father to earplugs, and Tillie resumed collecting for a rainy day.

So now with his mother gone Black Friday was erased from Sheldon's calendar, and the best he could do was sit around smoking cigarettes with a serious face. And although there was no love lost between Howie and Shelley, Howie took his cues from his brother, except for the smoking. Cigarettes are bad for the health, and Howie—don't ask Gross why—is for long life for Howie. Howie's wife Dowager Rae, the ramrod with the iron-gray hair, kept the servants at attention and the cookie plates filled.

But Shelley's Eleanor, that juicy piece for the rich—and also for some of the poor, she was democratic that way—cracked for my ear, "Dying should be illegal on Friday, shouldn't it, the way it kills the whole weekend?"

Lizzie of course ran straight to her mother sitting frozen in grief on the couch there, with that handsome face white and drawn, with red staring eyes, alone, even though the lovely Susan sat arm in arm with her. And Lizzie was right. The loss of a sister had softened my Charlotte. Liz pressed Mother's hand pressed to Mother's handkerchief pressed to Mother's mouth, Mother at least let Liz press. Liz whispered daughterly comfort, Mother at least only sat like a statue, Mother didn't sneer, or lash out, or stand up and walk. You want to know if that's soft, what's hard? You figure it out, Gross is too busy now watching Liz give sister Sue's hand a different kind of a squeeze, that real joy Liz had for Sue on account of sweet Charlie's announcement. And the beauteous, the grave-faced Sue, how did she react? She gave Liz a wink, as to say mission accomplished, fish hooked.

But later I asked Liz what she thought of that wink, and she said No, under the circumstances the wink simply meant thanks, with Mother so grief-stricken. So Gross has to be nuts, unless you ask Gross. Though Charlotte's grief I wouldn't dispute.

Yeh, she was Sister Tillie's chief mourner the next day at the funeral. Howie and Sheldon could switch on their mourners' expressions and their better-for-her-sake-this-way. And the husband could wipe a tear away, tough Henry Schwarzman, the barrel chest. But who was the one at the funeral caterer's, beside the bier, with the streaming eyes and the trembling mouth? Yeh, Charlotte.

"You don't remember her, you don't remember Tillie the way she used to be—"

I remember her, Missile Tillie, I remember the way she used to be. I remember her at one of her early hotels, the Oceanside, our first intro, looking me up and down like a rotten banana. So Gross gave good as he got and looked her up and down too. For looks Tillie was not bad if you like ice: tall, slim, with a handsome mug like sister Charlotte's but tougher. So I folded Tillie's hand over my room key and I spoke in her ear. "After your Henny's asleep." I also flipped 'er a wink, straight in the eye.

She dangled the key, for the whole world to take witness what a lemon the kid sister was picking. And she pushed those lips out that I could have pushed this fist in.

"And very funny," she made with the pursed lips, "into the bargain."

Hey, and if Gross was no bargain, couldn't you find better

for Charlotte in that pack of hoity-toi friends? Couldn't you steer Charlotte in the way of a nice well-lined wallet instead of letting the poor girl fall away to a Gross?

Could, yes. Would, never. But tell Charlotte that. I tried, when I was still trying for a woman not only a wife.

"So jealous! So abusive of his betters!"

Betters, worsers, God spoke, and the word rolled down from Sinai. In pain bring forth children, sweat! Listening, Sis?

Always listening.

Tillie said, in the early years of our marriage, "Why throw out your few pennies on a Catskill pigsty when you can stay in the mansion for the summer."

Charlotte's voice trembled with gratitude. "In Oceanside?"

Only, from Tillie, the icebox eye. "In Pittsville."

So what could Charlotte do but pack up the bags, bark the kids into line, and head for Pittsville, the heat, and the Jersey mosquitoes? And why not Oceanside, where the hotel was, with the beach and the ocean breeze? Plenty of room Tillie in the mansion there. Some joke. Congressman, shake hands with my sister that made bad and her stigma the painter. Don't wake me up let me dream—in the Pittsville Poor Wing.

Sure, Poor Wing. Philanthropic Tillie, the Eminent Jewish Clubwoman. She gave, she did give, even to third cousins twice removed. But Tillie'd had to suffer and work hard to get what she gave, so—champagne now being served in the drawing room, if you care for a little arsenic at the bottom of the glass—you suffer likewise while enjoying the charity. Have a wing of the mansion, Papa my boy, with a separate entrance all to yourself and no rules posted. Only no mingling with the guests!

And in summer, not even a guest not to mingle with.

Poor Charlotte, warm and she wilts, hot and she perishes. So the day before Pittsville Gross prayed for heat and God heard. Ninety degrees in the shade!

"Won't the temperature be too high for you, dear, in Pittsville?"

So she shot me the expected look, Charlotte. Yeh, between us, it was always one thing said and another meant. She knew my message was you can't say no to Pittsville and still hope for a chance some day to say yes to Oceanside, so fry sister, fry!

One thick belt of air from the middle of the Bronx to the middle of Jersey. And what stood in the sun in front of the mansion, like a scarecrow with a rake and a yokel straw hat, but my father-in-law Izzie, the lost soul, with his drooping mustache and his arthritic fingers. A hundred and three degrees, and he's manicuring the lawn!

"Izzie darling, are you out of your mind? You can get sunstroke."

"No," he tells me, "I don't mind the warm weather at all Moe, I'm used to it—"

When Torpedo Tillie was found detonated five years ago, the Schwarzmans to my heartfelt sorrow began coming apart at the seams. Barrel Henry the shrewd businesshead suddenly stopped ticking so fast without Tillie, and among the natives— the sons, I mean, Howie and Sheldon—there grew unrest. The boys, the family called them. Over forty, and still boys? If not men then, then when? So they figured, Howie and Sheldon, the time is ripe, let's grab hold of the pie. Only each one decided the whole pie for him. And there were the helpmates to egg 'em on. Like us and the Russians, all men are brothers. And Itchy Eleanor (Sheldon's) and Dowager Rae (Howard's) are of course sisters under the skin. So in the hotels the boys grabbed, Sheldon the front and Howard the back. And if Shelley could tell Howie, "Three kinds of cabbage on the dinner menu tonight?," Howie could answer Shelley, "You just keep on sneering at the guests." So instead of pie they got sticky fingers.

Each to his consolation. Howie ate, Sheldon drank. And the

cause of their troubles? Before you could ask, they'd tell you.
Mother.

Listen, they had to be right. With Torpedo Tillie a shell of
her former self, what business could be foolproof against such
fools?

One day at the mountains mansion—Tillie sprouted mansions the way they say the Hiroshima bomb sprouted weeds—
Sneering Sheldon sailed over and pulled me by the arm. This
you can imagine Gross loved. He stuck me that rummy mouth
of his in my face, and this I loved even more.

"Come on," he said, "I'll show you my mother."

"I've seen your mother, thanks all the same."

And what a sight, Come-Hither Tillie, up in bed with the
white curls and the white face, the knees doing their dance and
the whorehouse smirk. How old are you, doll? Sixty-six?
What's your name? You don't know that either? You don't
remember Eleanor right here, your daughter-in-law, that you
always used to bawl out—and get laughed in your face for
your pains—for chasing the golf pro or the dance pro or
whatever hotel pro would service her best? Well that look in
Eleanor's eyes when she'd see him, the stag she was chasing,
that look is in Tillie's eyes now. Gay Eleanor, Sheldon's horns
and he loved her. "No divorce," he'd beg 'er, "Eleanor,
please—" She could grin to me, Eleanor, "My mother-in-law
finally looks human, wouldn't you say?" Sure, beside a
torpedo, a monkey looks human. Only, for monkeys give
Gross the zoo.

But Sheldon never lets go. "What's wrong," he cracks at
me, "too delicate?" Fortunately for the Boy, my Lizzie was
present—yes yes, George Young was still in the future
then—and she saw from her father's face that one more pull on
my arm and a fist might explode in the Sheldon gut. So Lizzie
detached her Cousin Sheldon, and told him that she would visit
her aunt.

Sheldon let out a snicker. "Visit——"

And sensitive Liz came back indignant. "Do you know what he calls his mother? Exhibit A!" Me, gross Gross, I had to laugh, when wolves turn cannibal.

But the true Exhibit A, he should rest in peace these many years, was my father-in-law, Izzie, broken to harness by the good Tillie and still at it long after she ordered him "Enough!" Okay, raking the lawn—wealthy aged eccentric. But scrubbing the Poor Wing windows just when her cronies were arriving, or joining the laundress in the basement to do a wash with his three pair of socks and his two sets of underwear? Tillie would tell him, through iron lips, "We employ servants for that purpose, Papa." Papa was agreeable, he'd shake his head—and on to the next stunt the second she turned her back.

So that day, when Izzie grabbed his broom and got going on the porch, I grabbed the broom out of his hands. "Sit down, Izzie, rock, enjoy the green and the trees, it's too hot." Would you believe me, he jumped up like a jack-in-the-box, I had to push him back. "But the porch needs a sweeping, Moe," he pleaded with me, poor man.

"So what?" I said to him. "Who are you, the porter? Tillie's not here for you to aggravate. And Charlotte? After you finish sweeping the twenty rooms here you can come to The Bronx and sweep up her three rooms too for all she cares."

"Oh no, you've got me wrong, Moe—" still trying to get away but I wouldn't let 'im— "Why should I want to aggravate Tillie, they don't come any better than Tillie. Why if not for Tillie years ago, I could have become an idler, a burden on my family. You didn't know that, did you Moe? See how stiff, how withered the arm is? Well the first attack was the worst. I was away from the shop a month—what could I do, a cutter without a right hand?—over a month. And I'd never skipped a day's work in my life, since the age of twelve. Not that I fancied the factory, I hated it, the job, the surroundings, the grind. But I worked"—proud yet—"it's man's nature to work, and I worked! Then," he laughed, a joke, "maybe spring fever caught up to me toward the end of that month, I've never understood it—but I lost all desire to go back to the shop. You know how I'd spend the time?" And those poor old puppy-brown eyes lighted up, and he leaned back in the rocker so help me: my father-in-law, Izzie, relaxed! "I'd walk, I'd stroll down to the Battery and watch the sailing ships put out to sea. I'd sit there Moe by the hour, just watching: the ships, the gulls, the purple waves, and the whitecaps. I even forgot my pain, I was that fascinated. If I'd been a young man, I certainly would have signed on to one of those ships . . ."

And he rocked there on the porch, the dreamer, with his dream of ships that he had before Tillie woke him.

"No, Papa, we are not rich people. Hurt or no hurt, we cannot support you. You must go out and work, like everyone else."

That was how beloved Tillie, Izzie loved Tillie, straightened him out. Not the arm: that was crooked forever. But she headed him back to the shop, and it's a man's nature to work. Not as a cutter, with that bum wing. But he could manage a lefthanded iron, so he dropped down a notch and he pressed. He brought home less, they struggled—but Tillie held on to her own.

Her own, that she toiled for and hard, not yours remember, not mine, not her Papa's: Tillie's! Money is power: without those explosions, no rocket to the moon. What's on the moon? Ashes, but don't change the subject. Tillie's capital, little by little, sent her streaking across the sky. The millinery, the dressmaking. Then, with Barrel Henry the salami-slicer, her bargain delicatessen. They fell in love, Tillie and Henry, after matching their bank accounts. A honeymoon? Tillie—and don't you forget it—had no time for honeymoons. Right away they unloaded the delicatessen and they bought a hotel for the other honeymooners. What a location! Grass, trees, across the road a bubbling brook, and—before Tillie and Henry—Jews keep out! But they found their hungry Christian, and they bought. And the Jews rushed to get in there, like the Promised Land. And from hotel to hotel, bigger and bigger, ritzy and ritzier, the Christians sold and Tillie and Henry bought.

And ruined Charlotte with envy.

Now you think Tillie set Izzie straight? Wait till you hear what she did for her sister, and without benefit of consultation even. Izzie overheard this before the Poor Wing days, that sweet snooper. Hey, maybe Tillie confined him to quarters on account of security leaks? Anyhow, Charlotte was brand-new then, eighteen, nineteen, slim with those shoulders, and the burning eyes even in the snapshots, Princess Charlotte.

So along came Prince James the First and Last, Levy. This young man, hard as he tried—and he tried—he would have needed two lifetimes to run through his daddy's fortune in real estate: most of Queens, half The Bronx, and a little of Manhattan. To refresh his mind after a week's rubber-stamping, he took four-day weekends at the Mountainview. And Tillie, that summer, made a tactical error. She brought Charlotte up there as bookkeeper because family was cheaper than outsiders.

Penny wise pound foolish.

After Prince Levy's second weekend with Charlotte, he never even bothered to drive back to the gold mines, he just stayed put at Mountainview. Ten weeks of Charlotte for dinner, his bed to himself all night, and the golf course in the morning to try to work down the excitement, and this boy had to progress either into a husband or a driveling idiot. Charlotte, young as she was, she played him like a veteran. Hold hands, a dance now and then in the grillroom on Help's Night, giggles on the lower veranda where the upper-echelon help were permitted to sit and enjoy part of the stars: that's as far as she went. Poor girl, did she ever imagine that her worst enemy ran the hotel?

Tillie the Wise, she watched, she heard from her spies, and she kept her own counsel.

Until Prince James, already half out of his wits, invited himself to Tillie's rooms for champagne one afternoon when Papa Izzie was hidden in the bay window. Not that Izzie expected adventure. For the view.

Then Playboy Jim opened up.

"I'm thinking of joining your family, Tillie."

"My Stella?" Tillie played him. "You'll have to wait I'm afraid. She's only ten in September."

"Aw Tillie, you know I mean Charlotte."

"Charlotte? Congratulations. Now as your future sister-in-law, two questions. What does Father say, and have you picked your divorce lawyer?"

"Aw, Tillie—"

But the air became smoky with the wood burning, what his father would say to a pauper's match.

"Aw Tillie, she's your sister—"

So Tillie tossed another log on the fire. "And that's all she is." Then she said, "I presume my sister is a respectable girl?"

"For chrissakes Tillie, how can you——"

"You're right, that question was foolish. Why would you be so anxious about marrying otherwise? Here, have some more wine . . . Listen Jim, you go home, discuss it with Dad. Then if you're still interested, fine, you know her Bronx address. But your father is my friend and he's been my guest for many years. I can't have people supposing I entice their sons to my hotels as matrimonial prospects for members of my family I happen to give work to."

The next morning sharp, Prince James went back to the big

city to ink up his stamp pads, and Charlotte kept the Mountainview books with red eyes.

So Gross remembers, but Charlotte forgot? Yes, I believe it. Charlotte forgot. Who cried into Tillie's grave? Who stretched the arms out after the million-dollar box in mahogany carving? Charlotte, that's who. And no wonder, with her servants' quarters pass to the rich six feet down, that she'd nursed, that she'd waited on hand and foot, that she'd rushed to from The Bronx at a second's notice if only they gave her the nod. No wonder she had to lean there on her daughter Susan, the forlorn hope for affiliation with money. The other connection was downstairs, and the rich box gave the exact same hollow sound as Bella's Lou's poor box when the handful of pebbles was dropped down on it.

Then later, with the funeral crowd gone, we sat around with the two lonesome couches in the décor Hunting Lodge livingroom by Tillie's favorite decorator, with the antiqued knots on the floor, the beams on the ceiling, and a chill through the bones that made even the moose over the fireplace look depressed. And why was Gross there? Idiot Gross honestly thought that his wife would be wanting to come home to The Bronx again, now that Tillie was gone! It was cold, May Day in the mountains. Even that natural glacier Ramrod Rae Schwarzman crossed her arms over her chest, shivered, and barked her hubby an order.

"Howard, make a fire for God's sakes!"

Fatty went straight to work on the hearth, but when he had the match in his fingers Sheldon told him to wait.

"Her money just might be hidden in there."

"That's true," Howard said. "No sense lighting fires until we look."

Then they'd never found Tillie's treasure!

"My God," Henry said, "the earth is still loose on your mother's grave—"

And Charlotte took courage from him to whisper, "It's so soon—"

Gross, I leaned back on the cushions. "Finders keepers? Last one up the chimney's a rotten egg!" And if dark looks counted, we could have had an eclipse of the moon.

But when the treasure hunt began the bereaved husband kept quiet, and, with excited eyes, the bereaved sister joined in.

Gross? I'm sorry to report that without even discussing it the Schwarzmans kept me covered like the star end most likely to run off with the touchdown pass. Wherever Gross sauntered, there you saw one Schwarzman at least.

You can't be a star, enjoy the brawl as spectator.

The Schwarzmans watched one another too, they took good care. And thorough! Mattresses turned, suitcases sifted, drawers ransacked. What did they find? They found that her jewels also were missing.

Howard roared, "I'm bringing that maid over right now!" He picked up the housekeeper's phone, and this time he got no scornful looks. For deep misery, more than at the funeral that afternoon, those were the faces to see. Howard hung up the phone. "She's off duty."

Then Eleanor said, "And anyway, who'll search Dr. Greene? He was a half-hour alone with her every day of the week—and a lot of good he did her besides." And a lot of good he did Lady Eleanor Itch besides, when she made her play for him and he wouldn't play back.

But one suspect was right on the spot. Sitting up night after night with poor crazy Tillie that was scared of the dark, what candidate combined maximum need with top opportunity? A glance or two one to the other and you saw their verdict was Charlotte, in the first degree.

Innocent Charlotte happened to be poking just then in some dirty wash Howard'd already wrinkled his flat snout at. Dirty—only devotion like Charlotte's would have gone deeper in that. And right away, that bewitched one, she let loose her eureka.

Ever see eight, nine grand in five-dollar bills? That paper could have covered the walls of my whole three rooms, or else found me a shack in the country plus a dozen green acres and let the Schwarzmans have my three rooms. The jewels were there too, at the bottom of that bag that in every mansion poor Tillie must have stuck in the back of her closets to bank the rainy day bundle in.

Sheldon said, "I'll count . . ."

I commented to Charlotte, "You just gave away your favorite daughter's wedding at the Ritz."

"Low," she informed me, "you're the lowest."

Translation: she'd had that thought too, and it hurt. But her vote was cast and the Schwarzmans won and their petty cash lost.

"Like a lift back to The Bronx, dear?"

"I'm here in mourning for my sister!"

"Ta ta then. We should meet on better occasions."

Like at your funeral, dear.

So 8:00 A.M. MONDAY Gross rushed to Mrs. Amin's. Why the rush? God only knows. The lady was all combed and dressed, in the pink, a pink frock, and to see 'er this morning you'd never dream of suicides, birthday-cake celebrations, or tears.

Gross said, "You're ready to go to business? Go ahead. You can leave your castle with Gross. Gross brings nothing in, he takes nothing away."

And I started in with the plaster, to patch up, to redecorate. Meanwhile, you hear the walls falling away inside.

"I was expecting you Saturday, Gross."

I stood there in her foyer with my stick and my buckets, and my grin like an idiot.

"You're a mindreader?"

"See? What happened, another funeral?"

"What did you do," and this was only half-kidding I got to admit, "plant a private detective on Gross?"

"I didn't know that they grow such plants, except in the movies."

"They grow 'em, Gross can tell you from life."

"Were you the planter or the plantee?"

"The innocent bystander, that forgot that when you're

dealing with locomotives it's stop look and listen before crossing the tracks."

"Oh, just a traffic accident."

"Yeh, a small collision between Gross and a blonde. Excuse me, you're a blonde too—present company excepted. This happened years ago."

"What happened, Moe?"

I bent over my pail and resumed stirring.

"That's a long story, I may tell you some time. Meanwhile, you don't want to be late for business."

"I can be late for business, or even absent. My husband left me some money."

"Hey, you'd be a real catch for some bachelor."

"That's what my friends think. I've had all sorts of opportunities since Sol died."

Rupp, up and down, I gave first aid to the kitchen.

To Amin I said, "But nothing substantial, hah?"

"Well you saw, didn't you, Friday morning?"

I said, "You had a good marriage with Sol, eh, that nobody else measures up?"

"Sol didn't drink, he didn't gamble, he didn't run around with women. What more could a wife ask?"

"That's what he didn't do. How about what he did do?"

She gave me a smile, my middle-aged siren. "What do you do, as a husband?"

"Now, not much. But I used to bring home the bacon and tell jokes."

"Well that's what Sol did."

"So Gross is a reasonable facsimile thereof."

"Two men couldn't be more different."

I cracked, "You mean for better or worse, as they say under the canopy?"

She laughed with that nice sincere laugh of hers, if you can trust the sound of sincerity. "You could put it that way."

I dug in with the plaster knife, to get down to the bottom of things. And I said, while she watched me, "You want to hear about Gross's marital ties?"

"Sure Gross," she gave me a grin, this lady hard to pin down, "tell me about your marital ties," as if she's humoring me!

Still she asked for it, so let's let 'er have it. Then we'll see how chummy she stays when she sees what kind of marriage prospect she has here before her.

So I told her that long ago in my blissfully wedded career, it turned out my wife had a shortcoming, maybe two—but who counts? Susan must have been six then, my terror of the first grade. So that made Lizzie two. You quick in arithmetic? One killer plus one angel equals—? Two nuisances, they equaled. They were a nuisance to Mother, they interfered with her life. Her friends had husbands, so she'd had to have a husband. Her friends had children, so etcetera. And summertime, the slack season for paintners, Gross also was underfoot, good for what? So Mother decided on a vacation, minus her near and dear.

My mother never needed such a vacation, never dreamt of one. But let's say tempus fugits, and nowadays a woman requires time off, it's agreed.

So with no sleep lost except would her rich sister Tillie say Yes, my proud beauty swallowed her pride in a letter—with a hint tucked in here, another hint there—to Terrible Tillie, could she come freeload two weeks at Hotel Oceanside? Tillie flashed her the go-ahead sign, specifying a small room in Heaven alongside the hydraulic elevator shaft, where you shook like a malted with each up and down. Then what a change! Scowling Charlotte one second, and the next the old handsome Charlotte with that excited smile of hers. Sweet Sue was experienced, she never even bothered to look up from a fast ball-and-jacks on the floor there when Mother grabbed the valises. But the baby on my arm—you ever see worry on a baby's face two years old?—that one, with worry, folded and unfolded her hand good-by to Mother.

Charlotte sang out, "See you," and off to the Oceanside.

Two weeks later when she had to leave the rich, the song was over but the melody tore at her heart. And God, especially to afflict her, added a New York heat wave to the homecoming, a scorcher. Charlotte rammed the key in the prison lock, only she had to break in and be her own warden and chief convict, and the toddler Liz, she heard, she hurried to greet Mother. Gross-on-the-spot caught the child just as that door burst open, or so help me it would have been a skull fracture at least, the way that woman came crashing in, with the hot cheeks and the angry eyes! Lizzie, with arms upstretched to her? What Lizzie, who Lizzie? Sidestepped 'er, like ordure. She slammed herself into the bedroom, Lady Charlotte, and—Lizzie whimpered? let Lizzie whimper—was next seen in kimono, stamping to her showerbath.

"Hey Mommy," I took her by the arm, "you used up your hellos at Hotel Oceanside? Your child is speaking to you."

"That's right, Greatheart," she pulled loose, "go right on spoiling them."

I shushed the baby, I joked with her—Miss Button, Princess of the Bellybutton Club, my darling, my Liz. But even much later, when she was laughing, swinging up-we-go in the playground with Pop pushing, from nowhere a sob escaped, and she looked surprised.

Surprised.

Or else, say Sister Sue decided two kids in the family were one kid too many.

Charlotte and Susan, now they're buddies, the Grandview man-eaters. But in the good old days it was Walloping Charlotte and Susan the Rug, with the pot neighbors and their grub lapping it up from the sidelines.

"What are you?" Slam, bang. "You vicious thing!" Biff,

slam. "A child or an animal?" Bang. And Sue howling on the sidewalk, while Referee Moe rushed from the men to break it up. Then the mother, with the face white never red, as if a different kind of blood flowed in those veins, heading back to the mothers, with a leftover bark for the baby in the carriage Liz.

Now listen to this. Sue would jump up: click—like the noise was shut off with a button. And she'd smile. And the women became alert: the fun was over. Because Little Sue, the Joe Louis of her weight and age, was picking the next victim.

Shrewd little Sue, she was in no hurry. She'd wait till the guard was down, and the women were gabbing again, and the kids forgot. Then she'd start playing with one of 'em, she'd edge the sucker away. Not far, just a hard run from Mama. And bam—the shrieks, and you'd see Susan digging in, with the bright smile on her face, with the nails, with the fingers in the hair. Boys, girls: she took on all sexes, but from that day to this her infighting always was female.

So one nice hot Sunday I'll never forget, and not because that was the day the Nazis decided to wipe up the Reds, I stepped out of the building, and what I saw with my own eyes I could hardly believe.

First I thought they were dancing, Charlotte and Susan, in front of the usual audience. Yank, wallop, drag—like a dance. Then I saw some kind of stain on the child's dress, only it wasn't a stain, it was a thigh like a slab of butcher's meat, with the dress and the underpants ripped to shreds there from the sidewalk. I ran to Charlotte, I yelled was she out of her mind? And she gaped, with the burning eyes in the white face. The knuckles were white, with a grip on the child's arm like they were welded together. And never let go, my helpmate, till I pressed a thumb down against the vein of her wrist. Then *she* squirmed a little, and hissed, "Don't you have any shame for the neighbors?"

Now could Hitler have twisted words any better than that? But she let go.

Susan hustled up Grandview Place, the pretty little girl with the long legs and the black curls. So who had the last laugh but Charlotte.

"Go catch her, Greatheart."

Myself, I did stage a good show for the neighbors then, I got to admit. In buildings, out of alleys, in gutters, around cars. An auto screeched—I stood petrified—and just missed her. "Come to Pop, come Sue—" But when I stood she stood, with that little curl of the lip just like Mother's.

I finally hustled her back under my arm, like the animal Mother always called her: kicking, snarling, the whole works.

Upstairs I set her down and the screaming was turned off. I said to the mother, "You shouldn't have children. I'm talking to a lawyer about you."

"Talk," she told me, "who cares? Talk is cheap."

The rage in my heart and hands I pushed down, and I told the child—the mother was already lounging on the couch with her magazine—"Come Susie, we'll wash, we'll get out of those clothes."

Susie stood there.

But be a good father. "Come Susie—" I smiled, I stretched out my hand.

She ducked, Susan, with the glitter in the eye and the tight little cheeks that were as good as a yell Heyyy Stupid.

"I want Mommy to."

So the other's cheeks curled up like a twin—not that she budged to help Susan.

And that was just warmup time.

The same night, what made me look in the bedroom? A sound, a feeling? Too much quiet in Gehenna maybe?

On the bed being smothered under a pillow was the baby with her legs kicking; and leaning across the pillow—Susan.

To that moment I never laid a hand on that child, but then I laid a hand. I gave her a fling that only the wall stopped her. She took the count, but alert, watching, while I picked up the baby, poor red screaming Liz. And when she made her move, Susan Kid Speed, I grabbed 'er. "You know what dead is? Try that again and I'll beat the life out of you." And Susan? She grinned.

And the mother, when I sputtered out what happened? A wave of the hand.

"Nobody was smothering anybody. The fulltime father."

The next day Gross blew ten bucks on a lawyer. Like fifty today, yet mention divorce to my Lady and she says talk is cheap. What did the Clarence Darrow contribute? What I knew.

Is the wife willing to separate, let alone divorce? And if so, since the object is protection of the children, will she let them go? No judge, even in Reno, will take kids away from their mother merely because the father disagrees with her kind of spanking. That's incompatibility, not unfitness.

"Of course," he had to toss me something for my sawbuck, "if you could catch her *in flagrante delicto*——"

"Counselor, could you catch your briefcase there *in flagrante delicto*?"

So the counselor laughed.

A good joke.

Even then the canny Gross didn't say die. I told Charlotte that night, "Why should you be unhappy, tied down like this? Different people like to lead different lives. You've tried, you've done your best, no one could blame you." Tried. She should have lived so long like she tried, and Gross would have been a widower early. "So let's call it quits," was what I led up to, "I'll take the kids, you'll be free. You'll meet someone better than me, someone suitable—" Jack who was I kidding?

To plug twenty-nine years for the title *Mrs.* and then toss it away? She yawned in my face . . .

Meanwhile, now, I was zooming through Amin's front room, where her boy used to live before he ran into his fatal day at the altar. Across the street the houses looked gray, and rain splashed on the sidewalks, blue Monday for real.

"So," over my shoulder I told the tenant, "as the Talmud says, if a marriage is made in Heaven, it takes two to make a divorce. And that's how my marital ties stood, and that's how my marital ties stand."

And do my 20-20's deceive me, or is it a reflection from the weather outside, the wet in those eyes?

She said, "My God, what you've been through. And you're still with her?"

Aha, then that is the question!

"Not exactly with, not exactly without. And by now," let's see how she handles this one, "what's the difference?"

The plastering was done, Gross was ready to paint. I wiped the hands on the overalls and turned to look that answer straight in the face. And instead of the *Plenty of difference* I expected to hear, meaning Gross free is small game for somebody else, the Widow Amin for instance, while Gross attached is an entirely new question, I heard, "That's true." Absent-mindedly she said it. And again, shaking her head, "Treating children that way, my God!"

Then what, could it be Gross has run into one with a heart and no angles, the exception that proves the Folks, the first one since Mama she should rest in peace, and my Papa and Liz, that a person can talk to without posting sentries?

That same night I had my dream of the country, only this time there she was, Ruth Amin, like real life, on the little white porch. "What are you doing here?" I asked her. She laughed. "Why I live here. This is my house." Me, I was flabbergasted.

And woke up so happy!

Only, after watching Gross Monday all day to verify Gross ain't the pilfering type, on Tuesday why not leave Shmo Moe in your apartment alone, go down to business, and make some use of the day? That's just what she did, Lady Amin. And Gross, never too old to be fooled, you thought you found that paragon, that listens without angles and gives sympathy?

Ha ha!

By the time she strolled in with her bundles, with the May afternoon sun creeping back towards the windows, her paint job was done. She put a pot on the stove from the icebox and took a look around.

"You've made my house so bright!"

"Wasn't that what you wanted, twenty bucks extra a room?"

She laughed. "What I want, and what I usually get—" And she counted me out my eighty and good-by and good luck.

So Gross stuck the shoulder in under the ladder. "Well see you in three years lady, God, Washington D.C., and Moscow willing."

Or is Gross squirrel food, the way she looked at me what was I talking about?

"Three years? Supper's on the stove. Unless"—she gave me a shrug, but Gross knows those shrugs: to get your cold shoulder in first, before you're cold-shouldered—"you happen to be eating somewhere else—"

"My God, where else? In the cafeteria again?"

So I ran downstairs to stick the stuff in the cellar and change clothes. And while I was running, I ran to Jerome Avenue for a bottle of vino, I shouldn't come empty-handed.

"Wine?" she smiled. "I'll be drunk."

"What else is wine for?" Then I said, "You were busy in the office today?"

"That's why I went down, to make up the payroll."

So I sat down to her meal: that crisp-looking roast, and pan-browned potatoes that tickled your tongue just to look at 'em, and a table all colors with tomatoes and cucumber and lettuce and butter and a basket of bread. Then I put the meat in my mouth, and I couldn't believe it.

"What's this?"

She laughed, she was enjoying the vino I brought. "Not poison, I hope."

"It's my mother's exact pot roast!"

"Well that's a good start."

"Marvelous, the best I've tasted since Mama, she should rest in peace these thirty long years."

And could I help talking about Mama, that Mama always for Moe, with no strings attached, not even apron strings?

Ruth gave me a smile, "My apron's in the closet," with more vino.

"Yeh?" I grinned, then I got it: she'd changed her clothes too. "Then take care, that's a nice dress you got on."

So I told about Sadie, the love of my life, with Concord, and Cousin Joe, and the midnight ride of Paul Revere.

"Dopey Sadie," Ruth said.

"And dopier Moe. But appearances can be deceiving, and Gross was green, with pink cheeks. But you know what Mama said when the engaged man or should I say boy broke the news no more Sadie? Mama said, 'Yes Sadie no Sadie, I'll be bouncing your baby boys on my knee just the same, Morris.' Morris, she always called me, by my full name: Morris."

And look—what have we here? A hand on my hand, with her leaning towards me, smiling like sugar, right in my face.

"Who could blame her, Morris?"

So, a surprise, and Gross couldn't say pleasant. That forward, from this woman? Go figure.

Yeh, I chewed and where was the taste, appearances are deceiving. Four long months that Amin is defunct, and Gross happens to be handy? So let's have some Gross.

Quite a letdown, hah Gross, from your paragon?

So Gross said, "In my parents' time there was self-respect, and deportment. Not now. Why is that?"

"Was it so different then?" She leaned back, she smiled, she shrugged. "I suppose that it was. I suppose people feel that if you're going to be blown up any day, there isn't the time."

"You feel that way, hah, there isn't the time?"

"I'm usually scared stiff. But," with more sweet-eye, "not now."

Sure not now. Now you got other things on your mind, if I should place them that high. But let it pass, Gross, let's finish up without insults.

So we finished up, but then she stood with both hands on the back of her chair and that smile of hers down at me, or would you call it a leer? So me too, I stood, and started grabbing the dishes, to fill up the time before a quick exit, she shouldn't be able to say he ate then he ran, and he left me a sinkful.

And her? That grin, with the heat in the cheeks, in the eyes. And again the grab by the hand.

"The dishes won't run. Come inside, Morris—"

Again Morris? Okay Krupnick or Pupnick or Shtupnik, whatever your name is, Gross'll give you a Morris!

Gross took 'er to the hall, Gross made 'er a bow, Gross pointed the way to the bedroom. And Lady Innocence? She stood there and stared at me.

Gross sang out, "Come one, come all, amusement area next stop—tomorrow may be fast day again!"

Still she stared, so once more Gross bowed and Gross pointed. Then she went to the closet.

"Here's your hat, what's your hurry."

So I tipped it, and went.

And the hell with you too, Madam Bedstarved!

AND AFTER STAMPING ALL THE WAY HOME, just at Grandview, in front of my house, wouldn't I remember that I left the car parked back there in front of her house? So i fixed everybody and everything—I climbed upstairs and slammed the door hard.

And—"Excuse me," I had to mumble—there was Susan, looking up with entertained eyes from her nail polish to give Father the needles.

"Tough hunting?" she said.

"Speak for yourself, Sue. I found a parking space."

And look at that beauty, the long neck, the white even teeth, and go write on the blackboard one hundred times Morris: Seeing isn't believing.

Gross took his shower, he said good-night to his daughter, he shut his bedroom door and his light, and he stretched out to study the darkness. Now, once I said the word *shit* in the hearing of the young lady inside, and, assuming I'd meant her which in that instance I hadn't, and being a psychologist, she made a neat comment.

She said, "Where it's everywhere shit, there must be a taste for brown."

But what if brown ain't your color and the message is still

shit? Are you to blame then? Now tonight, were there hints, before Amin made her first move? And in my earlier career, did Sadie give hints? Or else maybe I sent for Nitzberger? Or for Charlotte? No Gross, maybe you been fooling yourself your whole life. Maybe you went out after 'em, your long string of man-eating tigers?

So let's see, first Heloise came. But wasn't she from your kid sister Sylvie the matchmaker, salving big brother's bruises from Sadie, and making a match? She was. And remember, green as you were, you thought Sylvie meant well too, with your interests at heart, not just making a match? Like the very day, in front of my eyes, I still see her, Heloise, and at first sight a broad better named than Heloise Nitzberger could you ever lay eyes on? That blubbery lip looked like hell. Nits are things that dig into you. And what's a berger? Warmed-over meat you get in a roll. And the blonde, the build, the sexy voice: what did it add up to, Gross? Remember, didn't it all add up to fifth-rate pelt?

But after all, a friend of your sister's. And remember the glad to meet me, how glad it was, straight in the face?

Right away, the second or third date, we were sitting in my chariot the end of the night, she told you did you know what your sister told her. Sylvia'd told her, "Heloise, I want you to come over and meet my brother. He needs a good wife."

Yet remember how your prick told you, it's a good something, but the word isn't wife? Then you sparred with a two-handed maneuver?

"Maybe I can convince you to stay single."

Heloise blocked that pass, and she told you that fortunate as she was in many respects—her good friends, her wonderful parents, since high school she'd never been out of a job—the truth was she was fed up with her kind of life. Every day pushed and insulted in the subway. Only her friends' babies to play with. And her place of business—three stories of furniture: wholesale-retail—her boss was nice, Monsieur Limber with a cute foreign accent, but the job, every day ringing up home sweet home for somebody else. She wanted a home sweet home of her own, a man she could love and trust, and her own babies to play with.

Just what the doctor ordered—didn't she sound like it?

Only just then she looked wistful, and out came that lip. So—"What's the rush, a kid like you"—Gross moved in tight for some body work.

Again she backpedaled, but with a laugh. Frank, friendly, open-faced. "A kid like me, I'm not such a kid any more."

Was Gross made of flint?

"Kiddo," I said, "I respect your viewpoint."

"I knew you would, from all Sylvia told me. That's why I wanted to meet you."

Would you believe, this brought mist to my eyes. I gave her a kiss like a brother.

At home I said, "Mama, what about Heloise?"

Mama laughed. "You must be her type. She's already asked me for recipes."

And not bad enough once, but history has to repeat itself and now Amin also with the recipes? And look, how just the thought of this last one gives Gross the shivers. Did Gross send for Amin? The same way Gross sent for Nitzberger!

And to meet Charlotte, all Gross had to do was arrange the 1930s Depression—with a little help from our Leader it's true. Sure, prosperity was just around the corner, and who could pay the rent? The tenants sold apples, the landlords turned honest and went back to work, and the banks took over the apartment houses. And what banker would deal with a Gross, in business for himself in the land of individual enterprise, just because Gross was cheaper and tops at his trade? You think they were out of their mind?

So Boss Gross laid off Painter Gross, and Gross went

painting for Super Paint Inc. And from the jolly little housewives (some did, some didn't), remember the difference in the offices downtown and the jolly little stenos (some didn't, some did)? You winked at 'em from the ladder, like always. Except one queen that wasn't so jolly, with black burning eyes, her you didn't wink at.

Why, to that one, did my heart open up right away? Yeh yeh, Charlotte always had looks, but it wasn't the looks: it was that look of unhappiness that got me, shmuck Gross.

You saw her discontent over those books, not to mention that narrow office where she sat hemmed in with the others, or the smell leaking through from the toilet door at one end and the printing presses murdering your eardrums from the other. For scenery she had an airshaft wall. Then there was that bookkeeper in charge with the thin hair, the steel face, and the desk full of papers—that seeing-eye dog!

Yeh, Gross knew those dogs, I met 'em head on, six long months as junior accountant back in the twenties, with the four walls and the gray faces watching while you dirty paper with tickmarks. And do it not just their way if you'd like some of their lip. Gross, he did it their way, because some of their lip to Gross would have been Gross's fist in the lip to them—and jail, who needs it? So I said toodle-oo to the punks, and how you been to my brushes and paints. Papa was disappointed at the time, he thought office work was a step up the ladder. But me, give me my stepladder any old time. Punks!

So it was easy to sympathize with the young lady.

"Dry, huh, those ledgers?"

Not even a glance. "What isn't?"

"Wet paint."

"Very funny," said Miss Morose.

"No jokes," I told her, "paint is good, not like them numbers. It has substance."

"Mr. Rembrandt," she gave a mutter.

"You seen that movie too?" I cracked good and sore. And then Gross added a neat twist of the blade. "I make no claims kiddo, I only like my work."

And as far as Gross was concerned, that was that.

Then she said, "I hate mine."

Good and loud she said it, and the man in charge shot her a dagger. Nose in your columns sweetheart! Charlotte's return dagger, she couldn't shoot it back in those good old days, not unless her aim was so-long to the job. She had to keep her dagger white-hot inside, and point it at the books.

"Cheer up," I told her, "some day your prince will come."

She let loose a cackle. "He'd better make it soon!"

Such desperation—pain has its charm, eh?—that again my heart melted to her, this damsel in distress. And Pink-Cheeks Gross, young innocence, I thought she meant me.

And did she set Gross straight?

Gross said, "How about Saturday night?"

Did Charlotte say No? To the contrary.

"Not that I mind work," Charlotte assured me the first time out, to make a good impression after the bad start in her office, "if it only would lead to something—"

"But kiddo," dumb Gross wanted to know, "if you don't like the work for itself, what can it lead to?"

Then the dam broke and flooded gold over the countryside. Limousines, town houses, country estates, like her rich sister Tillie.

Sure, now I can say that's where Gross should have tipped the hat and bowed out, like tonight. But back then I figured if wishes were horses then beggars would be kings, and you can't stop a girl from dreaming. Who didn't have dreams? Gross the loyal member of the Democratic Club dreamed then too, of municipal graft and fat cigars. And meanwhile did Charlotte refuse when you blew 'er to night clubs with her refined way of talking and her elegant build, shows, first-run movies, all on due bills, cut-rate big shot, that I got off my pals in the Club? King Gross, on the side I'd slip the headwaiter the discount ticket, and remember Miss Charlotte's big eyes to see Gross tip big?

But didn't Gross fence 'er? Wasn't Gross sharp right up to the gallows?

A few such dates and already Gross found himself subject to audit.

"I thought," said the subtle Charlotte, "painters are supposed to be poor."

So, "Some are," I'd wink at 'er, "some ain't."

"But is there a future in the painting business?"

"And what if there isn't?"

"No, Moe, is there?"

But Gross never told 'er his hopes, even when we were chummy already, when she let me kiss 'er good-night, Miss Freeze. Not that Gross looked for more from a bridal prospect. For more Gross had elsewhere. But first, future no future, show you're all out for Gross. *Then* Mrs. Gross.

Or else good-by and bad luck.

So next time she cooed in the restaurant, "Are you sure you can afford this expense, Moe?"—and was it impossible she meant it?—Gross explained about due bills.

She took it well. She said, "Why not, if you can get them. Why throw money away?"

"And who has money to throw?"

She laughed.

I laughed along with her, but I said, "It's only the truth. Here," I took out the bankbook, "read it yourself."

She read it—balance three dollars even, at the bottom of the Depression then—and if that rocky soul held water she would have wept. As it was she still smiled, like a corpse after worm treatment. But who knew? Not Slow-Learner Gross. I gave her a buzz at the end of the week, will you ever forget what she said?

She said, "What's the use?"

So did Gross beg and say please?

"The use?" didn't I say? "Search me," I said, "I'm short on philosophy. But come Rosh Hashonah I'll ask the rabbi, and as soon as he tells me I'll tell you."

And you dog you should live so long.

But who did God take? Not Charlotte. My Mama was the one He took. She had her attack—that dear, that funny woman, so rosy, so strapping—and a few days later she died. Papa and I stood there, next to her bed in the hospital, with my sisters in the hall crying.

"Mama," I begged her, "you must fight."

And Papa said, "You hear what our son says, Gussie? You must listen to him, Gussie, listen—"

Oh, there was a fighter, that listened, that made herself smile, that fought. The pain, it was like elephants trampling. The specialist said that, the biggest heart man in The Bronx. The life was dragged out of her, but she never quit, my Mama, never!

So was it a wonder, that I sat there stunned, in slippers, on boxes, weak as a baby the seven days' mourning with my father and my sisters, that I had to go lock myself in the toilet to bawl? What mattered then? Nothing mattered. Kind visitors stuck the papers in my hand to distract me, so I stared at the nausea of the day, Hitler and his Jewish laws, and what did it matter? And the great Roosevelt recovery I read about, only Moe Gross couldn't recover a business he ran from his hat, that didn't matter either. Death is a cure, hah? You sit alone in a desert, empty. So what could happen now, what could be worse?

So Heloise came, and brought comfort. Gross pulled a long

face, look long, it was okay by her. "Your mother meant a great deal to you, I know. It has to hurt." How many mothers does a person have? She tallied 'em for me: one each. Who can replace 'em when they're gone? She told me: nobody. A wife, yes. Even a child. But a mother, no.

Comfort? More than comfort. Because remember how you told her—you held nothing back—what a Mama that was, from your earliest childhood, like that winter in Essex Street, and how poor we were in those days, in a railroad flat that the wind whistled through, dark damp rooms, and Mama caught pneumonia? And that terrible week they wouldn't let me in to see Mama, and I hung on to my older sister, Maxine, like glue? Then Mama, you started getting better and Morris wanted to help, so you let me go to the grocery. How old was I then? Five, six years old. So, on the way back from the corner, making sure not to step on the sidewalk cracks, a short fella, a long trip—and boy did I trip! With the sugar all over the ground, and a dime change that dropped out of my fist, that was gone too. Papa was sore when I told them, with his face working, and right away my face started to work. But before the tears could get going, Mama, that Mama, she gathered me up and she said, "You brought home my sugar."

I was so surprised that I forgot about crying. I looked around at the torn bag on the table with the quarter of a pound of butter and the can of milk, and I asked Mama, "Where?"

"Here," she told me, "Master Foolishness, in my arms." And kissed me yet!

And remember then, after you told this to Heloise, how Heloise shone with wet eyes—and you're not off your nut yet Gross, that's exactly what happened!—and Heloise said, "Such love, such love Moe!"

So what could this mean, except that she felt, she understood?

And my sister Maxine and her doubts, did she push them?

Three days of mourning and three days of Heloise, and Maxine said to Sylvia, "That friend of yours must be a desperate case, conducting her courtship at a time like this."

Sylvia, she stood up for her match.

"Don't be jealous. What could be more natural than sympathy, at a time like this."

Maxine laughed, she hung her arm on my shoulders.

"Jealous, of this guy? I just don't want him monkeyed with."

Those days we were something, weren't we, me and Maxine? Nowadays of course it's like everything else. From Maxine in Denver airmail complaints. Papa the expense, Papa's ailments, she hasn't the strength, etcetera etcetera. Of Papa the graduate babysitter, the automatic dishwasher Papa all those years what do we hear? Zero, we hear. And Moe chipping in, with cost-of-living increases, any mention of that? Then I need Sylvia rushing to me, bitter, put out, with similar messages from Maxine? Poor Sylvia, her Phil died on her, a nice fella, and she's a widow with two young daughters she's sending through college and don't I have to admit that life is against her? I admit it, and for the sake of my health I don't ask who ain't life against. And what have I heard from my letter to Maxine last week that a man ninety years old just might not be a perfect specimen of health, and in any case find plane fare enclosed, send me Papa?

Yeh. More zero, that's what I've heard.

But back to the old days. Heloise wanted a husband. Was it an insult, that she decided to pick me? Finally I stopped looking so sick, unusual, from Mama's death; and Sylvie said, "Heloise is good for you, Moe." Yeh? Maybe. Only, you sorrow and you sorrow, and one day you wake up and an hour later you remember that you forgot. Still, Mama was gone, Papa was with Maxine, and what did I have to come home to? The furniture and my heart palpitations?

In the jalopy one night, outside her building before I took Heloise upstairs, you know, a kiss leads to a squeeze and a squeeze to a hold and so forth and so on. And the way she kissed back, the way that she gasped—I remember it to this day—it should have made a man think, shouldn't it? And Gross thought, didn't he?

Except all of a sudden she sagged in my arms.

"Moe," she gave me a gasp, "I want to give in but I can't, I wasn't brought up that way—"

Gross wanted virtue. Was he wrong to settle for virtue personified?

And with a little help from her mother she was a home girl too.

Yeh, she had a mother, a scared little woman that said Hello and hid in another room. But before the disappearance Mother took care of the props. She prepared the meals, all but the warmup; and also the knitting most likely. So Gross would ring the bell, and there would be the fair Heloise, all dolled up with one hand on the flanken of beef and the other on a sweater in process for Moe.

And was Moe that stupid? Moe wasn't that stupid. Two showings of this skit and I laughed out loud. So Heloise wanted to be let in on the joke.

"What joke? Such beauty and such talent, they bring joy to the eye and water to the mouth."

Heloise joined the laugh. "I'll learn," she promised me.

And the costume the next blowout included an apron, so I figured she's learning.

Look, let's be fair to her too after all these years. She wasn't a whore exactly, she— But hold it. A woman marries strictly for money, little as it is, and to be called Mrs., what is she? A whore, right? So what did this one do after the mishap with Gross? She married for money, little as it was, Sloppy Sammy, of the two Sammys that ran the corner cigar store. And while

Sammy ran the store, Heloise ran. And she had a baby—
Sammy's, somebody else's, who knew?—and she hired a
babysitter and ran. And one day the baby was sick, with a
terrible fever—and still she ran. She came back that night, and
no babysitter, no baby, nobody. The baby was in the hospital,
where Sammy'd brought him. Thank God the baby recovered
that time—yeh, Sylvia heard—he recovered, poor little boy,
God help him, wherever he is now.

So okay I'll be fair. Nitzie you were a whore. And if Gross
loves shit so, how come Sammy wound up with it? Luck? Your
good luck his bad? Then how about when you first ran into
her? Your bad luck his good!

Remember her rings and her bracelets and her silver fox
stole? Before, in winter, there was the Persian lamb coat. And
you asked. You didn't really think of shenanigans, and you
made it a joke—but you asked!

"Where'd you get 'em, Heloise? Where do you come to
such soft living in such hard times?"

But did Heloise flinch? Couldn't Heloise answer that, after
all, with her daddy's good living twenty years a printing
foreman and with her own nice little twenty-five-a-week
bundle, now and then she could stand the working girl to a
treat? And Heloise answered.

No, you weren't dumb, Gross, except to be trustful.

And then, smiling through, Miss Pathos: "Just to brighten
up life, Moe, when life isn't too bright—"

"Okay," I conceded, "but suppose—far-fetched—God or-
dained you should be stuck for life with a paintner, with a
dollar seventy-three liquid assets. How could he help you to
brighten up life?"

So Heloise laughed, and always when she laughed, deep
from the throat, downstairs told you it was beddy-by time. But
excitement over your wife is a drawback?

Drawback, draw forward, remember what a beautiful spring

night that was, with us parked on Riverside Drive, and down below was the river, shiny and black, and overhead the trees, and the air soft? And how she laid her hand on my arm, the High Voltage Queen, and she answered me, "By being just what he is, funny Moe."

So why not Mrs. Heloise Gross? She was sympathetic, she was attractive. The bust, the body, the swing of the hips: take her visiting and the family men gaped at her popeyed.

So with Heloise on the arm, you strutted into the jeweler's —wholesale, but that was all right with her—for the engagement paraphernalia, the ring, and the watch. She showed them and me off to her boss, Papa Limber, continental but nice. Fatherly, he was. With one arm on Heloise and the other on the cash register, he wished me well.

"Young man, your gain eez my verree bad loss."

Heloise sang out, "Isn't my boss a darling?" and I had to agree he was okay. He also presented her with a beautiful lamp.

Yeh, and I showed off Heloise to my clients, I was so proud! Five and a half days a week I was a Super Paint Inc. employee. My own private jobs I squeezed in on the weekends. So there was that Saturday afternoon on Fordham Road our Great Gray Way of The Bronx, on the way to dinner with the betrothed, and I took 'er up one short flight next door to the restaurant to kill two birds with one stone with Edmund Shannon and Son, Private Investigation, Divorce Our Specialty. That was 1935, with Shannon Senior, with the bull shoulders, the red face, and the bottle in the desk. Now I don't know if Shannon's is there. That was the last year I painted the place. So I showed off Heloise to Shannon, and I set him a Sunday for the paint job.

That day two weeks later, instead of taking off like always to wherever he went till the bars and grills opened, remember

Shannon hanging around with sad eyes and with grooves in the forehead?

How did I feel it, how did I feel what he was going to say? Even before he got started my legs were like water.

"You still with that blonde girl, Moe?"

Introduced him to my fiancée two weeks before, and was I still with that blonde girl.

But heart on the sleeve is a tidbit for vultures. "You know me Ed," I cracked, *"semper fidelis."*

"That's fine," he gave a laugh, "for the Marines, but—though, of course, it's none of my business—"

Yeh yeh, yeh yeh. And he knew how to enjoy my shame, with that light in his eyes dancing.

Monday on some case who did he spot but Gross's betrothed, yeh, and Monsieur de la Balloon-Head with the beret. Old enough to be her old man, Shannon said, but footsie over drinks with your old man at 6:00 P.M. in a Pelham Bay gin-mill?

Shit-seeker Gross, you set up that date for those two?

You know what Shannon expected: pallor, trembling. What? Help! It's a lie—gimme proof! Then right away he's my private eye, with a free paint job and maybe a few bucks extra thrown in. But not from Moe Gross you didn't, Shannon my boy.

"Down whose throat you say those drinks went Ed?" I made myself grin in his face. "Monday me and Heloise had supper at my sister's. You would have liked the pot roast, but no liquor was served."

"Moe, it's my pleasure to be wrong."

But when Irish eyes are smiling, it was his pleasure to be right.

And I had to smile too, until thank God he left and I could put back my teeth. Because what was there to smile, unless you like brown? Mondays and Thursdays we had off from the courtship, me and Heloise, by her suggestion. Though, be truthful, I didn't mind. Courtship or no courtship, it was a rest. So Gross rested, and Nitzberger nitzberged? Not to mention catch-as-catch-can maybe, breaking in upper loft mattresses in the Limber furniture house?

Sure I knew him, I knew who it was, the minute Shannon said. Her boss.

So I stood staring in Shannon's, like a man under death sentence. That's how much I liked brown. There was Fordham Road, curving downhill in the sunshine, I'll never forget it, Sunday morning, empty, like Gross. Then didn't I think she must still be asleep, with her sweet Limber dreams? So why not hop in the car, just like this, with the plaster knife in the back pocket, and ten minutes I'm there, in Pelham Parkway, in her house? She chopped me up, I'll chop her up!

And to think I really did go downstairs, yeh, I was in the car already, before I said Gross, what are you doing?

What was I doing, except making fun for Shannon?

About face, upstairs, and I started work on his loft.

Still it's true, give Gross time, he cools off. That night, when the loft was finished, I drove to Heloise in my blue serge suit and no knives. Because what did Shannon see? He saw Heloise, in her own neighborhood, having a drink with her boss. So on his way home Mr. Limber gave her a lift. And, she was quitting in a week to be married, he says Let's stop off Heloise, I'll buy you a drink. They reminisce, they laugh— after all, the girl is in the man's place eight years.

For this we commit murder?

In fact, truthful Gross, after the capon dinner the mother was still fussing with when I came in but, okay, Heloise wanted me to believe—innocent vanity—it was by her, I sat back on the couch with my cigar, and out of shame for that evil mind of mine that could so much as have given a second thought to friend Shannon's filth, with a laugh I told her the story. But of course only what Shannon said, not what I'd said. Because I was also ashamed of what I'd said.

You were ashamed, Gross.

And how about when she said, "How could he lie like that?," and said this with such sincerity, such indignation!

How could he lie like that?

And how could she lie like that?

No sleep for Gross that night, just like tonight, though tonight don't ask me why, for a nothing whose life I happened to save two or three days ago that gives me the shivers now. Back then, scene by scene, beginning with Act One, I reviewed Heloise's lies. The laughing lies, the loving-sounding lies, the indignant lies.

To be their fool always hurts most.

So find out for sure, you said to yourself. And then revenge. Revenge, Mr. Brownlicker? Yeh, revenge.

But supposing there were no lies? Supposing what Shannon said I should have kept to myself? Supposing Shannon made a mistake? Mistaken identity: hasn't it been heard of in courts of law? Or else, suppose she was there. Maybe she was surprised, embarrassed, to hear I knew. After all, with the boss in a bar, and it meant nothing so she'd said nothing?

But then couldn't she tell me that?

Or maybe she told one lie, out of embarrassment, one little white lie.

On the job the next morning the foreman said, "What's the matter Moe, aren't you feeling so good?"

"Yeh," I told him, "give me a minute," because I couldn't stand it no longer.

I ran downstairs and I phoned her.

No sooner did the word Shannon leave my lips but she said,

"He couldn't have been lying deliberately Moe, no one would be that vicious. So he must have simply made a mistake. But what a mistake!"

What happiness, what relief! I went back up in the best of health.

Only, that kind of happiness, it goes down like the sun. The shadows got thick in the offices we were painting, and me, I was full of shadows inside too. Five P.M. I sat in my jalopy sick again, spying on them, up the block from Limber's.

Heloise stepped out alone, right into the crowds, straight down into the hole.

Oh, thank God, thank God! I laughed and I sang, and I cursed Shannon. Tears of happiness danced in my eyes. And did I give it to myself good: Listen Gross—no more of this sickness, understand? And because I love brown I forced the doubt, the suspicion, out of my mind, definitely, finally, and I sat there in the car until I was calm.

Exit Limber, into his car—and good luck to him, what was he to me? Limber zoomed off in his Packard, Gross rattled along in his Ford, and I forgot all about him.

Then, a few subway entrances uptown, and Gross nearly crashed into the auto in front.

Her, hurrying into his car there, parked at the curb waiting.

So up in the Bronx meadows—you know, where the insurance projects block off the sky now, the prison yards with the picture windows from top to bottom? And what do the inmates see, those good Bronx citizens? Each other: That's why they look so sad.

In the meadows then, that's where the Packard stopped, at the side of the road, out in the open, brazen, not even under a tree. And the same mistake Shannon made the Monday before, Gross made the Monday after, only instead of a drink they went for their back seat tumble, my beloved and Limber. So gross Gross, he strolled over, no rush, and—what do you know?—at the crucial moment he politely knocked at the door and opened it up.

There was a picture: Varicose Limber and Wetlip Nitz. He turned and looked up at me, Monsieur Skinhead. Must have removed the beret before he got started, a born gent. So—Gross can be a gentleman too—I tipped my hat and calmly heaved him out of his pants, poor Limber, flipping like a fish, while he was also getting the heave-ho from the lady beneath. And as I strolled away with the pants over the shoulder, who chased after me but my fiancée.

And caught up too, and had the gall to grab at my arm, that shit that I have such a taste for.

"Oh Moe, I'm so lucky you saw us—he said he'd drive me home, and next, next he was trying to rape me!"

"Bravo!" I gave the little girl a big hand. "You should go great at the Palace."

So what does the bad guy do in the movie after the good guy shoots him and he's dead? He gets up and he dusts himself off and he goes to the commissary for a cup of coffee. But not Nitzie.

"Moe, what are you talking about?"

"The way you handled that line."

"Moe——"

So I said, "Dearie, I wouldn't screw you even with hees preeck."

And I gave the Limber pants one more heave, straight up, up in a tree, and from the Packard, where it was his turn to look sick, Monsieur Limber watched 'em sail. They caught on a good high branch too.

"And now," I told 'er, Miss Not-Brought-Up-That-Way, "there's a pair of pants to catch if you can."

"Oh, good riddance to bad rubbish," she said.

And what could I say but Amen?

So wasn't Charlotte enough, that I had to have Heloise

wished on me? And wasn't Heloise enough, that I had to have Charlotte in spades?

But Gross never forget, according to the prophet Psychological Sue, suffering's your dish. So maybe, Rosh Hashonah 1936, it was me that went after Charlotte again and sent her best wishes for a Happy and Prosperous New Year 5722? Or else was it Charlotte's greeting card that popped up in my mail box?

I picked my teeth with that card—remember?—I love to suffer so much, and I laughed. Then I threw it away. Because in all that clear message—she'd been around one more year, and next year she'd be thirty, in that office like arsenic, and, if I liked—what was in it for Gross?

So shouldn't that have been that?

But no, her phone call. Did I get the card?

"Yeh, I got the card."

Charlotte said, "I was thinking of you."

"What were you thinking? What's the use?"

"That's not nice, but you're right. I was awful." She started to cry right there on the phone. "I'm sorry, good-by Moe—"

And was Gross made of wood? She excited me too, with her tears.

"Wait a minute," I told her, "don't run—"

And funny, when we met, how that year, year and a half apart had made changes. We looked good to each other. Why? With the psychology department asleep in the livingroom, let Gross tell you why. We'd both had to happen to go and lose weight, that was why.

She still smiled and looked sad, but not so hard-driving, more . . . pensive, like a person that's suffered and learned. And me, I'd turned handsome in her eyes. Or so she told me, and when Gross laughed at that, she got sore, insisted I was playing myself down!

"With the same handsome three bucks, plus a fat ten cents interest," I lost no time testing her out.

"Money's not everything."

"Yeh? Tell Gross what else is there?"

She stuck her hand in my hand. "You know, Moe," she said.

One thing Moe knew was that my loyalty to the Democratic Club plus some peanut graft had matured just then to a small-sized contract to paint a small wing of the old County building. But that Gross kept under his hat.

I told her, "I know that a painter can just about make a living, that's all."

"Isn't that enough?"

"For me it's enough. How about for you?"

"Is this," she laughed, "a proposal, sir?"

"And what if it were?"

"Then two can live as cheaply as one, so they say."

So we kept company, but no due bills this time. Gross took her to the Saturday night local movie not the Paramount Times Square, and for snacks the Fordham Road Bickford's not the Broadway Trocadero. And handsome Charlotte, she never complained. Then, if we double-dated with my sister Sylvie the newlywed and her Phil—what a little doll Sylvia was in those days!—Gross saw two things. One: The gleam in Phil's eye was all for Moe's Charlotte! Two: Charlotte's sweet looks were only for Moe.

So one night over muffins at Bickford's, just us two, I said, "I've had some tough luck." And I told her about the Club and the contract. "Only now with Washington D.C. staging its Recession—thank God Depressions are outlawed—the City's canceled the contract, and at the Club I said how about a loan of my donation and they laughed in my face."

"Well," Charlotte said, "the muffins still are delicious."

"You mean that?"

She took another bite to prove it.

"You're sure?" I kept at her.

She shook her head sure.

What were you supposed to do, Gross, disembowel her and rummage inside for the truth? After the wedding march, and Susan was born, and Gross was hooked good, then Charlotte spoke.

"I have good news for you!"

My good news? Sister Tillie and brother-in-law Barrel Henry had just invaded the Adirondacks and captured the Royal Acres Hotel.

I said, "Mazeltov, should we send them a horseshoe bouquet?"

Charlotte said, "You don't understand. There's an opening for you! Tillie said so herself. You'll work your way up!"

"The way Mellush worked his way up?"

Remember Big Booby Mellush, that other poor relation, with a face a yard long, thin stooping shoulders and a hollow chest, that came to one of his Cousin Barrel Henry's palaces as front-desk man and for ten years took Henry's abuse? Yeh, then one day young Sheldon Schwarzman arrived with his Princeton diploma in hand—that meant four hard Jewish years when they didn't have Jews in the halls of Ivy—and his full-bloom sneer meant he was there to take over in the Promised Land. But with Henry his father robust hale and hearty: easy, boy. The first step—and to this day the last—was Mellush's job. But Mellush after all was a Schwarzman only one time removed. Could you go fire him like a stranger? No.

You shit on him till he quits.

"Goddam fool!" "Stupid bastard!" "Shmuck!"

Except patient Mellush, saving every nickel and in the splendor of his dreams a shit-dispensing magnate himself some day, you shit and he swallows.

Yeh, my father-in-law he should rest in peace used to tell

me, "It's a real shame, Moe, the way that that Mellush aggravates Henry. Why he makes him absolutely furious!"

"But what does Mellush actually do, Izzie? He trips Henry up in front of the guests? He plants him a hotfoot in the main lobby?"

"Now that I can't say—and there's another point about Mellush, the way he rumbles in that reasonable voice of his. Hard as you listen you can never get near enough to follow his side of the argument. But it stands to reason that he must be in the wrong, or why would Henry curse at him so?"

Oy Izzie, dear man, is God letting you play such tunes on your harp up in Heaven so He can smile too?

But even Izzie—for the final bout he managed to sneak himself a ringside location—had to admit he was shocked at the Mellush knockout: two against one!

A light left cross by Shelley the Sneer: "Hear you refused Mr. Lucksman the five-o-one suite."

And while he's sparring with Shelley—"But the guests in five-o-one have eleven days left of a three weeks' reservation, and Mr. Lucksman never even gave us a phone call. I did what I could, I put Mr. Lucksman in the identical"—Barrel Henry's finisher to the gut!

"Dumb prick! See Miss Hess for your pay and get out of my hotel."

The mouth gaped, the long face went white.

"I said get."

"But—"

"Get!"

So he got.

That was the gang Charlotte wanted to hang on dumb Gross. So when I brought up Mellush, she brought out flattery.

She said, "What comparison is there between you and Mellush? It's the chance of a lifetime, Moe!"

Her lifetime she meant: not as Mrs. Gross, but as wife of the Majordomo she hoped to Henry the Great, a Lady of the Palace, to consort with the rich, and no Bronx.

I said, "I'm sorry. That's a chance that I'll have to pass up."

"Think it over," she said, "you'll regret it."

And until the Royal Acres had its grand opening, Gross was force-fed her advice with each meal, between meals, and especially at lights out in bed. Then the Royal Acres did open up, with a different desk clerk than Gross, and you recall your wife's comment?

"You nothing," she told me, "you've always been a nothing, you're a nothing now, and you always will be a nothing!"

So Gross you were fooled, as sometimes happens in marriage. That meant you love brown?

My God, think of it—one after the other! And then this one, tonight . . .

Only how come it keeps jumping up in my mind, the faces and noises I made in her foyer there—and then I have shivers?

My own daughter, and she fakes the cheek for my kiss so my lips go pop in the expensive air. What do you think of that?

But the new Gross, Gross with the halo, tolerant Gross kind Gross Gross all smiles, you can't make him sore so easy. So I said, "Why be scared, Susie, we're related."

So Susan told me in the pleasantest tone in the world—after all, there, where she had to show off, at the grandfather-in-law's to be, old Axelrod's, with his dozen, his two dozen rooms, and downstairs the doorman and Park Avenue where to Susie's nose, God help her, even the automobile gas fumes smell better—"That's what I have in mind exactly, the relationship."

"Okay, I grant you. But can't things change for the better?"

And oy, poor beauty, wrapped up in that hate, what did she give me? The death grin, with the teeth and stretched cheeks. "That," she pronounced, "is my hope."

Clear as crystal—and she didn't mean me. The maid and the butler, the grand piano draped in a Spanish shawl so it shouldn't catch cold, the antique tables, and the up-to-date bar. That was her hope. Though of course—as she confided once to her mother—not in the taste of the late Mrs. Axelrod's interior decorator. And Susan hoped for such riches soon, very soon, from the Graveyard Stakes, maybe even next month as wedding gift number one at wedding number two. And look at her selection: Grandfather Axelrod. He looked like wax, a smoked and dried whitefish in a nice blue suit, as if the embalmers had been here already and done the job. Nurse Jolly was at his shoulder and Cousins Drool at his toes, and he sat, "Rodney's Clothing From Coast To Coast," with his little smile.

And like the laughing hyena that ate once a week, moved its bowels once a month, and had sexual intercourse once a year, why was he smiling?

A few Sundays back, in the Schwarzman mountains mansion when Tillie was still on this earth, Susan smiled to her mother, "What could that old man be smiling about, except that he's lasted through one more day?"

The other lady-in-waiting gritted her teeth in excitement then. "You'll be rich all right, you'll show them all!" Meaning she'd show 'em all, Tillie's volunteer slave and nursemaid Charlotte, hunched then under the gable in Schwarzman's attic for the indispensable poor, where you stooped in honor of wealth or hit your head on the ceiling.

"And Charlie?" Killjoy Gross butted in. "What'll she show Charlie?"

"Why don't you," said my daughter, "go away somewhere."

So Gross burned and Gross went, along the pine needles path to the hotel, a one-man rescue-squad for innocent Charles Davis.

Only there were those pines, so tall, so quiet, so dignified. And me? I should be part of the insect crawl underneath? So I filled up my lungs and my nostrils with God's blue air and warm sunshine. And far better. Later I ran into Charlie, on the veranda that hangs over the mountain, with the other mountains way off like purple mists on the ocean, and what were those poor magnified eyes of his full of, floating behind the thick lenses?

Sweet Sue.

Sweet-Suing old Axelrod that sat there in the wheelchair bundled up like a mummy in the hot sun, with his usual retinue. But Sue was the one straightening his lapels, smoothing down his blankets, and smiling closest into his smile. To me, dumb Gross, it was two sharks grinning, the old and the young, the full and the hungry, but the veteran killer was smiling to see fry the likes of Sue Gross hoping to fatten off him.

Charlie, leaning against the balustrade, admiring, when he saw me he smiled too. "Isn't she sweet, Moe?" With those dim eyes full of love, sweet fellow.

So kismet, what must be must be. Only I heard myself cracking, "But why do you let her waste her time over there?"

"Oh, my grandfather's dying, and she really likes him." Oy, Charlie. "Although why," he gave it a thought, "I must admit I can't understand."

"There might be a small downpour of gold?"

"From that tyrannical old man?"

"Not even," I suggested, "a drizzle?"

"Moe, my grandfather is a man of principal—and I mean cash. When my mother married poor, he told her, 'You want poor, then have poor. I will respect your wishes better than you respect mine.' So, Moe, from that direction the precipitation probability is zero."

"Then it looks like stormy weather for Susan, and for you, my boy, once Susan finds out."

"But Moe, I have no secrets from Susan—and my paycheck isn't that bad."

"Who said it was, Charles? But I'm afraid that from paychecks like yours don't come dreams like Susan's."

"Oh no, Susan's not at all like that, Moe, she's—"

And so forth and so on.

Yeh, it's true. She has sincere eyes, Susan Gross Meier.

I said, "She told you about her first husband, George Meier?"

"Poor fellow," poor Charlie said, "I can see how he couldn't resist her. And she was such a romantic kid—she still is—being proposed to by an older man, and a European at that . . ."

Oy, Charlie, oy oy oy oy oy!

But what does a man say, beyond what I said? Does he say Charles, my daughter is a ravening beast, run for your life?

George Meier was a runner—and fast. He ran away from Hitler and left an ocean between them. But Sweet Sue nailed 'im, and into his coffin.

Such a romantic kid!

"What's possessed you?" Yep, this was Charlotte speaking, five years ago. On George Meier with the sad eyes, the black mustache, the forty-two years, the wife, and the three children, my Unholy Two were not in agreement like on Charles Davis. "What's crept into that fine brain of yours? To want to throw yourself away on some dilapidated refugee?"

"Dr. Meier and I will do quite well, Mother."

"Doctor! That's no doctor, and he never will be!"

But he was, with the full M.D. that Susan was after by proxy, he was. Only not here, in Vienna. And here? Nothing here. Here he kept studying for the license exam, but study and study, George was never ready to take it. But one day he'd take it.

He'd take it—Susan would see to that. He'd take it, and he'd fail it. And once he failed it, and the sad eyes grew sadder, good-by George, you're too moody George, I'm not your mother George only your wife.

Susan told him that, towards the end of their quick little marriage. Right in my livingroom, I was there.

To the man that back in the rabbi's study, the newly wed

divorced man Susan promised to cherish till death did them part, had raved with damp eyes to me, "I'm so happy, Mr. Gross, so happy—like a person newborn!"

Gross so wise, know-it-all. But imagine yourself God forbid in the boots of poor Meier. First Hitler, and the Nazi thugs in Vienna to rip down your shingle. Then Hilda, the mother of your little brood, the born Frau Doktor Professor suddenly minus the title, with the former Doktor Professor a Laboratory Technician here in America, strapping down dogs for Certified Scientists. In the University cafeteria, with Meier sitting within earshot, one Professor said to the other Professor, "Do you have any techs in your department?" And the other Professor said, "No Czechs, but I do have one broken-down Viennese." Meier told me that story, as a joke. But to Hilda it was no joke. He'd struggle his way home in the subway, to Washington Heights, and she'd look at him doleful, glum, the dying swan with the sighs. So you're a good man, you love the two girls and the little boy, and there's even a tug in your heart for Hilda. But when the bright and shining psycholological student Susan strolls into the lab and shoots you a smile, what could it be but a brand new sun where gray was the everyday color to your dog's-eyes?

Six months after his second marriage black clouds again, worse than before. He came to my house to plead with Susan, to beg her to come back. One night he turned up, I was home by myself.

"She's out on a date?" George made me a smile sadder than tears.

Naturally you'll lie, you'll say she and her mother went shopping. But with the lie at the tip of my tongue, it was too much already, to see such pain for such nothing. So to get him to rage and storm, to curse her and hate her, I told him the truth, that he'd guessed it.

Some rage, some storm. He sat down with his spaniel eyes.

"Don't think harshly of her, Mr. Gross. You must remember, she's young."

I grabbed what hairs I have left, I yelled, I ranted. "Don't be stupid, forget 'er, study your English, be an M.D. again, crap on 'em all!"

He yawned, Meier.

"How can I forget her? Also, I miss my children."

And again he yawned.

And went home, and took pills, and stuck his head in a plastic bag. Three days later the neighbors complained of a smell. And quite a funeral: in the dead of winter, with frozen ruts in the ground, and the gravediggers standing with raw faces. And for final respects there were the rabbi, a professional mourner I rounded up for two dollars, and yours truly.

The two wives stayed away: number one too bitter, number two too sensitive. The day after though number two and my spouse really did go shopping together and they bought Susan a little outfit, very becoming, in black . . .

Now suppose, up in the mountains, I expounded all this to the new candidate for love. Would he have believed me, sweet Charlie Davis?

Better that I kept my mouth shut.

And besides, people change, couldn't Sue change, and couldn't the great Gross be wrong?

Oy could he be wrong, wrong on top of wrong! Shouldn't a man my age have known better than a horrible good-night like Tuesday with Ruth? By my dawn's early light of no sleep, even Gross had had to ask himself that. Here's a woman, the first time in your life, with a warm heart and some sense to go with it, a humorist too, that likes you. So Gross, dulled by a lifetime of bums, all you see is a bum? If your carcass was all that she wanted, would she have thrown you out of the house on account of a leer? Idiot, you leer at a Krupnick, Krupnick leers back!

There were the hands, no denying the hands. But she threw you out of the house! And I thought of her, what she actually looked like, with the thin nose that stuck out, but slim, nice, and my heart ached. What a shmuck. To have gone at her with fangs!

Sleep Gross, I said, try not to think of it. Don't think of it.

Who could sleep? So 7:00 A.M. Wednesday last beggar Gross stood at her door with a pail in my hand for camouflage, so if she gave me some sneer I deserved I could at least make believe the mission was business. Even so, three times I raised my hand to the button, before I found nerve to push it.

She opened, she gaped, and that trouble in her face—whatever it was, joy it was not.

"You!"

"Patchups, repairs maybe?"

"After last night?"

"Then at least an apology?"

She said, not happy at all, "Well, come in. But just for a minute. I have to get dressed. I go to work today."

She let me stand just inside her door, like a . . . like a paintner.

I said, "I know that I acted crazy, but it was crazy like a fox, that's been hunted, and caught, and skinned alive, and more than just once. You know, my on-the-job man-eaters."

"That's crazy all right," she let me have it. "What did I do to deserve that special sarcasm? Because I showed my feelings where I felt trust?"

What could Gross say? I blinked and I shrugged, I felt miserable. "I'm ashamed of myself," I did say.

Then she patted my hand. "Look, the end of the world may be near, but that wasn't it. Only," she gave a short laugh, "I've already had a lifetime of lunacy and sarcasm, and desperate I may be, but I couldn't take it again." And again that laugh. "Especially now that I've learned how to take pills."

"I feel worse," I said.

She said, "Put down that paint and sit down, we'll have coffee."

Gross went there ashamed? There unfolded a tale that taught Gross what real shame felt like.

She was born Ruth Rappaport, May 5, 1912, with a kid sister Sheila, and a nice father, oh Ruth'd loved her daddy, and a crazy mother. Crazy. But Daddy, Norman Rappaport, happy Norm, laughed and kidded Mother along, and in the great pre-Crash prosperity era, 1928, between clerking for the city by day and pushing shoes by night, a dollar here and the egg route there, he managed to keep them all going.

Then one Sunday night after supper, Daddy began making choking sounds and to Mother's put-out "What's the idea of that?" all he could do was tap at his chest.

Mother said, "Then go out of the room with your gas."

"Out of the room?" he had his last laugh. "You mean out of the world."

And that's where her daddy went. So where Daddy left off, Ruth picked up, hardly out of high school. She'd just begun a day job, but that wasn't enough. So she also typed envelopes a dollar a thousand at night. And she sent her sister, Sheila, through high school, someone had to do it. About this time, Mother got the idea her daughter Ruth was a prostitute, and she made that lamentation to the neighbors. Ruth started getting looks from the women in front of the house, so they moved, in those days it was easy.

Mother said, "You think you can shut me up. Well it won't work."

"It'll work," Ruth said. "You'll shut up, or you'll talk without me around."

"I always knew it," Mother said, "you want me to die."

And that part was true. Ruth had bad thoughts and looked pale. She'd just be falling asleep, and she'd see herself waking up in the morning, and instead of her mother muttering and puttering and cursing the pot that wouldn't make coffee right—sweet peace, heavenly silence! Then Ruth would see herself looking into the kitchen, the bathroom, and nobody there. Then, in the mother's room, the mother would be on her back with her eyes staring, dead.

So such thoughts gave Ruth a start, she'd wake up, and she'd lie awake hours feeling closed in like the night was her grave. She'd worry about sleeping, about the office, how tired she'd be the next day. She'd dream of happiness, it was her right as a citizen! And she'd really expected it one day.

In the meanwhile she was a girl with a plain face and a long nose, who the boys never looked at twice. Character? She asked me to tell her, do men look for character? Once in a while she did have a date and her mother's insane stare and dumb mouth were the reception committee to frighten them away. When Ruth got home, Mother would be waiting.

"Over my dead body you'll marry that one."

"Who's marrying?" Ruth would give a laugh of despair, "who asked anyone to marry?"

"Over my dead body."

And one boy—not such a bargain, just a date, that was all—called a few times. So Mother made a scene at the courtyard window.

"They're after me to kill me!"

"Nobody's after you, Mother, nobody's killing you."

"Then I'll take poison, I'll kill myself."

She never had to bother killing herself. God did it for her, slowly. "Ruth, why does my side hurt, why does my side keep hurting me so, Ruth? What kind of a doctor did you get me?"

Years of this—ten long years.

So dream of happiness, and what knocks on the door? Solomon the Wise Amin: he called himself that. But she—it was okay, he told her, he was democratic—she could call him

Sol. She wouldn't have called him at all, but the way she felt, anything, any change, and any date held hope for a change—until the date. He also happened to be crippled, so into the bargain you'd feel guilty going out with him once and then saying No.

"He's not so bad," Sister Sheila advised her, "he wants you to marry him, get married. It doesn't take long till you're busy with the children anyway."

By then little Sheila was married and busy with the children, two monsters that roared through the house while her husband munched peanuts and listened to the ball game. When Ruth visited, Sheila saw her worried look watching the nephew and niece.

"Obnoxious, aren't they?" Sheila laughed. "But—Marvin, Natalie!—I'm boss here. And it's better than nothing, and twice as good as worse than nothing which is our crazy mother. Seven years dying! Who knows how long she may last?"

Sol was an amputee, one arm to the elbow, and when Ruth said No to the first proposal, he laughed. "Ha ha, what's wrong? You think I'm not man enough for you?" He grabbed her by the arm as if he was going to twist, so she shrieked. But he didn't twist, he laughed, "Hah, all the man you can handle, maybe more." So she told him they'd better not meet again, and he laughed, "Ha ha!"

And he called her up every day, at home, in the office. She begged him to stop.

"They'll fire me," she said.

He laughed, "Ha ha, I'll give you a job—with plenty of night work."

At home when the phone rang and it was Sol, her mother let out long screams: "It's electricity, it's electricity, they're murdering me in the chair!"

Ruth told that to Sol, and he surprised her.

He said, "What am I calling you for, except that I want to get you away from all that."

Touching. Ruth was touched. She let him date her again, and she tried, she honestly tried to care for him, to ignore his jokes. Then they paid Sheila a visit, Sol tripped up obnoxious Marvin and Marvin dived on his face and broke his nose. Ruth had to agree with me that, looking back, this was the best gag Sol ever pulled. But at the time— So again Ruth said No.

Finally her mother died, and how Amin heard Ruth never found out, but there he was at the funeral, to tell her, "I wasn't so wise as I thought I was, but with your help I could be wiser, and I might even give you a hand too."

So, she was alone, worn out, empty. With tears in her eyes, over her mother's dead body, this time she said yes.

The marriage? Sol didn't complain, why should she?

"Although," she said, "here I sit complaining, throwing it all up to you."

"But I get your point," I told her, "Gross gets your point."

Their son Bobby, she said, had a right to complain, in the middle of a twenty-year skirmish between his mother and father. Not, to be fair to herself and Sol, that it went on every minute, or even most of the time. It was only the highlight of their married life. And not that Bobby complained, unless marrying his Jill was a kind of complaint. Jill had higher horizons, a bookmaker uncle in Miami. So that's where Bobby went for his honeymoon, the groom under voting age, to be transformed in two weeks from a good mechanic with money in the bank to an ex-junior bookmaker who'd lost all his savings. Of course, there were reasons, local politics down there last winter. They had bad luck, Jill told Ruth.

Ruth answered, "What do you care? His hands are his luck, and thank God he hasn't lost those."

Jill said, "Sure, but who wants to be a grease monkey all their life!"

"So," Ruth told me, "Jill's fierce, and the poor kid, he's so hunted."

I could see a reason she tried those pills. The kid's been her life. When he was four years old and he first tied his own shoelaces, he said, "Mommy, I don't need you any more."

"Okay," Ruth said.

That same night he said, "I do need you after all, Mommy."

"How come," Ruth said, "now that you can tie your own laces?"

"I still can't read, Mommy, I need you to read me to sleep."

The trouble was, the poor kid was born with a hearing impairment, so for fun Sol addressed him as Dummy. Ruth yelled and he still called him Dummy. So Ruth packed the bags and the baby, and Sol said, "Where's your sense of humor, what's all the fuss for?" And even then, for the rest of his life, he still had a joke: to call the boy Sir.

I said, "You're good, good to talk to me, after that . . . joke of mine."

"I just didn't sleep last night, Moe."

So I grabbed her by the hand, and later on I only worried two or three hours what she might have thought that committed me to.

See how Gross is improving already?

So, Kid Gross a week old, with new eyes to see with instead of seeing with hate, I wrung the paws of the engaged boy Charlie Davis's parents, that withered Rose that married for love, and Loverboy Davis with the paunch. Now twenty-two years ago Grandpa Axelrod, to celebrate or as Axelrod himself put it "out of pity" for the birth of his grandson Charles, let Davis Senior come in after a few years of floundering and work his way up to manager in one of the Rodney's From Coast To Coast stores. Now if Axelrod did that much for the father for the grandson's sake, how much more he was bound to do for the grandson in person! Also, observe the presence of the Ambassador from Mt. Schwarzman, that senior diplomat Fat Howard Schwarzman and his duchess the iron-backed Rae. Would they be here to celebrate poverty? No, Gross recruit to the optimist ranks, you had to conclude like the boy in the joke that with all this shit there must be a Shetland pony around somewhere! Or, in other words, money for Charles and money for Susan. And didn't I have to see likewise that money for Susan would be like a grease pack on my sensitive car: bumping, snarling before; quiet, smooth sailing after?

And next Gross Angel of Peace, with Liz there chatting with Charlie, and Sue now chatting with George— And yet with all the goodwill I had to stop and wonder why God in His wisdom couldn't have sent Charles to Liz first and George Young to Susan instead of vice versa, the sweet to the sweet and the sharp to the sharp? But that's life, and let bygones be bygones, even though this afternoon Georgie's first move was after old Axelrod and a share of the gold, and so fast he hardly had time for a hello to Mrs. Young's father.

Georgie's graduate school Project Excelsior was out to reclaim young colored hoods, but for a Jewish philanthropist like Mr. Axelrod he was prepared, given a modest grant, to scratch up some unkosher Jews. And the best of it was—a joy even to Gross!—the way this conman, this natural for a carnival old-style with three walnut shells, caught Axelrod's interest. Gross's imagination? The provident Susan went over, listened in, and, with her smile, drew Georgie away. The next gold-digger, some cousin, of course jumped into the breach. So, for the moment, Ulcers Georgie could only smile with Susan and trap drinks if the butler wandered into range with the tray.

Still and all Liz is our own flesh and blood and George is her husband.

"A happy occasion, Charlotte," I said. "And look, Liz's George is an educational doctor next week, another step closer to head of the college. Let's go over, let's slip him a hand-shake."

Handshake. In a life of distrust a halo is as bad as a scowl. A poison dart, that's what my wife shot him across the company, with another quick one for Gross.

"Don't think I didn't see you giving the Davises one of your earfuls."

And over she went to them with one of her facefuls, all white teeth and sugar, to show that at least half of their future in-laws wasn't a bum.

So me, with my friendly intentions toward Dr. George Young, I blundered over to give him my hand. But when I came within earshot, I was inundated with news I could have done better without. Because if Susan had outmaneuvered Georgie a minute, Georgie had a few maneuvers going of his own.

"Then"—he was smiling and she was smiling and how much was jokes?—"he definitely isn't providing you with the appreciation you deserve."

"Then," Susan shot right back, "I can call on you whenever in need of appreciation."

"Mohawk one one-thousand."

So I switched course to poor Liz, and she came to me from Charlie, on the plump side sure, but with the eyes bright this afternoon and the black hair full of glints. So where ignorance is bliss, a father should pull a long face?

I boomed: "Congratulations, Mrs. Ed.D.!"

And Dr. Young—still there with Susan—he's been a real education to Gross, for new twists of the entrails.

Lizzie laughed. "Giving credit where credit is due? All right, thanks."

"And you, how did you do in school this term?"

"Unsatisfyingly, Pop. I mean, the marks were good, but studying used to wake me up not put me to sleep."

"Yeh, like that last mouthful that gave the guy indigestion. Work all day with those sick little ones, then shop, cook, clean, and then study puts you to sleep and you wonder? But now that George is in the clear—"

And mention his name and he's there with the arm on your shoulders. I grabbed him by the loose hand so my pocket shouldn't be picked—you'll pardon the witticism—and gave him congratulations direct.

"And what next, George?"

"I'm offered," said Georgie aglow on Scotch, "and will probably accept, a three-thousand-dollar fellowship from the Golden Foundation."

"And what kind of a fellow do you have to be for that small pile of gold?"

"That's the beauty of it, Pop. No fellow at all. I promise them to sit in the library and read!"

"Now you're kidding an old workingman—or shouldn't I mention that four-letter word *work*?"

Georgie laughed, did he laugh. "Pop, you sound exactly like Liz!"

"Well, we're related. And what does Liz do, while you read?"

More laughing. "She's fully occupied."

You know the expression your blood boils? It boils, you feel it simmering in the veins and arteries, bubbling through the body, in the head, clotting the eyes so you can't see. But just when I would have boiled over, Lizzie spoke.

"He advises me to take peppy pills, but I don't believe in peppy pills—not even for others the way George does."

So—Lizzie razor-sharp to her George?—pardon my amazement.

George, he was calm. "Some of my best friends use them." And he fielded a drink from the drinks tray passing, only his happy hand fumbled a little.

"One too many, your lapel says," the father-in-law commented.

"Nothing in excess," Liz said, "if it's free."

So I should be happy, Gross also among the prophets? No, not Gross, that it gnaws on in the chest, in the stomach, the awakening of Liz. Depressing. I felt depressed. And there was that bastard, that mother—new leaves for Gross, old leaves for Gross—twisting her face to please a couple of strangers here, and when this daughter, this prize, this Liz, walked over to her with an open hand and a smile—my own eyes be my witness—to give a curt nod and then turn your back!

Suddenly Georgie went light green, like a sour apple, with a hic and the eyes slightly popping. And still, this actor, he could pass Liz his glass and wink, and say, "Mustn't disgrace Susan," before his twenty-yard dash to the toilet door.

"Pop," Liz laughed at me, "don't look so distressed. He'll be all right."

But how about Liz? Will she be all right?

And to crown my day's pleasure, when the party petered out that Gross stuck out to the end in the pose of beloved parent to give Susan her chance, my spouse produced half a closet of fat, loaded suitcases for me to carry downstairs.

"Going abroad?" dumb Gross asked her.

So I got a good glare.

"Home," Charlotte said. "Any objections?"

Home, away—who cares?

"Believe me, I'm honored my dear."

RUTH SAID, "What I'm worried about is my son."

"Sure," half-kidding, half to make her say one more time what I wanted to hear, "Liz is my worry, but your son is your son."

"Where's the comparison? He's an old-fashioned boy and she's a new-fashioned girl. He's a born victim, and she—her husband's on notice that he'd better reform, or else. Don't be dumb, Moe!"

So I had to laugh.

"Keep up the insults, it makes me feel right at home."

And she also laughed.

We had half a bench on top of Lookout Park for fresh air, where the auto fumes were a good distance away, floating up in the sunset, nothing right in your face. Around us the Golden Agers sat. Me and Ruth, we were each other's entertainment, and theirs too. I said park? Maybe when the Indians hung around here they could see a few trees. It's a rock like a skull with patches of grass alongside and a nice view of the tenements crawling east like incurable cancer. Also, just below on the sidewalk the teenage toughs were forgathering for a May evening's fun. But who looks? We talk, and the others ain't there.

And Ruth told me, oy, what was going on with her Bobby, her son—what a Jill that jack wound up with!

First, his squat pot, Jill, there was that bookmaking to make him broke in a hurry. Then she went and got herself knocked up. Sure, she came right out and told the mother-in-law, while Bobby-boy sat there quietly clutching his hair with both hands.

"We weren't planning on one so soon, but it's just as well having them and getting it over with."

"Them?" The papa-to-be just reached his majority let out a yelp. "How many we unplanning to have?"

"Three," Jill gave it her hefty shrug, "four—"

"And the Bomb makes five," Bobby let loose a wild laugh, "unless with luck it comes first."

"I wish you wouldn't speak in that crazy way," says the Mrs., "it's very unpleasant."

And besides being his family counselor, Diamond Jill also guides him on jobs. If by two months he ain't boss, then Jill tells him quit. And if you're Bobby Amin with Jill reminding you every sixty seconds on the minute that it's time to quit, you quit. Only, you're a little on the deaf side, so expert with tools though you may be, to the man in charge till he gets to know you—which with Jill is never—you sound slow on the uptake and not first in line for five-figure pay.

Meanwhile mother-bird Jill is building the nest: Italian Provincial furniture and thanks to the Almighty for the installment plan; not like Liz sit on the floor charmed in no-man's land Brooklyn and send hubby through graduate school.

That was what Ruth meant, that Liz lives differently. And the fact that our parents ran from addresses like where Liz lives, where the odds are even money you don't get home from the subway without being mugged?

"Those neighborhoods are different now," Ruth insists on it. "They're a new world."

"And Bobby's neighborhood, in Bayside Queens, that's the old world?"

"The same old world, Moe, that's learned nothing!"

So if they're a mistake, the Bayside gardenless garden apartments with a million little kids racing over moth-eaten grass, then wasn't it good that Jill wanted to get out?

Ruth laughed with tears. "Get out why? Get out where?"

And when I heard Jill's why, the pregnant woman, I had to laugh too.

"The schools," Jill said, "are too far away."

Also, Jill happened to want a house of her own—detached. Garden apartments, furniture with triple dressers, and framed mirrors: those all her friends had. None of 'em had a house.

She already had her eye on one, in Fairlawn New Jersey. And already Bobby was grabbing his hair and planning on 6:00 A.M. rising for a bus to New York, when he was saved by the Mortgage Companies of America. Who'll float you a house loan no money down and a new month a new job? So aside from expenses like the wife, the car, the furniture, and the obstetrician, Bobby was in the clear except for the food and the rent. The only trouble was that when Jill made up her mind, Jill's mind was made up. Fairlawn New Jersey. And for this, job counselor Jill advised him ten times a day and all day Sunday, our boy had to buckle down. Our boy had to find a good job and a steady job, and, above all, not like the job he happened to have.

So our boy buckles down, and if the palpitation and pale lips are a sign, soon he'll be buckling under.

And right now, in Lookout Park, the noises got loud enough so even engrossed Gross woke up to 'em. The younger generation was going for King of the Mountain, with rocks, and the rocks came up skittering through our Golden Age precinct.

An old man bleated, "Watch out down there—" and one

of our Hope of Tomorrow yelled back, "Twis', granpa, twis'!"

So Gross stood up to give that one a twis', but Ruth dragged me, shoved me down the opposite path. At the corner she phoned the cops to have a look-see at Lookout.

She said, "Those kids would murder you, Moe"—and with scared eyes too, like it mattered!

I said, "Ruth, let me talk about Bobby to Fox the Weasel, he's some character that I paint with an employment agency. How it is elsewhere in America don't ask Gross, but in this county pull doesn't do harm."

"Oh would you Moe!"

"Like it was my own son."

So WHY AM I LIVING in Grandview? Ten in the morning and the light sneaks in from the alley and goes and hides in the corner like it committed a crime. Is this a setting for the fine young Gross, that loves green air and sunshine?

And, maybe, also Ruth Amin?

Mornings I wake up, I blink—nothing special. Then into my mind, without me thinking, spreads that thought Ruth—and joy, through my whole being! So Gross fifty years old, that rated love a four-letter fake from the old-fashioned movies, you're in love?

Or else maybe it's the effect of a month of the Sue-Charlotte team and then privacy again?

Charlotte's second night home, and most evenings thereafter, Gross strolled in from being with Ruth, the first time to my Lady Prerogative's set of suspicious eyes.

And to the question, "Where have you been, may I ask?"

"Sure ask, with my paramour, dear. But you're ever in my heart."

I grabbed her and stuck a kiss on her neck, and she drew back and giggled, and that was that. Because her evenings also were occupied, with the trousseau for Susan and casing various weddings so they could fix on a place that was good, and expensive.

But once when I shut off my shower, they were discussing the sucker who'd pay for that wedding.

Charlotte said, "Oh, he goes out playing cards with his cronies."

"If it makes you happy to think so," Susan told her. "But if I were you, Mother, I'd break up that little game of Father's."

"Who cares?" Charlotte said.

"Why take chances?"

Then one day after work the good husband Moe comes home early—Ruth was having her Bobby and his Jill over for dinner, so Gross took the night off—and who was strolling out with valises but my loving spouse.

She was leaving me—oh joy! She'd found out about Ruth and she was going for good!

Gross, you better go get your head examined.

Charlotte said, "Oh, I wrote you a note. I'll be staying with Henry for the present at the Fifth Avenue mansion." And she reeled off her order of the day—ha ha, as if life never changes. "You'll be expected for dinner there Fri-Saturday six thirty sharp."

But what does that mean: with Henry? Ah, gross Gross, coarse must have been born in your blood, to face innocence like this and imagine corruption like that. Speculating with her pelt, Lady Icebox my consort of twenty-five years?

Years ago, Madam Purity's furrier—her furrier. My marriage and the black year '37 started together, and, with that loafer of a husband that deprived her even of such necessities, not till five Chanukkahs later did she graduate to the Persian lamb coat all the Concoursers wore then. Well, instead of coming home happy with those dead animal skins, she came home huffing and puffing, the eyes flashing, the face white. The furrier insulted her. How? How did he insult her? He said why rush the coat, come down in the evening, tell hubby they needed more fittings, they'd have a few drinks, they'd have a little fun.

"That," slow Gross wanted to know, "was the insult?"

"Isn't that enough?"

So I'd humored her, the maiden of thirty-five and a half then with two kids, I said that to a good-looking woman like her such talk is a compliment, or else laugh it off. Or, if not, then in one ear and out the other. Or, it still bothered her, then switch to another furrier for her mink.

You know what she wanted? Gross should roar down to the fur district and fight for her honor. Maybe a duel, with seconds?

"Some man I married."

"Too much man, for your taste."

That shut her up.

And now, at age fifty-four, a sudden reverse? Poor Henry is all I can say.

And yet—there's always that doubt as the joke goes—look at 'er, still handsome, with the shoulders, the chest, the slim waist, the face slightly dried out next to age twenty it was true, but altogether well-cared-for, you never would guess it was a poor man's wife, with the sun touching off gold on the black silk dress.

But the dress, she'd already told me, used to be Tillie's. And the ten G's Tillie left her, those I knew she hadn't seen yet because she was still after my life insurance to float Susan's wedding. So granted, between Tight-Fist Henry and Tight-Ass Charlotte the dogfight would be keen, and also granted to the king's bed every advantage, I was supposed to believe that for down payment of a secondhand dress . . . ? Nah.

But just to be sure, Gross tested.

"Saturday night, in the middle of your consolations? I thought two's company and three's a crowd."

The sneer went on like ringing a bell.

"Evil mind! Henry's been very sick."

"He looked fine at the funeral."

"Appearances are deceiving."

Deceiving and how! This motto I could embroider and hang over my bed. But look how she kept mum to the last minute, this dreamer, on poor Henry's poor health, to make believe that they wanted her for her good company, the rich.

"Then Nurse—last chance—you could use a divorce."

"That old refrain?"

"No no, I mean your last chance to get the things in life you're entitled to."

Did she throw me a glare! "Are you deaf? I said Henry is barely beginning to recover."

"Then the moment is ripe. He likes you, he's lonely. His children are in the mountains? . . . Then he's all yours in that great big house!" And see—my lady, that distant gleam in her eye, of wood burning. Now honestly, wasn't that alone worth a marriage to Gross? How many hubbies, after so many years, could kindle a wife up with her girlhood dreams? "Say," I kept at 'er, "if we weren't already hitched, I myself would be interested."

"You're a nut," Charlotte had to laugh.

"Subway, or cab?"

"I think I'd prefer the subway."

"No expense account even, from Henry, with those heavy bags? Never mind, I'll chauffeur you down, if you'll step into my Cadillac."

And in Eighty-fourth Street downtown, in front of a mansion with a white stone face just like the owner, stood Henry's actual Cadillac. So next to it I double-parked the jalopy, and I leaned to my lady.

"What, Mrs. Gross for life? Think, how much better you can do if you try. Last chance, think!"

She waved me away, but I watched her standing in front of the house till the butler opened the door—and she was thinking all right, she was thinking!

Ehh, poor Charlotte, it's a human after all, I felt sorry for her.

I gave a yell, past the black Cadillac perfect for following a hearse: "Forget it. Not Henry. It was a joke. Just try for your legacy."

"Oh yes?" she sailed me a smug smile back. "Don't be so sure of that, Mr. Gross—"

And she adventured into the black.

And after the blow of that departure, Gross suffered another. Mr. Rodney's From Coast To Coast Axelrod had taken a turn for the worse, so Susan was shifting quarters to the Davises' to place her unparalleled devotion to the old man within easy distance of his deathbed.

So good news all around, and for Gross most of all, like a bachelor again, the good old days, yeh, when Gross and Hitler were both in their prime. But friend Hitler is buried, and no worry now but friend H. Bomb. So today second youth, and tomorrow—tra la if we last—second childhood!

And this new run of luck spared me my promise to go see Fox the Weasel on Bobby Amin's behalf, with that agency waitingroom full of masks and hate daggers, mostly colored, that you walk through while they mark you down White Man Boss. Ruth tells me our government should stop reaching for the moon and spend for life here on earth. Me, I should grow wings and fly, and the air might be fresher upstairs. So I was set to face Fox's when the Angel Cheap waved his wand and in came a call from my cousin Sidney.

In the Depression Gross painted Sidney's candy store on Shakespeare Avenue for a dollar and a couple of free milkshakes, so Sidney's been living in hope ever since. Now big-shot, he's a home-owner with a factory, one car for him,

another for the Mrs., and car three for son Brian so
transportation should be easier for the boy searching from
college to college but still he ain't found himself—and still
every few years Sidney gives me a ring, to feel out Cousin
Gross on painting and decorating, low-cost.

"What's new?" I answered him. "New York, New Jersey
. . . Jersey's old, you're living there quite a while already? I
knew that too, from Bella . . . Yeh, I see Bella, your sister,
remember her? She's the one that throws funerals, like the one
you missed the other month for your brother-in-law Lou? Or
else to clean out Lou's stuff she holds one-man cleaning parties,
and the man's name is Moe Gross? . . . Ah, I see, the whole
family had the flu. A local epidemic it must have been . . .
Oh, I'm good-hearted, you wish you had those qualities? I'll let
you have 'em cheap, for a ten-dollar bill, like the one I found in
Lou's good suit . . . You'll bet I handed that ten over to Bella?
How much will you bet? . . . No, I never travel out your way.
Where is it again? . . . Pellworm? Yeh, I pass there
sometimes, on the way to the cemetery. That's some smell you
moved into out there boy, in Pellworm . . . They kicked the
pigs out three years ago? That's good, so it hardly must smell
any more . . . Listen, what are you doing, inviting me over?
You come to see me, with your three cars—you could drive
one with each hand and the third with your feet . . . You gave
up one car? Ah, heavy expenses with your boy in college.
Wait, I'll take up a collection . . . Sure I'm still a comedian,
but don't say it so loud, they might draft me for TV and I ain't
got the time . . . No, Sidney, I couldn't give you a
long-distance estimate on your paint job, but you go and ask a
local man for a short-distance estimate and it'll be the same as
me, minus carfare. And how's business? You still fooling the
Puerto Ricans? . . . Sure, I know you manufacture good cake,
I saw a piece in the garbage downstairs and the flies couldn't
get enough of it . . . Your customers can't get enough of it

either? Then keep up the good work, you're a real benefactor
. . . What kind of help is hard to find? . . . Oh, that kind?
You'll get more on the next plane from the Caribbean . . .
Your mechanic too? Then why didn't you give him another
dollar, he might have stayed . . . Oh, he got run over poor
fella . . . What do you mean you paid him plenty? What's
plenty? . . . You don't say? Well listen to your good
fortune—Cousin Moe has you a technician . . . You want an
expert, I got him up my sleeve . . . Yeh yeh, yeh yeh, yeh
yeh, yeh yeh . . . You're not sure you can begin him with that
much? Then go cry in your towel, not in my ear, with your
plant in Pellworm-by-the-Stink full of dying equipment plus
your fleet of broken-down trucks . . . Top running condition?
You can uncross your fingers when you say that, nobody's
looking. How many trucks you got now, half-a-dozen? . . .
Eight! For eight my man draws ten a week more!"

So Ruth sent Bobby out there, and from the boy's own lips
when he phoned to say thanks—a complete success. With
Frugal Sidney's three floors of secondhand machinery wheez-
ing and clanking, you couldn't hear yourself think let alone
speak: so it's all shouts or orders in writing and be as deaf as
you want as long as you aren't too dumb. Jill kissed Bobby
when she heard the pay, and Pellworm is only twenty minutes
by nose from the home of her heart's desire in Fairlawn.

"Gee," Bobby told me, "people you live with don't do that
much for you. You are something, Mr. Gross!"

He turned out to be a pleasant surprise, poor kid, not a sharp
chip off the old blockhead only with the joke always on him.

So, late yesterday afternoon in the zoo the sun poured like
gold over the ground, better than gold, through the treetops.
The grass around was like shining green light, and those petals
like pink fluff on the cherry blossom trees. And on the breeze
sometimes came a whiff from the animals, strong, good.
Everything full-grown, mature! And Ruth in pink—amazing,

that Gross should know such a woman—was thanking me in person on behalf of her son. I countered, since it seemed all in the family, with an invite to Cousin Bella's Lou's gravestone unveiling in the cemetery today.

"A family gathering?" she said. "I'd feel funny."

In the big cage those birds too—all sizes—were following the dictates of their nature, whatever they wanted, a good fly, a good squawk, a good splash in the mud. There, one gray-and-white lady plumped herself out with her boyfriend flapping on top, whistling while he worked, giving her a wonderful time.

Me, Old Man Suspicion, I ponder, I wonder. Gross is taking too much for granted? Is her angle first legally in the family and then family gatherings? Because from that famous night in her foyer, where she ended up throwing me out, say she's just after marriage and it all made clear sense. Bronx small-game trapping, time-tested and honored. You hang the cheese in the open, let him sniff, let him nibble—then you whisk it away. No rush, no hurry, till he walks into your cage—then spring the trap! And this one was working the old sport without even a new twist, with her frank and earnest, Frank here and Ernest in Chicago?

Gross likewise can set bait. I stood up from the bench, I struck up my cigar, and, "Did I mention," I let it drift out, on the smoke, the smoke screen, "my lady's considering divorce?"

Look, how her eyes lit!

"No kidding! How come, all of a sudden?"

So I drawled out this that and the other thing, and Charlotte and Henry. Once, to check on how anxious Ruth was, I interrupted myself.

"Look, in the cage there, see that short stocky guy dressed in brown, with the nice-sized beak also like Gross, gabbing away and all his pals go about their pursuits? Tedious, eh, a one-sided conversation?"

No no, she sat there all ears.

But in the end it was thumbs down on my story.

She said, "It sounds far-fetched to me, with a man like that."

"Then she'll be disappointed. But life is full of disappoint-ments," Gross continued diving for fish, like the gull in the pool, "wouldn't you say?"

She laughed. "Who cares about her disappointments? I have my own."

Aha! "Like what?"

She leaned back on the bench, smiling up like God's sunshine. "I don't remember offhand—but give me a minute."

So what do you want, Gross, that goes to love like a small animal to grass, with the ears perked up and every few seconds the nose sniffing air? Let the sun whisper in the trees, and scared Moe, he hustles for shelter on all fours. Then, from his hole in the ground, cagy rodent, he peeps out, he sniffs, to test if the coast is clear! So I knew all this, while we took a stroll next, and what good did it do? The worry was still there, like the shy giraffes with no place to hide, and the ugly flamingos with necks like up-to-date plumbing, and the tigers staring at you and licking their chops, and the late shadows creeping.

All of a sudden Ruth asked me, "Who do you suppose'll be at that unveiling tomorrow?"

"With crazy Bella? Crazy Moe and her rabbi, who else?"

"Okay," she said, "count crazy Ruth in."

Hey you—ha ha!—peacock in the path under the leaves hanging, what do *you* have to be so proud of, some feathers?

"I'M SO HAPPY!" Ruth said.

"Me too." I grabbed her hand. "It must be the weather!"

And she gave Gross's paw a squeeze.

"It's like the country—I love it!" she said.

There we were in the cemetery, with that baby-blue sky and the white baby clouds, the trees brand-new, and the grass.

And the way the leaves twinkled, like a laugh at the gravestones.

Ruth said, "Look—there's a funeral."

But way off, near an iron-spiked fence, with midget people and autos like toys.

"That? That's their funeral."

"Yes," Ruth said, "I don't feel it, either. And one short month ago—that was me?—I was taking suicide pills. Though," she looked worried, "it's bad luck to brag. Are you superstitious, Moe?"

I rapped on a tree. "God forbid, knock wood!" And ha ha ha ha, ah did we laugh, ha ha ha ha! "Did I tell you I told Bella, 'Bella, Jews don't have unveilings a month after the funeral,' and Bella said, 'The stone is all paid for, why not enjoy it?' "

Ah ha ha, ah ha ha ha ha!

Then Ruth gripped my hand hard, with a shudder. "Look at those two, on that bench at the top of the path—under that big tree."

And that was a pair, the old man with the beard and the woman in black, to chill sunshine itself. Woe, the way they were sitting there, one facing one way and one the other, they couldn't bear to look at each other even.

"Listen," what could I do but agree, "let me really knock wood. God forbid, God forbid such losses—what could it be, a young daughter? Or a son, a boy in the Army?"

When all of a sudden she spotted us, the lady in black—and up like a jack-in-the-box! Yeh, ha ha, some mourner, Bella, with the skinny arms flapping like some kind of scarecrow in a high wind, waving a big hello!

And the old man? A graveyard minstrel she picked up, two dollars a prayer.

"Hey you ain't Charlotte!" The bony finger stuck out, straight at Ruth, and the Bella eyes lit up happy and sly. "You couldn't fool me, bad as my sight is. Right away I says to myself, soon as I seen yez, 'That don't look like no Charlotte, Charlotte's better-looking than that,' I says!"

"I'm Ruth."

"Ruth who?"

"Just plain Ruth."

I had to guffaw, that came out so dry, smile and all.

"You're Moe's girlfriend I bet."

"That's one bet you win, Bella," said Ruth.

"Lou had a girlfriend, she was plain too, but God fixed her. She got run over."

"And God got away with it too," I had to butt in, "that hit-and-run job."

"Oh that ain't right to say, is it, Mr.—" she wanted a ruling from her assistant with the beard—"I forgot your name again."

The beard shrugged. "Melamed."

"Sure," Bella said, "that's sacrilege."

"Yeh? You see the Angel of Death beside me?"

Bella looked hard, but Ruth came in-between us. "Don't Bella," Ruth laughed, "I'm superstitious."

My God, and only yesterday I doubted this one?

"It's okay," Bella—as Lou he should rest in peace used to say—babbled on, "he ain't there. I know what he looks like, I seen him beside Lou."

"So," I sang out with joy, "he's entitled to a coffee break!"

"I don't drink coffee, it makes my headache worse."

Mr. Melamed said, "We're here for an unveiling?"

And Bella cackled, when Ruth looked around the green velvet plot with the shade trees, "What did you think, Lou was up here on Easy Street? He's down there, see, where them headstones are all jammed together? My family bought that plot in 1895, forty-five graves for ninety-five dollars. Where would you get a bargain like that today?" We commenced the walk down the other side of the slope. "There's my father over there, Moe's Uncle Frank—look at all them weeds and the way the stone tilts. I should pay 'em to take care of the grave, only it keeps slipping my mind. Not that he treated me so good. Gee, my head hurts."

Ruth took Bella by the arm. "Here are some aspirins."

And yeh, Lou was here too, out of the money as usual. But on Lou the weeds looked good, fresh blades of green, so silky and delicate, for that poor bruised soul underneath.

"No veil?"

From Melamed. And—the professional eye—Lou's name and Lou's dates sure enough, and no veil. Bella turned from her normal yellow to white, really scared. "Gee, I never notified them Stone people, it slipped my mind. God could punish me," with a glance right and left to see if God'd caught her redhanded.

Ruth cried out, "What would He want to do that for, Bella?" and she unknotted the summer scarf at her throat.

"Gee thanks, thanks," and to hang it around the stone Bella went to her knees in the dirt, Holy Bella, to pacify God that way, "God bless yiz, even if you are a married man's girlfriend—"

Melamed connected his thumbs behind his back and started to pray. And me too, didn't I know that prayer, over Lou, over Mama, over Sylvia's Phil, over how many others in my years, I knew it by heart, and I sang, with wet eyes, for Lou.

"May God remember—"

Rest Lou, sleep well . . .

Me, I was luckier than Lou, to walk out of the cemetery with the married man's girlfriend's arm in my arm—this Ruth. The second the praying was finished, Bella took Ruth's scarf from Melamed's fingers and calmly draped it around her own scrawny neck. My lips already were open for a Hey Bella, but Ruth laid her fingers across them.

"What do you think Ruth, she doesn't know what she's doing, that shrewd moron?"

"It's all right," Ruth said.

And virtue isn't rewarded? Back in The Bronx Bella says to me, "Come up for some cake and wine, Moe," and to Ruth, "You can come too."

Upstairs, of course, Bella remembered she never got to the bakery for cake today, and she was fresh out of wine. So we enjoyed instant coffee and a cracker instead, in her livingroom with the kitchenette on one wall, and in the great open spaces her TV, her card table, and her three folding chairs.

"I bet you're thinking the joint looks empty," Bella gave Ruth a grin, "that she can't afford no good furniture. I can afford all I want—"

"Yeh yeh," chipped in Cousin Gross.

"I ain't joking." Then, behind her hand, she gave us a whisper. "Stashed away in the mattress, don't tell no one." She brightened up. "All you hear of is crooks nowadays. Anyway, the more furniture the more housework, that's what I always say. My mother-in-law, let her rest in peace, she was a great one for housework, forever criticizing me I didn't slave hard enough. But where was she when I had her son for a cripple? She was dead, that's where she was. Though I must say Lou was good as a cripple, better than healthy. He never complained as a cripple, and he never socked me, the way he used to before. Though come to think of it he stopped socking me so much after my pal Nettie become his girlfriend, yeah, some pal she turned out to be, but God punished her, she got run over. So who wants to dust all that stuff, a sick woman like me. Though I still got a full bedroom-set. Come on in, look how nice it looks . . . Oops, I forgot, I never had time to make the bed this morning. See, that's where I saw the Angel of Death, right in front of that night table, he was next to Lou's head. But the place looks nice and fresh, not counting the bed, don't it? It oughtta, it was just painted last week. And who do you think done it, the landlord? Guess again. You know what he had the gall to tell me when I said a place ought to be painted after somebody dies there? He had the gall to tell me, 'That's your problem, poor fella.' What's he calling me fella for, I ain't no fella. So Moe did the painting last week free of charge. Ain't he nice, my cousin Moe, even if he does run around with a woman outside of his wife, the way my husband used to with Nettie?"

"I like him," Ruth said, but she looked at me not at Bella.

"And you ain't so bad either, considering," Bella said. "Another party would have yelled 'Hey, she's stealing my scarf,' but you never said nothing when I tried it on . . . Here, Ruthie, I just wanted to try it on. It's pretty, for just a cheap piece of gauze."

"Oh no," Ruth put up her hands like to an offer of arsenic, "I don't want it back! I mean, you keep it, Bella."

"Gee, you are nice! You can marry 'er Moe, providing ha ha ha ha you can get rid of your wife. I bet she ain't as easy to get rid of as I was."

"Yeh, you were a cinch. All Lou had to do was drop dead."

"Ha ha, that's true, that's true. Come to think of it, I wasn't so easy to get rid of either!"

THE SAME STREET, the parked autos the same, trash on the sidewalks, the pots marching their brats and bundles home from the supermarket, young ruffians racing around—left over from the public school next door to Bella's—and yelling to puncture your eardrums. Yet so wonderful!—a wonderful afternoon, with warm shadows.

Ruth beamed at me, coming out of Bella's house, and me at her.

"Saint!"

She called Gross that!

"Saint You, you mean, so patient with Bella."

"St. Gross, that's who I mean. It's easy to laugh at her when you tell the stories, but to go to her continually, to listen to her insults, and to do all that you do for her!"

In the street there we locked hands, finger between finger, let look who looked!

WHILE GROSS TIPTOED AROUND and by what sun stained the window frame and whitened the drape he gathered up the pants, the shoes, the rumpled-up socks, Ruth slept. A good sound sleeper, after her full night. Naked, but why not, in June?

Except, in this morning light, with the slim legs and belly and the neat pair of bubbies, couldn't you say she wasn't so plain after all, the face even, that looked smooth in the shadow, contented? And if after such a night, Gross standing a minute, looking, could start one more salute, someone else wouldn't?— and for one that wraps herself around you and keeps panting your name?

So maybe the naked truth was the truth? But in that case, why Gross in particular? Go down, wink at the butcher, the letter carrier, the grocery man. They'll give you that little extra service, all you want. Or maybe not all you want? Maybe for all you want—it must be a byword with the cows, up and down the building and all over the neighborhood—the ticket is Bull Gross, renovation with a bang?

So Gross said last night, when she snuggled up after round one, "You're the girl men never looked at?"

She gave a nice comfortable sigh. "That was me."

"And Bobby, he was an immaculate conception?"

She laughed. "Not exactly immaculate—"

Nice, a nice laugh. And didn't it remind Gross of other laughs in his life, of Sadie's, of Heloise Nitzberger's, and always the laugh was on him? But that's if you've had the misfortune to notice that with women there's a stock of laughs and expressions in common, especially in bed. And why not? Eat, and you feel better.

Then I said, "What would you really want?"

So she moved over, with those breasts crushed against me, and she stuck a kiss on my mouth. "What I've got." And she kissed Gross again—get this!—before she noticed there was no kissing back. Then she came up on her elbow, it was just getting dark, with the sunny eyes, but with the little crow's-feet of experience alongside. "Hey stupid," she smiled down at me, "don't you understand that I love you, and I could tell you the reasons why?"

But what did that mean, love? Lays prospective and actual? With Gross it's for love, but with Amin it was just in the line of duty? And with God knows who else?

So I said, "Yeh? Why?"

She laughed, she said "Shut up," and she started another long kiss.

And even apart from the kiss, Gross, he had to shut up, because that laugh—you could hear she thought I was kidding, and I was ashamed to insist.

But if she thought I was kidding, didn't that mean she really had all those reasons why? Then Gross, what next? Dial Emergency for the straitjacket? A Charlotte is too cold, so a Ruth is too warm? Feh Gross, honestly, would you be satisfied with an angel from God? Maybe, Lunatic, and then again maybe not.

Because here is this jewel, this last chance, and your one note should forever be What's her angle? What can you lose, precious Gross? And with the Kremlin Boy ready to blast for the East Nazis and the White House Boy for the West Nazis, how long do you ponder? Of course their Boy with the hangovers and our Boy with the backaches, they might just be irritable and it could be just talk. Still and all Gross, why not take a hint and try to live while you're inhaling?

So in the middle of the night, while Ruth slept quietly and Gross should have been sleeping, I decided—enough thoughts enough doubts enough craziness. Tomorrow sharp, make your move. Down to Mansion Schwarzman, to our homebred Florence Nightingale, and con 'er, tease 'er, edge 'er on, with her hope of Henry, towards a divorce. Then to your knees maniac, thankfully, before this one, with the proposal of marriage.

Then Gross was happy, and sleep came.

But now, by the dawn's early light at 11:00 A.M.? The happiness was in shreds, tatters, Old Glory shot full of holes. Say—and by the broad light of day this also was daydreams—Gross landed his divorce. He proposes. Mrs. Amin accepts. Then proven: He wasn't just a quick cure for what ailed 'er. So where would I get off then? Same as before, the Marriage Station, Booby Prize Gross, to be shown off to neighbors, family, and friends. Which could be at the bottom of her mind all the time: not Gross, only a husband.

Oy Gross, Gross, first smooth out your sixty years' wrinkles, then smooth out your brain. The one is as easy as the other. If you could stop being nutty, would you have these credentials of nut?

But listen, why all the fuss. At your age, even aside from the Big Boys and their games, another mistake more or less will make that much of a difference?

I LOOKED UP, Charlotte looked down. Grand, at the top of the grand staircase, like the sun on a mountain on a newborn day.

So with Tillie set in the west, Charlotte was rising in East Eighty-fourth Street.

That was my first thought, while the butler was lunging at the Gross chapeau: From a wisecrack by Gross, our Lady of Action went and nailed Hard As Nails Henry. Ha ha Henry, when the fox is outfoxed! Wait till Ruth heard this one.

Then, thinking of her, of Ruth, that worry, that sadness creeps into my heart.

Charlotte sailed down the stairs, trim as any man-o'-war gliding into the Bay—for her war you could see that the dispatches were good—and with the finger over the lips she motioned me into the drawingroom.

And quite a room, quite a room. I could imagine a wedding in here: young Gross and Ruth Rappaport—that's how it should have been—with the maid of honor the kid sister Sheila. And through the open French doors look at that garden in the courtyard, like a piece of the country with those blues pinks and greens. You got gold, it's the golden age. And this was going to that, that was shutting the door with such great care to be quiet, my Lady Slam. So if sucker Henry could even still totter, it had to be on his last legs.

Sure enough, she shot me the victory smile broadside. "Well, wise guy!" Another man might have been staggered. The weatherbeaten Gross, he just rolled with the blow.

"Congratulations."

"Huh, I'll bet you don't know for what." She dived deep in her bosom and came up with a check to tease poor Gross's eyes. What? A piddling three figures, signed Howard Schwarzman, out of her ten thousand inheritance. "And only a small down-payment—the balance next week!"

"That?" I dug in with a laugh. "That's the excitement?"

Ha ha, the sun vanished, clouds tumbled, winds chopped into the battle area.

"I just told you, didn't I, the rest next week!"

"Here, sit down, be calm, tell loving hubby—why not the rest this week? Henry's condition is so bad that his wallet can only stand minor surgery?"

"Nothing of the sort. Henry's fine—better every day! The account happened to be short of funds, if you're so smart. It's as simple as that."

Simple? Madam Simple and how!

To understand, you had to see Henry, better every day. That's Barrel Henry, that never spoke only grunted, or if you displeased him gave you a growl? Me, whenever I had the honor to accompany my Lady to her sister's hotels or mansions, Henry would never begrudge me one of his grunts unless he happened to be talking to money, in which case the dazzle would altogether blind him as far as Gross was concerned. But one day I caught him alone in the middle of his lobby, the Shelbourne oak. So I beat him to the grunt, and he who grunts first grunts best. Henry was so surprised that he said, "Hello, how are you?" But from then on you can be sure he was on guard against Gross. That was the Henry we knew and loved. But this? This gray withered ghost with the haunted eyes, this palsied beggar, studying your face for a clean bill of health?

Yeh, this is what's left of Henry. Well millionaire, cheer up, we all croak sooner or later, only better you sooner and me later.

Lunch was a farina orgy, and even that the onetime Barrel Henry had trouble keeping down, especially with the help of his little visit from son Howard and Howard's wife Rae and son Sheldon and Sheldon's wife Eleanor.

After lunch I asked Charlotte, "How that man looks is what you call better every day?"

She flashed out, the worshipper, "Of course. Couldn't you see for yourself!"

Yeh, I saw. She aimed to please, that's what I saw. And such dedication, if only to gold, ain't it a virtue and must virtue be only its own reward? So in this case the extra was five hundred dollars. A modest settlement, out of a millionaire that owes you ten grand? Tell me brother with your six feet of skin, you wanna spare Gross an inch? Likewise Henry and money.

What happened was, he was getting even with his near and dear, or else she wouldn't have seen five let alone five hundred.

Yeh Henry, take comfort, the clown Gross understands you. No one gives you a look, then you're dying and who cares. They look too hard, then you're sure that you're dying. And who did care of that bunch? Pompous Howie, with the fat face that looks like it's pondering? To that mind live, die—it's all hard to grab hold of. Besides, a hopeful for Chief of State, even slow and a long shot, don't he have to have daydreams? And his stiff-backed Rae with the iron eye? Years ago at the Oceanside when she thought no one was looking, who but Gross caught her priming herself for Great Lady in front of the grand ballroom mirror, looking grand, looking glacial, working up haughty glances—as if she needed the practice. Those two, Rae and Howie, they produced the creased brow of concern for poor Henry, suitable to the occasion. Eleanor, she was too merry. "Charlotte, why don't you feed Dad some real food? No wonder he looks peaked!" Or else she'd chatter on, the thirty-five-year-old young lady, that she was raiding DePinna's this afternoon for the October Charity Ball, while Henry sat brooding that for that event his charity would be to the worms. And Sheldon?

Sheldon—give credit where due, even named Sheldon—he did care, and he was worst of 'em all. Henry belched, Sheldon suffered. What his brother and sister-in-law pretended they had—fear, concern—Sheldon was loaded with. The worry poured out of his eyes, his face, every motion of his body, and whatever hope sprang eternal in Henry's chest Sheldon mangled at the roots.

So Henry searched in their faces and panned out their words, and what did he mine, the old desert rat? Clods for his coffin! The funeral march!

Only from his handmaiden Charlotte came the refrain he was longing to hear, that he wished he himself could believe the way she believed it.

Better every day.

Yeh, like in 1930, when our President, now one of our Elder Statesmen, kept making the same promise to poor sick U.S.A. Well, we got better, didn't we? With corpses—that's how we got better.

So, last week, after you sift out Lady Condescension's apologies for the rich—the good sincere Howard and his worries no matter how needless about Better Every Day, and Better Every Day's worries no matter how needless about the hotels under the Boys' star management while he's away for the time being—Howie turned up with the secretary Miss Hess, some ledgers, and the sickroom expression.

Henry opened up: "Hotel Henry just failed?"

"Why no, what makes you say that, Pop?"

"The length of your face."

Howard caught the hint and ran it the wrong way for an enemy touchdown. "No, business is fine, Pop"—hey, did you ever see Howard rubbing together those plump healthy paws?—"and I must say, you're looking fine!"

So Henry let loose a windbreaker, right to the heart. "You paid your Aunt Charlotte here your mother's bequest?" And my mate, God bless 'er, still thought they were talking business!

"But Pop, you yourself said there's nothing in Mother's estate."

Me, I asked Charlotte, "What did Howard mean by that, dear?"

"He was confused, obviously."

"Did you beg his pardon?"

"What are you talking about? Or is that supposed to be humor?"

Anyhow, Henry's next shot to Howard straightened him out.

"Get that Miss Hess, wherever she ran."

As Henry very well knew, wherever she ran, the emotional Miss Hess, she ran out, so as not to shed tears in poor Master's presence. Miss Hess, you should know Charlotte says, is a hypocrite, who stages this act with an eye to Henry's last will and testament. "Why?" I said. "Is he dying?" "I trust," Charlotte gave me a look, "Henry's will won't be read for many many years." And there at least—take it from Gross—spoke only sincerity. Miss Hess's little act annoyed Howard too, Charlotte assured me, especially since he was so anxious to rectify that oversight about the bequest. So he took it out on the butler.

"Get that Miss Hess!"

The time the butler took getting that Miss Hess Howie must have devoted to thought. One minute Miss Hess stood there red-eyed while Henry snapped orders to set up a check to Mrs. Gross and right now and she and Howie were dismissed to do it. The next minute the pair of 'em trooped back ladies last and delivered the five hundred plus their blue fairy tale of the account short of funds. Sick as he was and sore as he was, Henry Schwarzman must also have had time by then to figure why slice your nose to spite what's left of your face, because his comeback was only: "Then see you make a deposit for full payment next week."

To enchanted Charlotte the transaction was pure gold, and was it my job to argue? I pitched into 'er, again on the sofa there after lunch, with the garden sun pouring in but not for rich Henry's pleasure that they wheeled into the elevator and back up to bed. "See, he likes you, Henry."

And look at her, how she laps it up, flattered, that bitch, that nincompoop.

So Gross said, "We're old pals, thick and thin, ups and downs," and drop dead you dog, "so why should Gross harbor hard feelings and stand in your way? As a husband there may have been better, there have also been worse. But for your interests at heart I stand on the record. Did Gross wise you up or didn't he, when I chauffeured you down here, about your chances with Henry? Now see? Who's bringing him back to health, those R.N.'s upstairs? Charlotte, that's who. And who does he know he can't do without? The nurses, the Boys, the Boys' wives? He can't do without Charlotte. And half an hour ago at your luncheon, the couple of smiles that he gave—who to? Ramrod Rae? Gloomy Shelley? Who-Gives-a-Damn Ellie? The butler? Or maybe the guest Gross? Who?" And no yawns now. Now the schoolgirl's eyes shone, at such high praise. "You know who."

I smiled, I winked, "What do you think," friendly, with a hand on her thigh—my shoe twitched to kick that fine ass—"Gross is nuts, huh, crazy Moe with the wild imagination?"

She lifted my hand away like dead fish, and she patted her hair. "Oh I don't believe in hiding my light under a bushel. Henry knows my value to him."

"Sure, but between knowledge and action there's still a big step. And what are you here for, if not to give the convalescent a hand? Henry follows you with his eyes, and on his lips is a question. But go pop the question to a married lady, a respectable man like that? Naturally not."

"So I go get divorced I suppose."

"What can Gross teach, with a pupil so gifted?"

"Well I'll tell you something. I've given good thought to all this—and first things first."

"That's what I'm telling you."

"Oh no it isn't. First Henry proposes, then I divorce."

Then you divorce. And Gross is no factor, Gross doesn't exist? Ah, slice this one up Gross, chop 'er to bits!

"Sure, boy meets girl, that makes sense. But think, the way Henry must think. Much as he likes you, nurse par excellence, best nurse in the world, you're still here as nurse not as girlfriend. First you nursed Tillie, now you nurse him. Is Henry a fool, a man that likes to look foolish? He may have this wish, this dream, but you keep mum and what can he say? A man wants a hint before he opens his mouth." And look—cogitation, with the eyes slightly crossed from her big mental effort. "Now listen. Today Howard was here, but where was the balance due on your ten thousand dollars? . . . Of course he's a busy man, and so is Henry, running the business long-distance and with all these doctors and nurses underfoot. By the way, as Mrs. Schwarzman you should show them the door, those crooks! So the next time Howard drives down off the mountain, you remind Henry about the inheritance, but tactfully, that your poor sister, poor Tillie, wanted you to have. You'll say it isn't the money, it's—then you'll blush, you'll play dumb. Play? It's real, your real feeling. 'It isn't the money?' he'll say. 'What then?' Three, four, a dozen what-thens, then you'll tell him. 'For Reno.' 'Reno?' He may look gruff, don't be scared, his heart'll be bursting with joy. 'Why Reno?' 'Because,' then you'll say, 'I'm spoiled for my old life, with my husband I mean, and I can't stay here either.' Then he'll answer, 'Why not, why can't you stay here? What's wrong with it here?' 'Because,' then you'll spill the beans, you like 'im too much. Now thank God that he's better, you'd better leave. 'Don't be silly,' he'll say, 'I need you.' 'Me? How can you need me? You have the boys, you have Rae, you have Ellie.' 'Them?' he'll say. 'Stay.' You'll shake your head no, he'll keep saying Yes. Yes no no yes. And between the noes and the yeses he won't let you go. He'll get you your divorce and he'll marry you."

She said, "What do you get out of all this?"

In the poolroom they have sharks, that fumble around the table dumb as a herring, easy pickings, watch 'em and drool! Only just jump in for a small friendly bet, and one bet you're safe with is that a short hour later the picked bones won't be them. So sucker, you know there are sharks. Why jump?

Blind with greed, that's why they jump!

"I might make a small touch for business expansion, nothing extreme."

She thought. Then she laughed, wistful, and she had the gall to say to me, Gross, "It sounds almost too good to be true!"

"Well, you make it come true, Charlotte, and it'll be true."

And she saw me to the door in a dream of happiness where Gross didn't exist, not even as a memory.

When just then she remembered.

"Did you bring the insurance along, Moe?"

She meant my life policy, that I said maybe I'd let 'er cash for that worthy cause the wedding of Susan. All right, I said that I'd let 'er cash it, and now maybe I changed my mind.

I went through the motions patting the pockets. "Gee, and I thought that I brought it."

"Well don't forget next time."

"Don't worry, kiddo."

And don't worry, there won't be a next time you bastard. And when your Henry boots you out into the gutter there where you belong, don't look for Gross either—his door'll be locked!

Only, Gross— I came to outside. Did I really say all that stuff? Did that talk really happen? It was like a depressing dream. And what was accomplished? Who cared about Charlotte, one way or the other? And say I had a divorce.

Then off to the wedding—Here comes the gloom, all dressed
in ruin—and the lady that gasped under Gross last night in the
dark, like with anybody?

Bright sunshine danced through the trees there between
Madison Avenue and the park, and the shadows fell in those
nice patterns on the sidewalk. I mean I knew they were nice,
but what did I feel? I felt nothing.

Gross walked along empty, in his own gray day.

EVEN GOING UPSTAIRS I could hear she was after me, Ruth, my
new leech already, with the phone ringing before I could get
so far as to fit the key in the door.

I gave it a bark, "Leave me live," and I let it ring.

Eventually she quit.

My God, does it ever once fail? You go to bed with some
cunt, and right away they got a lien on your carcass. So hide,
Gross, and not here in this dump that's dark in broad daylight
with every shade up as high as they'll go. Find a mountain and
dig in, with green leaves for camouflage. Be friends with the
trees and the grass, and talk to the birds, and let the wolves and
the vultures back home rip each other apart or else go boom all
together in one big explosion.

Only, shmuck, how will you find a mountain? In our age,
mountains take cash.

Grrrr!

Look, they got me growling, and pacing like an animal!

Oyyy . . .

And that goddam phone again? Okay, she asked for it,
Gross is letting 'er have it!

"What? Who? . . . Oh, Barney, Barney Frankel. Was
that you that just called? . . . No, huh?" Then she is after
me, Amin, it ain't just my mania. "I sound sore? Well, I been
pummeled, so I'm a little bit sore. And what's with you?
How's married life the second time around?"

What a question. But God is good. No matter how bad things are, He'll show you they can always be worse. Here was a man, Frankel, Old Graycloud with his white mane of hair, a sweet man. So, late in life— Late in life. He was in his fifties then, like I am now, and he married a widow, a nice normal lady, with a family of nice grown daughters that treated him like a father. Better, in fact, than some fathers get treated. I knew the first Mrs. Frankel, from the pinochle at Barney's. Also, she happened to be a sister of my cousin Bella's Lou, and we'd meet in the hospital sometimes, or in Bella's house, after Lou had his stroke. So the daughters, they married, they moved out, and the wife, poor woman, one day without warning she dropped dead on him, still in her forties. So Barney felt lonely and he went to Miami and he looked for a wife. And, God forbid, he found one, a Betty, likewise a widow, even better looking than the first, with marcelled blue hair, a bright expression, and could she make chopped liver! Only, when the honeymoon was over and he got to know 'er, Barney's liver began to feel like part of the chop.

Easygoing Barney, whatever she wanted was okay by him. Stay home? He'd stay home. Go out? Out they'd go. The pinochle game was too raucous, okay no more pinochle. But fulltime attention, twenty-four hours a day? That he was in no position to give this Betty of his. So she'd pout at him, and she'd whine in her baby voice.

"Didn't you tell me, down in Miami, that you could take off from your business whenever you liked?"

Sure, but he'd assumed that she understood, within reason, like a vacation. After all, in his business, in real estate, you got to be there in the office, in the store, or else business goes elsewhere. Then there are days when you leg it around looking for business.

"Well my husband"—her good husband the dead one, she

meant—"was in insurance, and *he* didn't have to leg it around looking for business."

Naturally you dumb bunny—not that her bad husband Barney ever would say such harsh words to her—Husband One's percentages on old sales kept coming in anyway, and how can you leg it without legs or with what's just as bad: a heart so leaky that all that there's left for you to do is sit with your wife and slowly expire. And wouldn't I bet that that one sliced years off the few he had left!

All this in public, the night of her pinochle ultimatum, before Gross and the other two could grab their coats and get out of her house.

Seek wives.

"No use grumbling," Barney still could try shrugging it off. Me, I'd grumble. But lucky him, he ain't me. He didn't call to grumble. Gross has mountains on the mind, and like telepathy here's Frankel to offer me the best kind, his own place, that he bought in hopes of pleasing his Betty.

"So why ain't she pleased?"

"There's insects."

"In the house?"

"Oh no. Outdoors."

A Betty-and-a-half, that Betty. But what could I say after thank you? He knows Gross and the country, that's why he tried me first. Only I'm bare.

"Nobody's bare. I'll lend you the key, try it a weekend, a week, as long as you want. Then, say it suits you, there always can be terms."

"Barney, why ain't you a lady, you good soul, so I could propose marriage and we'd go up there together and you'd cook and I'd clean and we'd live happily ever after."

We laughed, but me, I'm laughing with tears in my eyes. Because that longing of mine for God's green earth and a pure sky overhead, when'll it come true? I'll tell you when. When I cash in on my payments to the Young Kishinever Social and Burial Society, and settle down in my six-by-three footage near Flushing Meadows Bay. And even there, with all the new highways, it still has to be gas fumes.

And still the phone!

Did you ever see such a persecution?

"Moe?" she checked up on me.

"With your kind permission."

"Spare me your wisecracks. I've been trying long enough to reach you, and your sister too, all day long. Papa's dying, so now of course he must see his other children, his dear once-a-year ones."

My throat stuck together, my head spun. "Who, who's this?" But I knew, I knew before she spoke again even, with more sarcasm, I knew it was my sister Maxine, phoning to vent long-distance spleen on me. My sister Sylvie's good luck—because Maxine would have to make believe Sylvie was a lady of leisure that if not for her social life could have taken in Papa long ago—Sylvie's good luck was to be in the office till five and miss Maxine's phone calls. Though why—with Papa dying, our dear, our only Papa after all—Maxine had to be brimming with bitterness, that God only knew. But all right, after years with a daughter a dying man should feel like also saying good-by to his other two children? An insult, it's true.

Jet Age Moe, short of breath and cash, I phoned the airlines and then went hunting for the only greenery that counts—in my pants pockets, in the old shoe in the clothes closet, in the cracked cup in the kitchen. Even so I had to run down and borrow a twenty off Murray in the grocery store. Then I phoned Sylvie at her place of business, and I held the wire listening to her wail right there in her office, with the others gathering around her asking, exclaiming.

"Oh, I've been a bad daughter Moe—" meaning Papa with Maxine and never with her all that time.

You think this was strictly sorrow for Papa? Have a second thought, on me. Age thirty-seven and an attractive woman, and you decide to settle down with two daughters and three rooms as a 100 percent widow famous among family and friends for refusing all offers both honorable and otherwise, where could you have put Papa, on a shelf in your foyer? Nah, when Sylvie's Phil passed away on her ten long years ago, he left her poor in money but rich in tears. Look at her and she cries—her privilege and fine, but what if you yourself have a shrinking in the intestines and a cold sweat breaking out thinking of Papa?

But let me laugh, since I forgot how to cry after age ten when I broke open my knee on the sidewalk on Rivington Street and the other kids roared like comedy at the National Burlesque.

At the airport Sylvia grabbed me with tears in her eyes.

"Ten years and five months ago to the day this coming Wednesday I lost my poor Phil. How can I stand another such blow?"

"Try sitting down."

So at least I could listen in airport comfort to the rest of the tune, how good poor Phil was and everybody loved him and how he suffered with his twisted rheumatism and never complained, and his walking pneumonia and never complained, and though he never smoked a cigarette in his life his lung cancer—"At least if he'd smoked," she threw up her hands and wailed—and still never complained, until he had to groan on his deathbed, after the operation, "Sylvie, they're murdering me—" And now Papa. Was there ever another woman with good luck like hers?

Everybody loved Phil? Phil had friends, who don't? I liked him, complaints and all. Not that he wasn't more than entitled to a complaint, the way life fell on him. And when I heard him complain, Sylvia didn't?

"I heard you," she used to sing out to him, "I heard you the first time and I heard you the tenth time."

So, what was so terrible? It ain't fun with an invalid, a dying man. But to milk a bad year—okay two, three bad years—for the rest of your life? Whatever the shortcomings, did you see the other widow, the Widow Amin, pull that? Suicide, sure. But remember those jokes she had for her sorrows? And ears for another too, not like Sylvia, just to hear yourself talk.

Warped, my sister Sylvia.

And me, I'm better, with these eyes that shift and trust no one? One Ruth listens, but a different Ruth wants you in bed?

"Excuse me a second Sylvie, I got to make a call."

And eager as a boychik I ran to dial Ruth's number.

Say, to sit while the lady's phone rings twenty-five times, do I earn a good mark for patience? Oh she don't let the grass grow under her feet, that one.

Back at Gate 3 my sister was pacing the floor. "Moe, something awful's going to happen, I feel it in my bones!"

And right on cue came my name through the public-address system: Gross wanted at the main desk!

"Moe I feel faint—"

And me, I didn't feel faint? I gave her a look faint then you dog. But at their main desk with her still whimpering behind me, and again it was long distance, what, what did I hear?

"That's what he wants," Maxine was snapping at me, "that's what you want, and that's what he's doing!"

I couldn't believe it. "What? Who? What did you say?"

"Are you deaf at a dollar a minute? I said he's flying to you."

My throat choked. Did she mean in a box?

"Please Maxine, don't joke. Is this a joke?"

"Victor drove him to Stapleton Airport, he'll be in New York in three hours, and I'm hanging up."

"But how can he, so sick?"

"Let him explain that."

And she did hang up, right in my ear. I called back and in luck: My brother-in-law Victor picked up the phone.

"I won't say Papa looks robust, Moe, but it's hard to believe he's the same man who was in bed this morning."

"And the doctor? What did he say about Papa flying east?"

"I don't believe they consulted the doctor, Moe."

And you, Mr. College Man, Mr. I Don't Believe, you couldn't give the dial a twist to consult the doctor? But on this I kept mum. If he don't drag down no medals for Brother-in-law of the Year, slow-motion Victor, he's still in the family and I run into worse in my time. But Maxine, my big sister that used to help me do algebra when we were kids? And after that business with Nitzberger, the Maxine with an angry laugh whenever she heard an injustice was done: "Thank your lucky stars you slipped loose from that one, kid." And now heartless? Where, what happened to her?

And the other, our Sylvie, that we called our Little Woman on account of the smile and the way she liked to take care and take charge in the house? All the way back to Lucky 11 for the long wait for the incoming flight, "Oh my God I can't face it, how could she, how will he look, oh I can't, I—"

"Shut up!"

I never yelled like that at Sylvie before, not even when we were kids, and she was shocked. And me too.

She said, "You abuse me like this, your sister, after all that I've been through?"

Feh, feh on life. The airport was shiny all over, everywhere gloss and chromium and marble floors, with artificial air and sweet music in your ears from the loudspeakers. But underneath, feh, a world shriveled up, dust, black night. Bring on the pills, the plastic bag for the head, the Bomb, who cares?

I begged her pardon, and at the gorgeous magazine stand I bought her a *Good Housekeeping* to distract her mind. Me, I entertained myself with the papers. Arms buildup over Berlin, theirs and ours. Our Leader tells us build bomb shelters and burrow down deep. In Havana Señor Castro states that a man equals more than a tractor, he equals a tank or a bulldozer at least. So he'll hold on to the Made in U.S.A. freedom-fighters we sent down to put 'im out of business only he put them out of business and threw the ones still breathing in jail. Later maybe, pending the bulldozers, he'll shoot those too. Meanwhile, look at the bright side. There under Weather they claimed cloudy with showers, and here's God's golden sunshine pouring through the glass.

Sylvia likewise must have picked up good news in *Good Housekeeping*, maybe a bulletin on family life the last hope, because when I said how about a coffee break, she never blinked out a tear. She just pulled a long face and said, "I could use a cup of coffee."

"Me too. How about a coffee break?"

She gave me a funny look.

"Did anyone ever tell you, Moe, you're becoming eccentric?"

I felt ashamed, teasing her so. So in the snack bar I tried making her happy and asked what was new with my niece Carol Ann. That's her older girl, very bright—not even out of college and already engaged. But true charity hurts. The high marks Carol Ann got last term, all right, that chicken of nineteen with every grace of a cow thirty-five. And okay too with the fiancé hitting it small on the stock market, with capital gains, quick profits, and his always the right guess. But to tell me that the one worry, heh heh, was he was such an observant Jew even Carol Ann might have trouble keeping up with him in that respect? And rubbing it in, in case the message hadn't come through, "How's Lizzie, and Fu Young?"

"George. Fu is an omelette."

"She still works and he goes to school?"

The opposite, if anything, according to Liz on the phone last week. "I'm going back during the day next fall and getting my degree, Pop, no matter what." But no matter what what she didn't say. Black years, black days, and minstrel George.

These thoughts however we don't share with the public at large.

"What do you mean?" I told Sylvia. "My son-in-law the doctor, even if he won't be taking my pulse. But listen, and no waterworks please. Soon Papa will be landing, even if God is kind a sick man—"

"Oh God!"

I warned her with my finger, the way you do a child. "All the better. Maxine is worn out, and here he has us."

"My God, if only I had the room!"

"I have the room. Charlotte's away and the house is empty except for Moe. But me alone, Moe Nightingale the short-order cook, fried eggs our feature, how could I take care of him?"

"I'll cook."

"God bless you. Then, say Papa ain't well and I have to go out on a job. You got vacation coming?"

"Ye-es . . ."

"But then you might be busy in the office, even though it is Papa."

"The hell with the office! Papa comes first."

Fine, so I shamed her into it.

Optimist, infant, idiot Moe!

The plane pulled up, the passengers debarked, there came Papa eager but hamstrung, with baby steps. One look and Sylvia's eyes rolled. She went limp, she sagged to the floor.

I would have let her lay there, with her spectators, her steward, and her smelling salts. But Papa, weak as he was, shrunken and creased even since last year—and remember what a husky little man he used to be—he wanted to bend down and help, only how could he bend?

"Chafing the wrists is good, chafe her wrists Moe—"

Meanwhile they brought her to, they gave her water to sip, they sat her in a chair. Now Papa could pat her wrist and smile at the baby.

"How's my young lady?"

One look and Sylvia's eyes rolled. Again she passed out, this time with me holding the smelling salts.

"I thought," Papa said, not so happy, "I had the Angel of Death fooled and left him in Denver for a day or two, but it must show in my face he flew in on the same flight, huh Moe?"

"Papa, forget it. In this part of the country only cousin Bella can see the Angel of Death. You know Sylvie."

"Ah, she's a good girl."

Was, Papa meant, a long time ago. Right now, another message seeped through to slow-learner Gross. Find help, but quick. And where would a man turn for help, if not to his helpmate? So forget pride, and give in.

Gross brought Sylvia to with some slaps in the face that I had to hold back on so they shouldn't be punches.

"Oh I can't, I'm sorry," she moaned for me, "where's Papa—"

"Never mind Papa. You just take a cab home and give us a ring some time."

She shook her head that she would, and I went and gave Charlotte a ring.

"Why you know that I couldn't leave Henry."

And why did I call up this nothing when the same dime could have gotten me the Home Nursing Service? Going on sixty, and I pull stunts, and the reasons are still a mystery to me. But you start, like a losing hand in the pinochle game, so you play it out.

"Trust me, Henry's needs will be filled. My candidate

however don't have such facilities. And after all Charlotte, we're still man and wife."

"For the time being, as you advised me today."

Twist-your-guts Charlotte. But that I been hoist on my own petard, that I can't argue with. So what do you say, let's unhoist yourself Gross.

"Charlotte, I'm apologizing, that was a gag. To become Henry's heiress you'd have to drag every Schwarzman through cousin-five-times-removed into your parlor like the spider and the fly, and serve them tea with an arsenic Danish. Henry's business now is with caskets, not brides, Charlotte, and even if—"

"That's a lie!"

"God should second the motion, believe me. But say if he lived to a hundred. You know Henry, better than I do. Even with all your merits, would he propose to a woman without money?"

"So that's your opinion, and the other was a joke?"

"Honest and truly I'm sorry, I must have been out of my mind. So what do you say Charlotte, I—"

"I say you'll discover that she who laughs last laughs best!"

And bang!—again in my ear, the pastime today with the ladies of my family.

As long as I was in that sweatbox anyway with the little plastic fan blowing free hot air in my face, I contributed another ten cents to AT&T and chatted with Home Nursing. The woman said they had a slight backlog of requests, which are acceptable only in writing, and four to six weeks were required for processing. But what, I asked her, if the client God forbid entered the next world for lack of care those four to six weeks? She said she was sorry.

Here let me put in a good word for Our Times, for Science and Technology, that besides the Smog, the Bomb, and paint rollers for shoemakers to smear walls with, have also invented a young lady with pilot wings over the bubbies, that steers an electric cart in the airport. You're too old or feeble to make it on foot, and you paid for a plane fare, she'll run you down to the baggage pickup. Papa, he qualified on all counts and she ran him.

But who's going to run him up my three flights of stairs, who'll cook, who'll clean, who'll hand him his medicine? Papa comes first, but cash comes second. So what's left? Find a free-of-charge housekeeper, like Liz? Sure she would, gladly. But what, you got one good one so you pile it on heavy? First I'll ask Susan my eldest—that's never; then I'll ask Liz.

Such were my happy thoughts in the station wagon all the way home, while easygoing Sam Gross beside me was laughing off Maxine. Child play, he called it. He was dying this morning, such weakness that it was hard not to give in. "So heavy Moe, your bones hurt, and you want to shift for a little relief, yet you can't raise an arm to move yourself." But he prayed, he implored God for a few more hours till I'd get there, and Sylvia. Then—isn't God wonderful!—he must have slept, because he opened his eyes, and, "You know what, Moe? I thought I was dreaming," he could turn. He could even sit up. So he tried standing. "I didn't find myself set for a kazatsky, but I didn't fall down either." He managed to get dressed, and he went over for a look out of the window at Maxine's beautiful backyard, with her trees and her flowers. Then a scream like death: his heart almost stopped. That was Maxine. What was he doing? Get back to bed!

"I answered her," Papa looked sheepish, "with an unfortunate choice of words."

"Cursed her up and down, huh Papa?"

Papa laughed, that I never heard use a curse word in his whole life, not even the years I was his apprentice, working together with my fellow-ruffian paintners.

"I said, 'What's the rush? I got a long rest coming.'"

To me that sounded like a brave man, in contrast to a bully his lifetime the great Henry Schwarzman that in the end is scared shitless.

But my sister Maxine translated as follows: "You mean I'm rushing you into your grave? Me? I'm killing you?" And however Papa could laugh, whatever Papa could say, Maxine wasn't listening. "Go to your other children," she screamed at him, "where you want to go, where you'll get better care than I know how to give!"

I asked Papa, "Where was your son-in-law Victor meanwhile? Downstairs reading a magazine?"

That also struck Papa funny. "Self-preservation, Moe."

Papa tried to thank Maxine, to assure her no man ever had had a better daughter, and Maxine screamed, "But not as good as your son!" Then she went running to throw the fare I sent for Papa down on his bed.

"So," Papa said, "I could argue to myself it's hard, catering day-in day-out to a sick man, a dying man, the way she caters to me. And if she thought that last week was the end already, why not? Didn't I think so myself? Only the shoe fits the wearer just the same, and to hear her, from her own mouth, rushing me into the grave? And if I felt that resentment now, how would I feel if I gave in and went back to bed to die? I love Maxine, Moe, that good child, that good unhappy woman, and my dying thoughts should be bitterness towards her? No. Better, if I could do it, to do what she said in her hysteria, to go. Besides, I finish up here, I rest in peace next to your Mama. In Denver, who knows?"

"What, we'd have brought you back, Papa. Don't have such thoughts."

"And I honestly did figure," Papa could grin, "maybe, if I keep going so he thinks that I'm well, I could fool the Angel a little while longer."

"You'll fool him more than a little while longer, Papa, if you can live through my cooking. And how do you like your eggs, scrambled or sunnyside?"

Now ain't Papa the best-natured man in the world, to laugh at that too? But driving into my block I wasn't laughing.

And when I double-parked, who's guarding the building but La Amin! Gross full of anxieties, and here's Madam Itch? But wait, you'll see 'er run fast, like my gem of a sister out at the airport.

I told Papa just a minute and got out, and sure enough she was there with the hands. Gross stuck his in his pockets.

She said, "Boy, am I glad to see you!"

"Then you're glad to see trouble, hah? Eager to help, in God you'll trust, Gross has no cash?"

"But what"—she honestly went white, she pressed her hand to her chest—"what is it Moe!"

"Just my father there in the car, though to some it's like cholera."

But when I got through the plot of the Airline Follies, and Sylvia and Charlotte and the Home Nursing Department, I didn't see this one disappearing into the sunset with deepest regrets.

She said, "I'll keep house."

Only— What did she have in mind? Because we'd be in the house together then, her and me, it would be one long party like last night? But Gross kept mum. If that was her angle—in front of Papa especially—she had another guess coming!

HEY, YOU WANT TO KNOW what it'll be like here when you're underground, what the Folks will think about you, what they'll say? Okay, I'll tell you. Nothing, that's what they'll think. Here today gone tomorrow, out of sight out of mind, good-night sweetheart good-by and good luck! Unless, of course, between Their Side and Our Side, the boys, the brave men, blow up the whole shebang, including Hotel Fancy and the contestants in my daughter Sue's wedding. What then? Then, according to the Scientists—who after all have lifted us to the topmost peak of human development so shouldn't they know?—then, the crickets will rub their wings together and there'll still be chirping: the same conversation as now. Would that be so bad?

Invisible Man Gross!

For Gross's three G's insurance money Hotel Fancy not only caters a ballroom medium-to-small for the wedding festivities, but another made into an instant synagogue for sanctification of the crime, and on top of that a two-room suite for the bride to change costume in and flash the prebout victory smile at well-wishers. Also—free!—the happy couple can spend the wedding night in this suite if they want.

If pains equals genius, count Sue in.

Her week's mourning in advance for Rodney's From Coast To Coast Axelrod would go without saying, in his bedroom every night with a sad face waiting for Nurse to announce his last breath, or with a sweet face when every last breath was followed by the next. As to God's opinion—or Axelrod's—of the premature sorrow, we won't know until Axelrod's will is opened, and for this he first has to die. But her impression on Charles Davis I do know, because poor Charlie told me. Such devotion he'd never seen, and he fears for my daughter's health. The fact is Sue always was late to bed, and between the job, her diets, and her few hours' sleep, the face is pale and spiritual, a saint's among saints, with the eyes slightly marked underneath. Now, at his Grandfather Axelrod's, where he has to sit because she sits there, Susan is Charlie's only scenery and in his eyes all she lacks is the halo.

Also, starting the bridal party from Schwarzman's Fifth Avenue to slip Uncle Henry a blossom from the corsage and a daughterly kiss, that was a masterstroke that might not occur to every young lady on the verge of matrimony even the second time around. But Henry was likewise teetering over the grave, and granted Sue's expectations in that direction couldn't amount to more than a fat check for the wedding, still he likewise would leave a will—and who knows?

But what, besides genius, could explain her skipping an hour at Axelrod's last week to visit her Dad (that's what she called me that visit: Dad) and (that's what she called him) Grampa Gross? Because even if she thought Papa was God forbid a dying man—and I was happy to tell her, when she began her mournful effusions over him, that he still made it downstairs for his morning sunshine—all of his property, the six feet next to Mama, he was sure to take with him.

When Susan and Charlie left, Papa said he didn't know, she seemed like a sincere, goodhearted girl. And the man that sold Papa the underwater Florida real estate in 1921, he seemed like a sincere, goodhearted boy. Goodhearted Papa, he laughed, and he repeated all of Susan's excuses: shopping for her house, added Clinic cases with the late summer vacation schedule, and Axelrod. She was good, Papa said, to the young man's grandfather. And how about to the young lady's grandfather? It hadn't taken a wedding to make Lizzie visit—and all laden with her touch-and-go marriage. It should only end go, but Ruth says shut up, Liz'll do fine by herself. She should only do fine, and meanwhile I can enjoy the heartache, Liz's and mine. Just the same Liz came to pay her respects to her grandfather right away back in June and more than once afterward, while the other pops up over two months later with her sincerity, her good heart, and her orders of the day what I should wear, where I should report, for her wedding.

Papa said, "Be reasonable, Moe, till she came today you never let the child know you were attending the wedding."

"I didn't know if I was attending. And if not for that boy Charles, I wouldn't be attending."

So St. Susan, the affectionate loving daughter and grand-daughter, she could smile in her Grampa's eyes, laugh at his jokes, invite him to the affair, and even make him think she really wanted him there. Was it a wonder Papa was conned? He wasn't the first, and he won't be the last. And if she fooled Papa in the space of a half hour, she couldn't manage old Axelrod on an intensive-care basis? She'll find her inheritance, Sweet Sue, and some men rob and they throw 'em in jail, and others work away their whole life painting walls like a horse.

But—go ruffle a sick man—I should argue with Papa? So I kept still and burned.

After Ruth helped Papa back to bed again, then I could unburden myself to her. She understood, but she took me by the hand and reminded me I myself said the more money for Susan the more hope for Charles. Still it eats you, such money, because even if you want nothing, say a cottage small way out of sight of the waterfall, it costs.

The con girl. One wedding prop was a father in full dress, so she staged her visiting act. On the wedding night though she sailed into that suite with her mother carrying the wedding gown and Liz the overnight case, and my son-in-law for protection. Who needed protection? I did, from the son-in-law. But that came a minute later. Out of the side of her eye Susan checked the old man dumped in a soft chair with the hard collar biting, on hand as required. So down went the curtain on Act II and we were back to Act I. She breezed straight into the bedroom, never paused!—though she did give a tilt to her cheek to see this prop was in place. Charlotte went next, and then—it hurt, it hurt—Lizzie.

Like I'm not there.

George Young didn't overlook me though, the Duke of Taiwan. He slapped me on the back, stuck a cigar in my face—"Genuine Havana, Pop, invasion or no invasion. I have relatives in Cuba, and in Florida too, in the restaurant business"—and right away went to milk me for twenty.

"What for?" I asked him. "The bar is free in the ballroom."

George laughed. "I'm off liquor, Pop. The ulcers object."

"So how come the place smells like a distillery since the second you walked in?"

"Not me, Pop." And before I could grab my nose he blew me a breath specimen to prove it. "Sue had one or two. You know, for a girl's nervous moments."

What George had was a letter he'd written to an artist Franz Cigar—famous, George assured me—conning Cigar for a scrawl, a line, a dot, that wouldn't run more than fifty dollars or a C-note, that his poor and desperate admirer could cherish forever. So Cigar, being one of those born every minute like most of us, free of charge drew a cow with sidelocks on the back of the letter, and on the bottom he drew his name Cigar—absolutely authentic, George said—with even a curl of smoke drifting up.

George needed the twenty to frame this masterpiece.

"No pay at the University, Doctor?"

George gave a sad little smile. "The stipend comes small and infrequently, Pop."

"Stipend? I thought you were appointed Professor?"

"Pop, that didn't pan out."

He lowered his voice and from the bedroom we could hear Susan: "Ow, for chrissakes Mother! Why this mad haste?"

"The truth is," George started to get confidential, so I took a tighter grip on my wallet, "Lizzie and I have just reached an understanding on that, and I'd like to have this framed as a gift for Liz. She's crazy about Cigar."

Gross, if right ever won and wrong ever lost, could you live through the shock?

The long and short was I gave him the twenty, only let him get out of my sight. With his mission accomplished he beamed me a smile no extra charge and off to the ballroom for bigger game.

I sat, and Susan's complaints from the dress-changing through the door that they left ajar turned into the other two's ohs, ahs, and beautifuls. There was a kiss, and Lizzie spoke; and how could you not love the lilt of that voice? "Good luck, Susie!" At the same time, me, I missed Ruth.

"It's all speculation." I couldn't believe my own ears. That was Susan? A truth from those lips, even in jest? How? From excitement? Too little sleep? Whisky? "Mother, run get me a Scotch and water before the Greeks arrive bearing gifts. Wouldn't they all love to see me eat crow, those bastards my friends."

Whisky, it was.

Susan's number-one fan, Mrs. Young, couldn't believe her hearing either.

"Susie, are you well?"

"Oh I'm well," the big sister laughed, "and I'd be even better if my beloved grandfather-in-law were just a little bit worse. You should have seen him last night, heard him. Like ashes, and gasping for air. But he didn't die, and that was his last chance before the wedding."

"But why must he die, Sue?"

The barmaid Charlotte—in fancy dress on my money— rushed by me and the other furniture again with first aid for Sue. For two cents I had a good urge to open my Lady High Tone's legs eyes and mouth right on the rug here to who's who and what's what.

Inside, with a gulp at the mother's milk, Susan laughed. "Till he dies, where do I stand?"

In a small voice, Liz said, "Isn't Charlie enough?"

"Ha ha"—again gulp—"what do you think?"

Lizzie said, in a voice even smaller, "I like him."

"Oh, like him. Who doesn't like him? What distresses me most is this foreboding I have about the old man's duplicity, especially his endearments." Next came an old man's talk, high, shaking, with an accent. " 'You're like sunshine, dolling. It is a fect, I've learned, and I feel it more, now that I'm . . . an old man, that the best things really are free.' Now is that, or is that not, a turn of the knife . . . in the entrails?"

Was Charlotte sore! "Don't be ridiculous! And even if it were so, the money is bound to come anyway, through the Davises."

"You're like sunshine, dolling," said Sue, "but haven't you heard? We live more for now nowadays, not a dim distant future. And your Davises have never realized a nickel out of Axelrod yet. Only jobs he gives them—Charles, and his father—with timeclocks attached." She giggled. "I'll bet he'd give me one of those too, to have another live soul in bondage, if I begged pretty please. But, cheers! At least jobs are behind me, and Clinic brats. So here's to marriage, from this day forward, in wealth and in health, the richer the surer, till debt do us part!"

The guests began strolling in, Sue's Greeks, with their smirks and good wishes, and Lizzie sneaked out. This time I reached and grabbed her by the hand.

What a face—slim again, dark, good-looking—that even a Georgie should love. And those eyes, full, to break Gross's heart.

"Tears, for that?"

"You heard, Pop? I feel so sad for her!"

"Good heart. But it could be worse, in these times. Behind her there are no armies marching."

"But Pop, in these times people should surely be decent in their own lives. What about Charlie?"

But look, edging into the room with the mother and friends: the virgin bride and her sweet laughter. Widow, I mean? Look at 'er, in the crown of white: a beauty, with shy eyes.

"See," out of the side of my mouth, "what Charlie sees."

Liz shook her head. "Incredible." And you, when you look at George, that's credible?

"So," I gave my hands a clap: insincere, what was there to applaud? "And how about you, Liz? Ready for college again?"

"Didn't I tell you, Pop? I'm putting it off this term."

Babbled away, what a good talk she and George had had, how it really had cleared the air. And last June she'd completely misunderstood what the new research offer they'd made him meant. Oh—proud of him!—George already was an authority on educating the oy underprivileged. What should be done he knew all about. But what could be done?—that was the question. Very significant: political, social, financial. Me, I

would have given Dr. Young's stipend to an underprivileged
mother and let her buy lollipops for the kids at least. But never
mind, Dr. Young was making a study of the situation. That's
what Georgie was working on now.

"And harder than ever! Do you know"—the eyes shone
with love, for him, for the world—"how much what he's doing
will mean to these millions of children, Pop!"

My dear fool, I know. But when will you know, with the
bill of goods that he sold you?

And Charles Davis, with the sentence pronounced and me
an accessory before and after the fact, what did he do? Did he
yell beat it crook, howl murderer away?

He smiled like an angel. He promised me lots of grandchil-
dren, all with brown eyes like Susie.

To PAPA—why upset him while his warm milk and sleeping
pill began taking effect?—I mentioned only the bright side
minus the drinks, with him it's always been Prohibition: the
chopped-liver tureen, the cute little knishes, the chrysanthe-
mum vase on the tables, and above all my sister Sylvia
concealing her sorrow in merriment, after the ceremony not a
tear the whole night! My tale of woe was reserved for Ruth as
usual, while I was driving her home.

"Wanting children now," she only could shake her head.
"You've got to be out of your mind, or braver than I am."

Lately even the ride home she kept the radio on. What for?
The threats on the hour, the half hour? She listened in spite of
herself: the Megatons with the broken windows in Siberia; the
Berlin Wall; our good Germans that we got to protect, the
world drifting toward war Tito says.

But I sang, "What's the use of worrying?" while I reached
to switch off God's deputy, subbasement department. Only
look at that scared face, those clenched hands. "Ah, Ruth—"

"I can't help it. I'm terrified, Moe."

So at her door I said I'd come in for a minute, and she said, "What about your father?"

She believes all Gross's lies.

The day Papa got here, she believed Gross's lie that in the morning, from her house, I just ran home to shave, I thought that I'd be right back. Sure, I phoned her later, the way I said. But how much later, that I didn't say. And I didn't say either what beautiful thoughts Great Gross had when he condescended to call and Amin wasn't right there to answer! Ruth? *She* apologized that that must have been—except mum Gross knew different—just the moment she ran down to see if my car was still there after she woke up and saw that I wasn't.

Or else, I introduced her to Papa, did I say even my friend Mrs. Amin? No, crafty Gross. The last thing you wanted was that Papa should know what you had there, not that you knew it yourself. So let Papa be old-fashioned—couldn't that have been mentioned to Mrs. Amin beforehand?

Deaf Ruth ain't, and dumb she ain't either. I said to Papa, "Here's Mrs. Amin, she'll help in the house while Charlotte's away." So when I drove her home that first night, she said, "You feel funny about us, don't you, in front of your father, letting him think I'm a housekeeper?"

And did that make Gross ashamed at least, being caught in the act? What ashamed! Put out, Gross felt, at her presumption, her "us"!

Gross said then, "I better straighten him out, hah, give credit where due?"

And her, she put her head on my shoulder, she laughed. "That's all right, your cousin Bella gave me all the credit I need, yesterday."

So Gross, you must have been grateful, to hear her say that? Gross sat there stiff, with her leaning on me, and telling himself aha, with this one one minute the favor and the obligation the next. Bull Gross back in bed was what she was after!

So Bull Gross fixed her that night, and every night thereafter—whether I liked it or not. I'd bring her up to her door, and then—didn't Gross have to hustle right home to Papa?

Who had to hustle right home to Papa? Papa always slept fine the first couple of hours. But Lunatic Gross was still testing.

My sister Maxine phones every evening, long distance.

"Papa, are you taking your medicine?"

"Would you let me forget?" Papa laughs.

But who sees to his medicine, plus his airings, plus his meals, from early morning till 10:00 P.M., and later if there's a wedding on? Yeh. The lady that Gross was still testing.

So a few Sundays ago, while Sylvie was visiting, and a couple of others, I couldn't help it: all of a sudden like a madman I jumped up, I told Sylvie, "I'll be back in a while, I got to give a job estimate." Like a madman I cursed and ranted at the traffic in my way the half a mile over to Ruth's, and I rushed upstairs panting there to grab her in my arms.

She opened the door, and her eyes opened wide, then with joy. But I reached out, she raised up a finger. That was the Sunday Gross met Ruth's sister Sheila, ha ha ha!

But it was worth the trip, more than worth it. I was leaving after an hour, Ruth pressed my hand in the hall, and, "Gee, I love you, Moe," she thanked me for the visit!

And tonight when I got home before, with the stink of that wedding still in my nose, what did I find?

Papa in bed, Ruth next to the bed, and the cards—what do cards mean to her?—spread out between them. The radio, with the end of the world blow by blow, that was for Ruth's ears; Papa didn't even hear it was on. He grinned, he apologized.

"I couldn't sleep, so I'm teaching her pinochle."

And Ruth made a smile!

So now lie number ten thousand in answer to her what about Papa—that Ginzburg (I asked him today) guaranteed sleep from the pills.

We went in, she asked me did I want coffee.

"Ruth, I want."

She shrugged, poor kid, so doleful, so tired out. She said, "The world situation's too much for me."

"In that case, I'll make coffee." I helped her off with her coat, I sat her down at the table, I started the coffee pot.

Ruth said, "You're a good lover, Moe."

Me, that she hadn't had to bed since a week ago Sunday?

"Kidding the kidder, huh, Ruth?"

"No, you're a dream, my dream. Considerate, everything."

"Not a nightmare? Well, romance runs in the family."

And those blue eyes looked up at me.

"You mean your father? I don't believe it!"

"What father? Grampa Aaron, the Kramnitz Casanova in the old country! I mean, after my grandmother died. See, Grandma Gertie wasn't my grandma. The real Grandma Gross they picked for Grampa Aaron when he was thirteen, she died a young woman. After that it was field day. He had a smile like his chest expansion—wide: and the ladies came running. And money!—a village captain of industry junior only to his partner, and the partner had a daughter named Gertie. So, free agent, with women tripping over each other for years for the honor, or dishonor, as case may have been, what made him pick Yackety Gertie as legal wife number two? In a well-filled-out world, Aaron preferred slim, and slimmer and peppier than Gertie couldn't be found."

Ah, Ruth sat smiling already; I stood at the closet with the cups and the saucers and she sat smiling up at me with her face on her hands.

"Reasons run in the family," she said. "Your father told me that as a young man you only went after good-looking girls and your biggest misfortune was when you finally caught up to one."

"He told you that?" I stood stunned. I thought I'd always thought beauty was skin-deep. "And he never told me!"

"He said he did tell you, but you only laughed."

"And how about luck, that sent that bunch my way? Luck don't count?"

She jumped up and kissed me and hung there. "Without luck there's nothing!" And she smiled with damp eyes.

"See, you'll have me crying too—and who needs tears at home? Now, sit down, Gross is still serving . . . What really appealed to Aaron was that then he could wisecrack that the boss's daughter was the secret of his success. But then came bad times, no more boss, and no more business, so Grampa Aaron laughed he still had the daughter. But," I poured out the coffee, "that was the last laugh Gertie was good for. The figure, the chatter, the pep: they were old news to Grampa. I remember Grandma Gertie. When she used to visit us, I'd hide in the closet. Then Grampa and Papa and Uncle Dave would settle down at the kitchen table for a game of pinochle, while boychik Moe lost to Grandma at hide-and-go-seek. She was tiny, but wherever you hid she found you and dragged you out. Then kiss kiss kiss, hug hug hug, with Moechik trapped on her lap while she talked poor Mama's ear off. There was only one way to handle her, Grampa's way. If they were together, he made believe she wasn't there. Like my cousin Irving's bar mitzvah, Grandma talked straight through the first forty pages of Irving's greeting to parents, friends, and guests, but you think Grampa listened? He sat there like a Chinaman with his big face and yellow complexion, thinking up a joke. Then he said, 'By the time the boy finishes his speech, he'll be fourteen years old.' Whoever heard tittered, so an echo must have reached Grandma. She said, 'What did you say Aaron, what did you say?' Grampa said, 'I said drink up dear, whisky is good for you.' But back in Kramnitz, one bright day after he turned fifty, the same age as me now, he disappeared altogether, with a message on the table. 'Good-by dear. I have run away with a brunette.' "

"Gertie was blonde!"

"You guessed it. So Gertie raved and she moaned, and she sent stepson Papa to find him and bring him back. Papa finally found him in Wladkow, the big town, in a café, sitting like a gentile and swallowing down vodka. Papa said, 'Gertie's taking it very hard.' So Grampa could wisecrack, 'Let her be like me and take it like a man!' 'You're still with that brunette then?' Papa asked him. Grampa gave him a grin. 'What brunette? Her name was Quiet.' He lived at an inn, but that he kept from his ladyfriends. 'Otherwise,' Grampa laughed, 'honesty pays. I tell them I'm married, so I'm always the guest.' And Papa had to go back to Kramnitz without him."

"Poor Gertie," Ruth grinned. "That's one story I didn't hear from your father."

"Not proper for ladies' ears."

"That's what you say."

"No," I could honestly tell her, "Papa would say that."

"But how did Gertie get Grampa back?"

"Cirrhosis."

"His, or hers?"

We started and we couldn't stop laughing, we grabbed hands, we got up from the table, we danced, we kissed, and we hugged. I unbuttoned Ruth's blouse, I choked out, "His naturally ha ha ha, what would Grampa Aaron care about hers? He needed somebody ha ha ha to keep hiding the schnapps and take care of his diet, so he went back ha ha ha!" Oh how Ruth laughed, we laughed our way to the bedroom, and how proud I was she was laughing!

So East Nazis, West Nazis, both sides of your Wall, you should grow like onions, with your head in the ground and your feet in the air! And when you're down in Gehenna that crowing you'll hear—that's Moe Gross here with Ruth!

So WHATEVER WE GIVE THANKS for this Thanksgiving night it won't be the cranberries. The H-Bomb factories poisoned this year's crop and from that you could get cancer if you live long enough. Outside the rain splashed and the wind moaned; inside Papa dozed and moaned. While I dressed to enjoy the fine weather, my sister Sylvia muttered that my TV reception was the worst bar none she'd ever seen in her life.

Well, torn from home hearth and perfect reception to sit an hour with her father the third time in three weeks, could you blame her for muttering? After all, Butterfly Gross would flit here and there in pursuit of pleasure: to Ruth in her sickbed, to Bella in her hospital bed, or now to Ruth's boy in the hospital in New Jersey. So that's good, keep muttering, Sylvia, so your brother can appreciate what he missed the six months that Ruth took care of Papa.

God punishes pride.

Last June home from the airport I remember me asking, "How are you on stairs, Papa?"

"Better going down," Papa laughed.

And what a climb that turned out to be, with me on one side and Ruth on the other, and Papa between us without strength. And inside a few days Ruth had him taking round trips to the street and the sunshine under his own steam, blocks away to the park even.

"Doc," I asked Ginzburg then, "what gives? It seems like a miracle."

Ginzie said, "Moe, let your father live and be well—life is a miracle."

So I went and bragged to myself: Dying at Maxine's my dear Papa, and here at my house he's rejuvenated, a picture of health!

Like a blight it hit us, almost from the day Ruth had to stop coming, the way Papa started to fail. Now, mornings he's still okay for awhile, but every morning a shorter while. The day wears on and that little strength drains, and the afternoons and nights, they're hard, very hard for Papa.

This time I wasted no phone calls on Home Nursing Services or Charlottes. Right away I found Mrs. Schultz. What does she charge? She charges plenty, and no chip-ins from Sylvia either, though my sister Maxine's guilty conscience in Denver's been mailing me five-dollar checks that I endorse and pass over to Bella to bribe the ward nurses with so if she gives a call they might give a listen. But Mrs. Schultz here, she earns her pay, a nice gray-haired German lady with as much patience as heft. Papa groans give him a pillow, she gives him a pillow; take it away, she takes it away. Or else she'll smooth back that beautiful white hair of his that gets matted from the fever the pain brings. Between groans, good soul, Papa apologizes, and Mrs. Schultz says, "Not at all, Mr. Gross. That's what I'm here for." But I know what Papa means when he jokes, "If she only could play pinochle."

So who told that dumb kid Bobby to go set himself up for a heart attack, so first his mother had to race out there to Jersey, and then make herself sick over him? Long before the attack, you asked Ruth how was Bobby, she'd say, "Fine, suffering in comfort."

The young marrieds owned their— Owned? Jill proposes, the credit company disposes. They had their two-car garage in Fairlawn and the two cars to go with it. They kept one car in the garage, Jill's late-model Olds for her trips to the shopping center. Bobby's early-model Ford that he drove to work he kept on the street, and after his day in the bakery he used the other half of the garage as a machine shop to make extra cash to keep up payments on the garage, the house, the Olds, the Fifth Avenue obstetrician until baby was born, and the Park Avenue pediatrician after. Bobby's New Jersey medical plan didn't reimburse you for New York doctors? Too bad for the medical plan, his wife let him know. Health first, medical plans last, no contest. But there were plenty of good local doctors, Bobby heard? Then let Bobby use them, if they were so good. And how could they afford an agency nurse for when Jill came home from the hospital? She informed him she was only the mother. He was the breadwinner. So that was his problem. He suggested why not let her mother come stay and help, or his mother, they'd both volunteered? Well Jill wasn't having the child spoiled by grandmothers playing nurse its first month home.

"Did you say month?" Bobby said.

Jill said, "Month, as in thirty days hath November, April June and etcetera."

Give Jill credit. She married a baby, and she turned him into a man. He'd make his points, she'd steamroller 'em down, and he'd toddle back to his shop, a quiet, twenty-year-old man. Jill would drop in now and then to make sure the welding wasn't scarring her Olds, but Bobby was very skillful with sparks. He worked like a horse, only the debts were like the stick on his neck that the carrot hung from that the horse could never catch up to.

The night baby was born Bobby shut up shop, chauffeured

Jill to New York in the Ford (hands off Jill's Olds except Jill), clocked in at the factory, back to the hospital at night, and still found a few hours to moonlight in the garage. Then, with the little family home ten days with the twenty-four-hour nurse, he had to send away nurse or bust. So first he put his foot down and sent away nurse. Two A.M. the baby began whimpering, crying, howling. Jill, she slept. Bobby, he got out of bed and fed baby. Then again at six. So he busted in the end anyway.

They took him off oxygen, he smiled at his mother.

"It's nice, you just lie around and they take care of you here."

His mother smiled back. The tears and the virus came later.

"Please Moe," I sat next to Ruth's bed, she grabbed me by the wrist, "go to that bitch, make her stop killing him!"

How, with a demolition charge?

And into the bargain this gorgeous weather.

So Gross tuned in Sylvia's program to get good reception, pulled on the rubbers, pushed the umbrella into the wind, and splashed off to convert the man-eating chieftess, visiting hours from seven to eight.

On the bright side, the kid had a nice room there in Jersey, not Bella's Mt. Eden Hospital ward. Semiprivate, and the roomie a hernia that was out watching TV, and on the wall facing the bed a nice country scene with cows and no humans around. But to make Jill stop killing him, I'd have to sue for divorce, and I ain't her husband thank God.

The boy looked young, a child, with pale smiling cheeks. The wife, the same age maybe younger, was a mature woman, plump and pink and why not, that lived off raw meat.

After I introduced myself she gave me a dinosaur squint and she said, "Are you a widower, Mr. Gross."

"Grass."

"I meant Mr. Grass."

"Gross is the name, you were right the first time. Yeh, I'm a widower."

Because who wanted her to pile on the boy because her mother-in-law's friend had the wrong marital status? All the time I made chatter with Bobby, Jill kept consulting her watch.

"Miss baby?" I asked her.

"I have a very qualified babysitter. I just don't enjoy hospitals."

"You would," piped Bobby, "if you were here on my medical plan."

Jill said, "You'd better get a grip on yourself. Life isn't a medical plan."

"I wish it was," Bobby said.

"Well it's not, and the sooner you realize that you have to work like anyone else, the better you'll feel about it."

Why, you dog! So Gross cut in with that story about my painter pal Leo Blum long ago and his medical plan.

"A shmearer," I told the kid, "but fast, and you've ever met nuts? Leo was king of the squirrels. You'd phone him to the candy store, 'Come to work Leo,' and he'd tell you, 'What for? My insurance is paid up.'"

The wife began looking grim at bad influence Gross, but the kid, he gave a giggle.

"'For laughs Leo,' I'd say. He'd say, 'Thanks, but my caseworker Miss Abelson was here with the supplementary relief check this morning and I been laughing all day. Listen Moe, I got art work to do and you want me to go out painting apartments?' His art work was country scenes, like that one hanging there Bobby, only as follows. He'd take a picture postcard somebody mailed him the summer before and he'd paint it ten thousand times enlarged on his bedroom wall facing garbage alley, the Leonardo da Vinci of Kelly Street, in red like fever and nauseous green. Then he'd take the cow from a milk bottle cap and work 'er up to life-size in the foreground, like a monster cat with two horns. There was also a resemblance to Jenny, his wife, except, of course, Jenny didn't have horns. You'd say to her, 'Jenny, you're gonna let him stand there all day, making pictures?' So Jenny would look fat and laugh, 'Ha ha ha, what can I do with him? Did you ever in your life see such a man?' And then he'd start a new picture over the old one. Once in a while his Miss Abelson smelled a rat and cut off the supplementary relief, he'd work a little bit and then he was flush—he'd pay up his insurance and bet on the horses. How he made out he kept to himself, but once he did say, 'Moe, you know what they do down in the Argentine when a favorite loses? The owner comes down to the finish line and shoots the horse personally.' "

Bobby grinned. "He couldn't have done worse than we did when we tried bookmaking once."

"Because you didn't even know how to pay off a cop in Miami," his love let him have it.

"Sure, honesty's the worst policy," I said. "Leo knew that. Came summer, and no work even for painters like me those days, Leo switched quarters to Manida Hospital. 'Keep it under your hat,' he'd tell me, 'if Miss Abelson finds out I'm here between calls, my relief check's a goner.' 'What are you in for? How do you fool the doctor?' 'Well,' he'd say, 'my hay fever I got, and then there's my possible TB.' You'd look at him, a big strapping man, with a chest like those horses he played. So he'd whisper, 'What should I do? Draw it for you, on the bottom of a bedpan?' Him, the M.D., and the hospital, they were a three-way dairy farm, milking the insurance company. 'Besides, Moe, I need the rest.' And his wife Jenny would visit him with homemade chicken soup to keep up his strength."

You know how you make jokes for a child, and the child

laughs and you smile? That's how this kid laughed and I smiled, only my heart ached for him.

Jill said, "I don't see the humor of that story."

"It's no disgrace," I told her, "everyone has their own idea of a laugh."

So she said, "I don't see where disgrace enters into it."

Let the boy bite my head off, I made up my mind to give him some advice after all. Jill and I rode down to the lobby, the two silent enemies, and there we both saw that I'd forgotten my umbrella. We politely wished each other good-night, and I went back upstairs.

The kid slept, almost like dead, with the lips blue and apart, and no smiles now or even a vestige of a smile, all fagged out from that pile driver. So the next time I'll tell him.

Get back your health, Kid, then run!

Oh, was I mad! And driving through Pellworm, where my dear cousin Sidney lives, Bella's dear brother, I got even madder. What are these vermin stinking up God's earth like the stinklands of Jersey in the black rain?

Gross, keep control, don't madden yourself into a muddy ditch by the side of the road.

A month ago already that I got that phone call from Bella early in the morning with the sun barely rising. "Moe, I think I'm going blind." So, crazy Bella, what'll she think of next?

"Did you pull up the shades?"

"No kidding Moe, I'm scared."

"I'll call up my doctor for you."

"Don't, Moe, I'm scared what he'd say. Please come over, okay Moe?"

"How about brother Sidney in Pellworm? Did you phone him at six in the morning?"

"I phoned him when I got this last week, and he laughed at me, he said that I'm nuts. Then he mailed me one of his twenty-dollar bills, but he can't fool me. That's just hush money my relatives send, so's they won't have to bother with me. I don't need their dough, I just stick it in my mattress. I'm on Relief!"

"What you have went away last week? Don't worry. It'll go away this week."

"Gee Moe, you're the only person that's nice to me. Come over just for a minute—"

So what should I do, laugh, like her brother? Feh, be human, or why live? After Ruth came to take care of Papa, I dropped over at Bella's.

I rang the bell, and—what, she picked up a cat for company now? Miaow, miaow. Only it wasn't a cat, it was Bella.

"Moe, help . . . Moe, help . . ."

"What, what?"

"Moe, help . . ."

You think Bella would trust the super with a key? Not Bella. Her valuables might be stolen: that side chair with the leg broken, or else her winter coat with the rat collar. Up, over and down, me and the super climbed, the stairs, the roof, and the fire escape. Bella's bedroom window naturally was locked. But the shade was up.

Oy, inside—

Bella was dragging herself along on the floor, with a blind hand up in front of her, going in circles. "Moe, Moe—"

Ginzburg came in a hurry when he got my message, and he kidded Bella. "I know your kind. Get yourself potted the night before, what do you expect but to wake up blind and fall on the floor the morning after?"

"Come on doc, what've I got, what've I got?"

"You've got the heebie-jeebies."

"Then why you sending me to the hospital?"

"You expect this poor man to hang around all day while you sober up?"

"Aw, I never touched a drop in my life, except a couple of

times after I got married, but I hated the taste. What've I got, doc?"

"How do I know what you've got? I'm only a doctor, not a fortune-teller." But behind his hand, Ginzburg said in my ear after I had Bella dressed and in the jalopy with her other nightgown and her toothbrush in a paper bag, "Moe, my guess is so rotten if I'm right that I'd rather not say. Let's wait for the tests."

So we waited for the tests, and when I called up Sidney last month and said, "Sidney, your sister is dying, in room so and so in such and such a hospital," and Sidney said, "Oh this is awful, just a second Moe, let me write it down," I honestly believed that guy was about to drop everything, jump in one of his three cars, and rush to poor Bella.

You know something, in God we trust Gross all others pay cash? You're an innocent.

I said to Bella one night, "And how's brother Sidney?"

"Him? Never see hide nor hair of 'im."

But a shame as it is to say, who could believe Bella even when her brain was intact? So Private Eye Gross began the interrogations: patients in neighboring beds, orderlies, nurses, even an interne or two. It was true: no hide, no hair.

I phoned Sidney again and said, "Shmuck—"

"What did you say?"

"I said you're in luck, they just extended the visiting hours at Eden till eight P.M. every night."

"But that's what you said they were before."

"Then you were lucky before, and as far as visiting goes, your luck still holds."

"Why the sarcasm Moe? You know I'm in bed with the grippe."

"Hey, you're the grippiest man in North Bergen County. It's a wonder with your health that you manage to run a factory. But take care of yourself, live and be well, get on your feet again soon, and if she's still breathing air go say hello to your sister."

Sidney laughed. "You're a rare one, Moe. Do you think I need a sermon to make me want to do just that?"

Liar.

Back from Jersey I dropped in on Ruth a minute, and one bright spot in a dark night: she was up on her feet again. Pale yes, drawn, with black pinches under the eyes, but without fever, better physically if not mentally. So over our cup of coffee in the kitchen I gave her scheme one, the daredevil escape from Jolly Jill the Cement Mixer. Ruth didn't think so.

"He'll never go, I know him. She'll hound him to death Moe."

"Why shouldn't he go, out of reach of that hound? What does he need her for, companionship, care? And meanwhile, when she's dishing out her advice he can tune down the hearing aid."

So Ruth smiled, but only to humor me. Then she said, "It's late, you'd better go, Moe." But how could I go, with her blue like that? So I held her, while she cried on my shoulder, and in the end I had to go anyway, like tearing yourself from yourself.

In my house, with my sister the sport as caretaker, the lights burned in all three rooms—and dead silence. Right away, even at a glance, my insides felt empty. But if Papa God forbid died the little time I was gone, the body would be here.

Unless, unless Sylvie called Ginzburg with the number I left her, and Ginzburg sent Papa to the hospital . . . I called Ginzie quick, but all this was news to him.

What could she have managed to pull, my sister, how could I have foreseen this, in three short hours?

At least leave a note, a message with the neighbors. Nothing. I went down and around the back alley in the black and the wet into the basement, but the super was out. I even traded pidgin English there with the new porter just landed from Russia, only what I said was a mystery to him and what he answered was a mystery to me. He kept bowing and smiling, a nice man.

Upstairs I took turns dialing Sylvia's number and grabbing at the few hairs I have left on my head. Then, between a grab and a dial, the phone rang, long distance from Maxine.

"How is Papa, Moe—"

"It ain't how, it's where. Nutty Sylvia—"

But I'd never imagined nutty Maxine.

"What's wrong with that woman?" She sounded desperate too. "Hasn't she called you back either?"

Slowly it emerged, how Papa woke up in pain, and the Bronx nut phoned not the doctor but the Denver nut. The one blubbered "dying" and the other barked "hospital." Hospital? Sure hospital, where he'd get emergency treatment.

What world was Maxine living in to believe this?

The two specialists held their long-distance consultation, Papa was hustled into the night on a stretcher, and all Gross had to find out was which hospital.

I nailed 'em at Eden, God is good, where Bella was, so I could see two of my four patients at one blow. Papa was dying and Sylvia was crying. But who wouldn't be dying, running around in such weather? The kid himself, yeh me, Perpetual Motion Gross, was beginning to feel achy and dull.

Only was Papa dying? Sylvia of course sat right on top of him where he'd be sure not to miss one handkerchief-twist or wipe of the eye, but he was busy consoling her, with a pat on the hands and a "Sha, sha—" till I sent her home.

Me, I stood shivering in that steam loft with my hands in my overcoat and my collar up. "Well Papa, how's the hospital boy?"

Papa still had a joke left. "There's a method in their

madness, keeping you in the hall here for an hour. You get a chance to recover."

And when Ginzie strolled in a half hour later, he agreed with me that if Papa didn't look good he didn't look worse.

"What medical plan you on, Moe?"

"More or less the Gross plan, what else?"

"Then he could have stayed home. Still, he's here. And how about you?"

"What about me?"

"You look lousy."

"You're a judge in a beauty contest?"

But Ginzie pushed a thermometer in my face, grabbed hold of my pulse, and ordered me home with an aspirin.

I was there in the hospital, how could I bypass Bella? So I phoned Mrs. Schultz about Papa, she shouldn't show up tomorrow, then I sneaked a flight down—up I could never have made it—winked at the desk nurse since it was slightly past visiting time by four and a half hours, and dropped in on the women's ward.

Thin as Bella was in health and sallow, now, dying, she was yellow, and down to the bone, like a woman of seventy. She was whimpering, she was in pain, she was blind. But Sixth Sense Bella, she suddenly listened, she knew she had company.

"Whozzat, whozzat?" She clutched me by the hand. "Moe? Is it visiting hours already? You're an angel, Moe!"

"Angel, I feel more like the devil."

"Nah, never mind, you're a real angel. You're the only one in my life that ever liked me, and I ain't no chicken no more, I'm seventy-one years old next August."

"I'll hit ya, seventy-one years old. Your Lou was fifty-eight when he died, and he was older than you."

We were whispering, but the woman in the next bed was bothered. "Who cares how old, why don't you shut up in the middle of the night!"

Bella cackled for spite. "Middle of the night—she's got a screw loose, poor thing, because she never gets any visitors. Sure I'm that old, though it's none of her business. I never told Lou, I never told anybody but you just now, Moe. Lou thought he put one over on me, marrying me for my dough, but I put one over on him. He never knew my right age. I always looked younger, don't I, Moe?"

"Absolutely."

"But what good do my looks do me now?" She gave a little sob. "I'm a goner, Moe. Ow!" I cranked up the bed, I fixed the pillow, I gave her water to sip from the straw. "Thanks, Moe, that's better. You think that I'll go to heaven?"

"Why what's heaven for, Bella? Everybody should be as sure of heaven as you are."

"C'm'ere Moe, come closer. . . Moe," she whispered in my ear, "I'm gonna leave you my money."

"Thanks, Bella."

"No, I mean now. Go get some paper Moe, and write it all down."

I could hardly hold up my head one in the morning, and now I should write wills. "Tomorrow, Bella."

And oy, Bella began to cry.

So I took out my job pad and pencil and wrote. You think Bella was satisfied then? Nah. Wills have to have witnesses, everybody knows that. A dollar each and I found a couple of orderlies in that acre of misery. Bella signed, and they signed.

So my fortune is made.

WHILE I WAS SICK, Ruth visited our sick ones, and the look in her eyes after the first visit to Papa, it was like an icy claw on my heart. "What?" I grabbed hold of her arm.

"No," she said, "I hate hospitals."

But Papa was in good hands, Mrs. Schultz's, Ruth told me. So I dragged this fine story out of her, how his first lunch they gave Papa pork chops.

Papa said, "I'm on a kosher diet."

And the Nazi answered, "Pork is good food."

Ruth heard that, she brought in Mrs. Schultz for day duty there with Papa. Then Mrs. Schultz in her white uniform took off her coat, the R.N. in charge said, "Only nurses wear white."

God forbid—a helper in white, somebody might think she was a nurse! "Not if they catch her working," Mrs. Schultz gave a mumble, and then did Florence Nightingale get up on her high horse! Who knows if she would ever have come down if Ruth hadn't gotten sore too, and mentioned talking it all over with the Administrator.

Oy, murderers! And Papa was there on account of me, in that cruel charnelhouse. Ruth said don't be dumb, my fever was talking. But it was my fault, it was mine. Right away my mind was made up, Papa was coming home where he belonged, where I'd be there beside him. Ruth, she looked so unhappy about that idea, whether because she was afraid I'd expect 'er to watch Papa again or else because I was there at her house and I might try to move him in on her too, that I had to ask—because trust, need I say, can also be carried too far—was there any objection.

"No no," she told me, "just get well."

Yeh, after that famous Thanksgiving night, Gross reeled home a case himself. Such heat in the apartment that night! But the radiators were ice-cold 2:00 A.M., the heat was in Gross. Next came the shivering, then the headache, the nausea, the hacking, all night long on the couch, under blankets, my overcoat, whatever I could grab to pile on before I collapsed. Worst were the dreams, everywhere looking for Ruth, and finding her nowhere. Then I'd wake and I'd thank God I was dreaming. When light broke, with gray in the window, I thought soon, soon I can phone her. But later I tried, and between the quaking and shaking I couldn't. So I prayed in my cave of fever: "God, let her phone me please, just let her give me a ring on the phone—"

Since God talked to Moses we've had a lot of water under the bridge, and Science teaches us that to count miracles nowadays you don't need the use of your toes. So listen to this. The phone went off and I fumbled it under the covers with me.

Ruth said, "You okay?"

"N.G."

"My God," she said, "what woke me? I heard you calling my name—"

Then she was there, in that hot little room, pressing that cool cheek to my face. "What I've done—giving you this, then sending you to Jersey in the freezing rain!" Gentleman Moe I wanted to say No, but the teeth chattered too fast. She wrapped me up like a jewel in wadding and she carried me home with her, Gross, this fine trembling specimen of manhood.

A week I dozed or I tossed, with the shades drawn even in daytime because the light made my eyes ache.

Then the fever began going down, and ah, that was nice, with the shades up where I lay, that used to be Bobby's room, with the green plants on the windowsill and a thick snow falling. And the sun was nice after that, like butter on the snow banked up against the window in front of a bright blue sky.

Only it ate me about Papa. So I telephoned Ginzburg to leave a checkout order at the hospital for Papa, and the next day I'd go pick him up.

"How will you go," Ginzie said, "on your back? Ask me again in two weeks."

And it was true, Gross tried standing up, he fell down like a baby. And meanwhile the whole burden was on Ruth.

Papa, and Bella, and Bobby, and me—and then to keep busy three times a week she went to the office. Exhilaration you couldn't say that she had.

Bella, even with an insult or two for identification purposes when Ruth visited her, was a short-term proposition for the funeral caterers, poor thing.

And then Bobby.

He was up now, our New Jersey convalescent. His mother held him by the hands, her darling, her dear. Sure, soon he'd be leaving the hospital.

Him? He grinned like a maniac.

"Yep, back to the old routine!"

So Ruth jumped in and begged, "Don't go back."

She reasoned with him.

You think Bobby listened?

"Ha ha, what's wrong with routine? Everyone has a routine, from the cradle to the grave. It's well-known, especially around Fairlawn, or why would the grave jump out of bed at one A.M. to serve the cradle its bottle? But you know, Ma, kidding aside, what I'd like? A South Sea island, all to myself—ha ha ha!"

"Then go darling! There's Hawaii—"

Bobby made a face, our paterfamilias, "Aw come on, Ma," Master Tall and Skinny with coronary one just behind him.

Ruth grabbed at straws. "Moe says you should."

"A message from Heaven." Then, "I'm sorry, Ma, he's a nice man. I'm glad that you met him."

You can imagine the lip bites and wet eyes when Ma brought these tidings back to The Bronx. I have a daughter, I know how Ruth feels.

A couple of times during my siege I phoned Liz—"What's wrong? You sound funny, Pop." "A code in the node"—so she shouldn't lose sleep over the old man.

And with her too—to these ears—the drift was from bad to worse.

She was telling me about her sister's inheritance. Yeh, Rodney's From Coast To Coast Goldenrod finally staged his last gala opening, six feet downstairs!

Ready?

> *To my granddaughter-in-law Susan, the Bechstein piano she liked so much in my apartment, and the wish that God should provide her with everything else to go with it.*

Ha ha ha, sheet music he meant?

Then Susan blew into Liz's drunk and full of her grievance. "Bechstein piano, the fake, the fraud. Why didn't he shove it up his dry husk of an ass and take it along with him."

And if a live fraud could sue a dead fraud for fraud, Susan had a good case. Rodney's turned out to be an empty shell, from coast to coast, with creditors in the woodpile, talk of sale, liquidation. I bet Axelrod finally died laughing, the old bloodsucker, to think of Sweet Sue the young bloodsucker, along with the other assorted bloodsuckers.

"And now," Susan said, "I'm stuck."

"Stuck?" Lizzie answered her. "With the sweetest boy in the world?"

So hey Liz, where does George Young rank for sweetness then? Second? Seventh? Fifteenth? But let's call it a figure of speech that means nothing.

Liz said Sue said, "That's all that he is, a boy!" Then Sue said, "He's getting the can, by the way, now that Rodney's is going kaput."

"So what? There are other jobs, and you have a job."

" 'I see,' said the blind man's wife, and do you know what I see?" laughed the sister. "I see that it would have been an all-around boon if you'd seen the blind I mean the sweetest boy first."

"Have you told your analyst that?"

"I've given analysis up, what do you think of that? I'm completely adjusted. My vocation come rain come moonshine beginning next June is motherhood."

Liz rushed to Mother-to-be for a kiss and a hug, but Susan, our repository for the future in case there's a future, she fended Liz off. "You're so . . . old-fashioned. Make mine bourbon and water instead, ha ha, no ice . . ."

After Susan tottered along, Liz called their mother at Schwarzman's.

I asked Liz, "What did your mother say?"

"Pop," Liz said, "I feel blue."

And what color was sick-at-heart Gross?

"Ah, you know your mother. It must be her disappointment too, Susan's bequest."

"That it most definitely is, Pop."

"Sure. And Susan? She'll drink while it suits her, and then she'll quit drinking. Susan's a practical girl."

"But Mother's abuse, Pop. I know what she said was irrational, my marriage a reason Axelrod left Sue nothing, though it seems to me a good Bechstein can hardly be called nothing, but—"

"Sure, but who listens to such talk when you know what the cause is. Five cents says the words your father also were mentioned."

"It's your nickel. But such hatred, such fury. Do you know, Pop, if it wasn't for you, I'd feel lonely?"

Oy Lizzie, did you hear what you just now said? But to that too I kept mum while my heart ached inside me.

Then, one afternoon when I'd just begun to sit up in bed, Ruth brought me home from my mailbox, along with my gas company fan mail, an afterthought from Liz on a scrap of paper without an envelope even.

Thanks for the closet space, Pop. I'll be in touch soon. I love you.

Ruth grinned. "I couldn't stand the suspense, I went up and looked."

"What was there?"

"Her suitcases! She's left him!"

"God should be listening. But why are you so sure?"

Rashi interpreted the Talmud, Ruth Amin interpreted that note.

1. *Closet space.* They have your Mark Cigar on the wall and your hi-fi on the floor, and that's about all. And are their rooms small? Some small—they built big when Jungle Edge Brooklyn was a country town with Americans under the elms in the good old days, while in Brownsville Jews fell like flies from consumption. And how many closets? Galore. With space? To house elephants.

"Then what does she need your closet space for?"

2. *I'll.* When a married couple do something together, do they call themselves I'll?

"They say 'we'll.' "

3. *Be in touch.* Do you call up Liz? Once, twice a week, some weeks more. And sometimes she calls you? That's correct.

"Then if she's home, why must only she be in touch?"

4. *I love you.* If that's just regards, where are George's regards? Nowhere. Then where's George?

"Home, where she left him," my Talmudist wound up, "and all of a sudden, I bet. Once you start thinking, you're stuck. That's Bobby's trouble, he comes from a short line of thinkers . . . You're lucky, Moe—"

"Well if she's really done it," Gross babbled—"but it seems too good to be true—why shouldn't Bobby?" Ruth shook her head No, but I wouldn't listen. "So let's test, let's call up George."

And ain't Liz also a thinker, and couldn't the joy have been premature? Once, twice, six times I called him—and no George.

So how about an alternative theory?

Lizzie feels blue, with a sister a drunk, a mother I won't even speak of, and a husband attentive once-a-week when it's paycheck time at the Clinic where Liz works. George is no fool. George may not care, but George sees. Does he want to hold on to Liz? Do I want to hold on to my brush arm? So he smiles at her, with all his smooth teeth. Christmas is a-coming and the geese are getting fat, please to put a penny in the young man's hat. And that Foundation, the way they slave him there from ten in the morning to three in the afternoon, he's worn out from his exertions anyway. So he proposes to my poor fool, how about a little jaunt out of town, just you and me and your paycheck makes three? Gross's closet? George has Liz store his Mark Cigar there with the frame courtesy Gross and a few more small treasures he figures safer uptown than in their empty apartment.

Gross with all your new resolutions, already my hackles were beginning to rise at the way how, in the face of she's wrong, Ruth kept insisting she was right. Then the next day, "Look!," she picked up a postcard, once more signed Liz, that came from my mailbox, a picture postcard, from out of the blue, with a jet liner sailing in front.

I'm growing wings Pop and it's scary—but gee, the elation!

So what was it? One set of wings for two, or Fly United to Reno and come back divorced?

Ruth went to Jersey to drive Bobby home from the hospital, her daughter-in-law wouldn't, with the new Olds, or the old Ford. Jill had her own worries: an infant, cooking, cleaning. She should put herself out to bring back her husband and his imaginary ailments from a four-week vacation? So me, I devoted the afternoon to calling my son-in-law every half hour, that bastard.

And lo! All of a sudden an answer!

But no answer. Giggling—then that would be Liz, and the wings had been just a weekend in Boston, or Washington, to see a museum, like they did: the alternative theory. I heard scuffling with the giggles, then crash—oy right in my ear, their bell, landing on the floor.

What? You call up, and without asking who, they got to prove that they're married? I know that they're married.

So much for the hopes.

But George came on and he answered my hello: "Pop? Where have you been? I've been phoning you three days now— Hey cut it out, Sue! Will you cut that out I tell you— Pop, where's Liz?"

Oh shake the timbrels, let the trumpets sound—this woman Ruth is first with the prophets!

Between the gigglings and the cut-it-out-Sues—what Sue? he had to go find a consolation of the same name this brazen bastard? but who cares now!—George sang me his tribulations and his trials. Liz fled from him like Israel from Egypt, early in the morning, while he still slept. And don't ask him why, he hadn't the faintest idea—never a cross word between them. "I've been the happiest man on earth with that girl, Pop— I'm telling you, Sue, I'm giving you fair warning!" At eleven, as usual, he went to the Foundation that day. As usual, our hard worker, he was back home by three. Six, or even seven o'clock, he wasn't unduly alarmed. Liz sometimes came home that late if she decided to do the marketing after work instead of on Saturday. "Hey, Sue!"

So hurry to market boy for TV dinner why don't you with suppertime near, now that cook's gone! Ha ha ha!

"Listen Pop, would you speak to Sue. Her insobriety is very distressing, especially now—"

"You mean my Sue?"

That's who he meant all right. But like most of my conversations with Sue, this one turned out to be one-sided, all Susan, speaking up good and loud, but from a distance, for George and the telephone.

"Never mind, you cold clam, I'll be on my way now. No wonder my sister left—two years at the Pole, without even a fur coat! So ta ta Georgie, stew in your juice, if you can manage to heat up to a simmer . . . And give my regards to Mother, Father, ha ha!"

George's door slammed.

George said, as if Sue never existed, "You can imagine my feelings. By nine I was worried, and by midnight—why I was frantic."

"You must have been hungry, too."

"No, I threw something together. There were cold cuts in the fridge."

George ended up phoning the cops that night, and at the break of day 10:00 A.M. the next morning he called up Liz's

Clinic and what do you know? Mrs. Young had resigned—also by telephone!

George asked me what I knew and I didn't hold back either the bags or the postcard. All I held back was that clear blue sky for Liz and the smile that filled my whole heart, and those I held back for Ruth.

But joy, it ain't always catching. Ruth said Bobby shook hands all around at the hospital, and he tried to be cheerful on the drive to his house, but he only was brave.

So what could I do but shake my head, pat her hand?

But me Liz's run gave new strength, and the next day, sly Gross, as soon as Ruth went to business, I got up, I dressed with my trembling hands, and I went to straighten out my apartment, and then to get Papa, and at the same time relieve Ruth of my burdens at least.

Where the car was I hadn't dared ask her, or else she would have stayed home all day to push Gross back into bed. But cabs also operate, and thank God one came along right away on the Concourse, because that bitter cold was like a knife down my chest.

At Grandview Place I didn't need the climb three flights up to find out how weak in the knees I still was. But not to be able to fit the key in the lock? Did I go one flight too many?

Peculiar, those couple of weeks at Ruth's house went by like days, yet Grandview here seems like from a lifetime ago.

The door was my number.

So steady fingers boy, it's your Castle Ugly.

I tried the key, and I tried, and once more I tried. Then, like a double for Papa with the banister for a crutch all the way down, I went to Mr. Guchkov the super to powder the key.

He was surprised.

"Old key? She no open door. What for change lock, I say wife. Good lock."

What lock, what wife?

Would you believe it? Gross had his lock changed on him, by that third-story woman still signing herself Mrs. Gross!

Other day, Mr. Guchkov clean snow, porter drunk, no come, in taxi Mrs. Gross come with suitcases. Mr. Guchkov say hello, Mrs. Gross no say hello. What can do? Snow make shoe wet to Mrs. Gross? God send snow, Mr. Guchkov no send. Next locksmith come. What for change lock?

In the gray biting cold outside the alley, with my teeth rattling and my wrists pushed way down in my pockets, I stood staring at Guchkov like at news from the crazy house.

Lock Gross out when Gross pays the rent?

And make Gross sore enough and the legs ain't so shaky no more. Up I flew by the overland route: the roof, the fire escape, then in through the window I figured.

Till I saw what my Lady Charlotte has planned. Not a divorce for her weird scheme of marrying Henry, but widowhood—with Gross succumbing to stomach cancer.

That's how my insides ground then.

Iron bars in the window!

But—I crouched squinting there on the fire escape—past the bars a catastrophe. Clothing strewn, torn: a knocked-over chair. Some thug got in and beat me to the punch? Was that Charlotte crumpled up in the livingroom shadows there? I felt slightly sick.

It was only some ex-shirts of Gross's mangled and dead on the floor. Still, who knew what horror was out of sight inside, that you wouldn't wish even on Charlotte?

Down at the super's again when I said, "I got to use your phone, Mr. Guchkov, Mrs. Gross could be dead upstairs," Mr. Guchkov laughed.

"No worry. Wife no upstairs. Wife go 'way, yet with suitcases."

To come in, tear up my clothes, and spend my money to lock me out of my house? You know what a spasm is? I got one, that made me take a deep breath. I took a look at my watch, but what the time was I couldn't have told you. And before I got to the hospital, I still had to get to the hardware store, for him to unlock the undoor.

The undoor?

Gross that can't even think straight, you've got strength for a hardware store, and to bring Papa back? Charlotte sure took care of the new strength, and even the old.

But I had to see Papa.

And even Papa, I flagged a cab on the Concourse, I came close to telling the driver home not the hospital.

And up in Papa's room in the hospital, where I stood with stiff knees so I shouldn't fall down, Papa was sleeping, early as it was, and Mrs. Schultz looked up from her paper.

"Do you feel well, Mr. Gross? You look pale."

Me, I blinked.

So she said, "He's under sedation."

"How is he?"

"Well, you know. About the same, Mr. Gross."

So I sat for an hour while Papa breathed and he groaned, till I couldn't hold my head up any more. Then I went home and crawled back into bed, and I hoped, Crazy Gross, that I hadn't gone and gotten myself sick all over again, on top of all that trouble I'd given Ruth already.

Later, she came in, I couldn't keep my antics a secret, I had to tell her we needed that locksmith. But there was no scolding. She just shook her head from one side to another, with that message in her eyes that I knew was about Papa. I waited with that shriveling inside, that ice on my heart.

"You can't take your father home, Moe. Didn't you see? He's barely alive."

"Then you been keeping"—that was my voice?—"secrets from me?"

"It was Ginzburg's advice, to keep you in bed. But he was right. Look at you now."

And who could be sore at her? Poor Papa. I only could twist up my face and start crying like a baby, not that I wanted to, while she held me in her arms, while she shook her head Yes.

Now I'll tell you what's outstanding about Gross. He's son to a hero. Listen to what Ginzburg told me in the hospital hallway.

"Moe, when you go into that room, you're going to find your father in pain. That's because he refused sedation this morning. He said that he expected you, and he wanted his head clear."

My sister Sylvie was present, and this time she had a real reason for tears. Me, my own eyes were far from dry, looking across the other beds to Papa stretched out on the bed in the corner. The words in pain from a doctor are one thing, those piercing gasps at the top of each breath are another. And Papa kept grabbing the covers, and then he'd let go. He looked smaller, and, oh Papa, the sickness had crossed one eye on him. He saw me, he wanted to give me his hand, and he couldn't. But he managed a weak squeeze when I stuck my fingers in his.

"All these years with this body of mine—and suddenly it don't like me no more." Then, oy, Papa made himself smile. "Now Moe, with Sylvie all right," he touched her hand too, "a woman cries. But wet eyes from you, Moe? Ain't God good, to let me wake one more morning and see my children again?"

That was my Papa!

HE DIED LATE THAT NIGHT, and poor Sylvie, she fell completely apart. We sat in the solarium there in the hospital with the windowpanes black and hardly a light in the houses across the way, Ruth, me, Sylvie, and Sylvie's two girls. And did my sister carry on! It was a shame for the sick people, starving for sleep in the middle of the night. But what can you do, grief is grief. Her daughters kept shushing her, wiping her face. Me, I sat too stunned to help. What a loss. Never to see him no more. All of a sudden I sobbed, and I stuck my hand in Ruth's sitting next to me there. She gave my fingers a press, I took my deep breath, I blew out a sigh.

And would you believe that the next thing I saw was my sister shaking her head?

"That's not right Moe, especially not now."

Yeh, she'd controlled that uncontrollable grief and sat pouring her long face at me.

She said, "Papa wouldn't have liked it."

Give credit to her Carol Ann and her Sandra, they at least looked confused. Me, I asked Ruth, "Am I dreaming, or are you hearing this too?"

Ruth said, "Unfortunately, we're all still awake—and it's time that we weren't."

We put our coats on, Sylvia watched.

And at the solarium door I heard Sylvia in her sweet affliction call after me, "It's all right, Moe, we'll find a cab—"

"WHO CARES ABOUT MY FAMILY? Now that Papa's dead, I don't have any family!" I stood in front of the mirror, but I couldn't knot up my tie right. "You're my family, goddammit!"

Ruth sat there and laughed, so I turned around to her, I said,

"What's the joke?" Then I said, "What, the one that belongs next to me at my father's funeral should stay away because my sister Sylvia won't like it?"

"Who needs to fight her? But finish dressing, we'll see."

So we were first at the funeral parlor, to see.

And what do you do with those catering guys? How many times did I tell them no rouge and no lipstick, and they went and smeared Papa up just the same. A smooth fatface kept spilling explanations into my ear, except the one explanation that the cosmetics would also show on the bill, till I barked, "Close the box!"

But Ruth said, "Otherwise he looks nice, Moe. The suffering's over, that's what counts. Let them leave it open. Your sister Sylvia might want to see him once more, and"—Ruth's mouth trembled: to cry? no, a smile, barely but a smile—"and shed a tear."

And would you believe this, alongside of my Papa's bier?—I found myself smiling too.

Ruth said, "Then you'll be all right?"

"All right, all right."

So she looked at Papa once more, she gave me a pat, and she left.

To tell the truth, even with the bier and the box, the rouge and the lipstick, the caterer's fakes with the striped pants and pasted-on solemn faces, the friends and relatives and sighs and low voices, "Better occasions . . ." "Better occasions . . ." "Ah Moe, we should meet on better occasions . . . ," I couldn't imagine Papa was dead. Later at home I'd tell him about the makeup and Papa would smile.

"As long as they didn't paint me a mustache, Moe. Maybe I'll win the beauty contest downstairs."

"Downstairs? You couldn't get a foot in the door downstairs, Papa."

That was how proud I felt. Sure, in there it was all gloom, as thick as the wall-to-wall carpeting. But outside God knew better, with a heaven like spring, April in January, a miracle, His last smile for Papa, that good kind man that hurt no one, that left his son not beating my breast what a bad son I was, but what luck to have had such a father!

How many could you explain this to? A Ruth? An Elizabeth? And they weren't there. Certainly not to a Charlotte, who was.

She showed up, Charlotte, dressed in black, with a veil, I was almost bowled over. An outsider would have taken her for my wife! And she was surprised too, how well I was bearing up.

But even if you could explain that pride I felt, that joy almost, could you explain the heartache the next minute of missing Papa? So who could yell Fake when my sister Sylvia went to the coffin and collapsed in her daughters' arms? Even if first she did stop off to abuse me?

"Your wife hasn't been at Schwarzman's a whole week. Wasting my Carol Ann's time on fool's-errand phone-calls trying to let Charlotte know about," she sobbed, "Papa, while you flaunt your shenanigans at a time like this!"

With Charlotte there on the couch alongside me! So I had to figure that mentally Papa's death had altogether finished Sylvia off, that she should have taken Charlotte for Ruth, even under a veil. Charlotte, she gave me a new look, sad but resigned.

She said, "So it's public news."

The Martyred Wife!

Yeh, that was her line, our wayfarer suddenly returned with a pious face and a squeeze on my arm. Twenty-five years a devoted spouse, here at her bereaved husband's side, and shenanigans. But she was willing to sigh, and let bygones be bygones.

So between the departure from Schwarzman's, her one-day

Grandview Place blitz, and her arrival at the funeral parlor, Gross concluded as follows.

Number one: Charlotte's number one man was done, Henry Schwarzman. Two: and she wasn't two cents the richer for all her pains. Three: that day that she installed the locks and the bars in the apartment was Humiliation Day for this poor dreamer of riches, the return, she had to figure, to mornings noons and even nights with Gross. But four: this depressing thought infuriated her so, she locked Gross out. Only what was left then? Castle Ugly. And to add injury to insult, she heard from one of my charming neighbors, or the super maybe, that Gross wasn't exactly pining away in her absence. So five: she ripped up my four or five shirts and stormed away altogether. Except six: or with Tillie and Henry both six feet under maybe it should add up to twelve—either way, a late number in life for Charlotte—where do you storm? To a hotel for the time being, then to a new apartment you'll have to support with a job? When to get rid of the job was a main reason you swallowed Gross in the first place? Then thirteen, the unluckiest number of all: where could she have gone but to Susan? And where would Susan have pushed her but right back towards Gross?

But who wants to push Gross let them push. In the olden days you'd see me bristling and growling, with the chest expanded for battle. No more. I'm light as a feather now, life is too short.

So to Charlotte's public-news crack I answered, "How's things with Sue?"

"Her cold is better. I was taking care of her the past few days . . . And do you know that meanwhile someone broke into our apartment?"

Ah, thank you Papa, to have left me with so much life that on such a day I could be biting my cheeks to keep from laughing out loud!

I said, "So, healthy a man as he was, Henry died."

The shock! "Who told you that?"

"I assumed, God forbid."

"He was perfectly well when *I* left him!"

Then I was all wrong? She really was up here to show Gross respect at the loss of his father?

Hey Moe—you getting soft in the brain?

I said, "Then you'll be going back to the townhouse."

"I certainly will not. I've been away from home too long as it is. Or," and again that aggrieved look, "you might not think so?"

"Charlotte, the place is all yours."

But shoo fly, pooh hint: they're both the same to this lady. In the chapel, Sylvia sat down beside me and said through her handkerchief, "Moe, don't pay attention to anything I said. I'm half out of my mind, on account of Papa." So we became brother and sister again, and on the way to the cemetery Charlotte expressed surprise that the mourning would take place at Sylvia's.

"Where else?" I said. "I was locked out of my house."

"Didn't the super give you that set of keys I left with him for you?"

In a sense it takes courage, to tell lies like that in back of a hearse. But then Charlotte always believed a story the minute she made it up. Her conscience was clear, the subject was closed, and she was enjoying the scenery, I mean the gas stations flicking by in the sunlight. In the limousine back seat it was Charlotte, Susan, and me, in spite of the furious look Charlotte shot at her daughter when Susan and Charles first walked into the funeral parlor. So between the services and the trip, reconciliation also took place between mother and daughter—and I could make a shrewd guess what about.

Yeh, Susan turned up, perfumed, she smelled beautiful. She gave me a kiss on the cheek, and liquor? Not one drop. And that slim black dress I knew very well, even if the hemline was up since she bought it for George Meier's suicide. In the olden days it was new occasion new outfit, and now No. So, she wanted children, couldn't she make a real helpmeet after all with such economy and the breath free of booze? Charlie still thought so. If he was only a boy to her, that good honest young man, she was a girl-and-a-half in his shining eyes.

He filled me with her at Sylvia's when he paid his condolence call: brains, looks, housekeeping, and motherhood next—his woman of valor! Papa died Sunday, the funeral was Monday, and after lunch sharp Tuesday Wednesday and Thursday Charlotte would make her appearance at Sylvie's as Mrs. Gross, with Susan pasted like glue alongside to make sure she played the part right. I sat in a corner with Charles, Susan came tripping over to censor the conversation. No harm done, it was all praise of Susan. She curtsied and went back to Charlotte and Sylvie and Carol Ann.

Then I put out a feeler to Charlie, "So Schwarzman gave your mother-in-law the heave-ho."

He laughed. "Wasn't that more like a hundred-yard kick, Moe? But you should have seen Susie's firmness when she tried moving in on us."

"You heard what happened exactly? At Schwarzman's, I mean."

"Yes, I heard, I overheard." Charles looked at me worried a second. "Moe, I don't want to put my foot in it between you and Mrs. Gross."

"Between us there's room for a lot more than one foot."

"But listen, you very well might get together again?"

"For our sins maybe later, but not in this world."

"In that case— Poor Howard, I'm grinning and shouldn't. But—"

Then, between what Charlie heard or overheard, and what Gross could figure out for himself, there unfolded a tale that I could see me and Ruth up half the night laughing when I got home and told her. Which reminds me, what are they all so excited about in the ads and the commercials, with their sex and big bubbies? Listen, Gross knows his way around on a mattress as well as the next one, but as the old gag goes if a man ain't made of wood he ain't made of iron either, and you know what I like when Ruth and I go to bed at night? That there's so much to tell each other. When all's said and done it's true, from the talk comes the other thing. But that there could be so much to say between a man and a woman, that's what I never imagined . . .

A man is dying that goes pale even at the sound of the word *die*—Henry Schwarzman, I mean—and one snowy morning he wakes up with a little fresh strength. Is it possible? Slow fella, slow. He lifts up his head. He eases himself up in bed. He pushes the bell and the deathwatch comes running: the nurse, the butler, his son Howard guard-designate from their Palm Beach hotel. What greets them, besides the new gleam in the corpse's eye? The old curl of the lip!

"Gedada here. Where's Mrs. Gross."

Only one qualifies to wash him, to dress him, to get him into the wheelchair, that one that assures him ten times a day how much better he's looking and means what she says. Charlotte, who else?

She brings him down in the elevator, with her own hands she prepares his cereal because Henry won't put up with lumps. And Charlotte wheeled Henry to the French doors, where he could enjoy the snowfall caking his trees and his garden: the best property east of the Park—he'd said it before and he'd say it again!

"I'll say it again! It's a happy day. Till today, I hoped. And now here I am!"

Oy Charlotte. That message from Headquarters triggered her Battle Plan Number One. The Henry that gave his son

marching orders from the sickroom before was the Henry of
yore. Now he still needed her. But up on his feet? She'd be
shipped back to the Bronx, buried alive without hope. So if this
wasn't D-Day, when would be?

She said, "I'm so glad, Henry. Although now you won't
need me much longer—"

"Heh heh, don't run yet."

Did mortal ears ever hear such encouragement from on
high?

Charlotte said to Henry, "It's better, really, that I go—"

. . . "Now come on," Ruth said when I finally got to
telling her this story, "she didn't actually say that Moe, you
made it up."

"Word for word Ruth—that was her defense to Susan,
music by Charlotte but lyrics by Gross."

"You mean you advised her to say such things?"

"I sure must have had a hate on, that day. Now, I can't
understand why—like a crazy man returned to his
senses" . . .

Yeh, Charlotte said, "The longer I stay, the more involved I
become, and it's not fair to anyone, not to me, not to———"
—the blank, that stood for yours truly—"and especially not to
you."

First Henry barks, then he bites: Charlotte had to know
that. But dreams and schemes, they clutter the vision.

He gave a bark then: "What are you talking about?"

"I mean," and no truer words ever were said in grim
earnest, "you've become my whole life—"

"Thanks. Anything else?"

"I've decided to get a divorce."

"I'd think twice about that."

She said from the heart, "How many times haven't I
thought about it! Anyway, I, I'll use the money, that is, if . . .
you can—"

Henry heard the word *money*.

"What money?"

"I was thinking . . . of Tillie's legacy. But if you're short right now—"

Henry said, "Now I see daylight. The same as the rest of them." And in his fresh strength he jerked his wheelchair around and he roared, "Howard!"

Even Charlotte began to sense trouble then. "Henry—"

"Never mind! I'll see to your money. Howard! Where is that fat— You see to your bags."

What could she do but stand there with her tears and her handkerchief and watch Howard come lumbering into the grand lobby.

Henry let him have it straight to the gut.

"Make out her bequest, you hear me? Every last cent!"

Howard heard, but he couldn't believe.

"Every cent?"

"Are you deaf? And then she gets off the premises, quick!"

To the buts, from Howard for the cash, from Charlotte for mercy, Henry barked out another "Quick!"

So Howard disappeared, and Charlotte sobbed on one of the sofas behind the great man. Finally, without even the smell of wood burning, Howard came back with limp hands.

You can imagine the look he must've gotten from his father, and the grunt. "Where's her check?"

"You didn't say how much is deductible for her room and board Pop—"

"You see some health in my face so you're trying to aggravate it away? What's the matter with you, Harvard Business School!"

"I don't know, Pop. I don't feel just right—"

And before Charlotte's very eyes Howard sagged to a chair with his face like cream cheese gone sour. Next he was squeezing the chair arms and sucking air like a fish. And next—slack, like a big bag of matzo meal. One minute a man a picture of health, unless you counted that little rash he always had on his lip, and the next—in spite of the doctor, the nurse, the oxygen, the butler, the maid, and the cook—finished.

By the time the tumult died down and Henry noticed his nurse on his payroll waving smelling salts under Charlotte's nose, most of his starch was gone. But he could still tilt up his jaw and mumble at Charlotte, and Charlotte could still jump to her feet at the sound of her master's voice. She went to him, she bent over to hear the word of forgiveness, peace at any price—ten thousand, ten million—only let her stay.

"I said," he said, "five minutes to get yourself out—unless you want the police."

So if Henry lost a son, he gained $9,500.

Poor Charles, he still confides in his wife, and some tongue-lashing he must have taken for that story he told Gross. The day after, Susan said to me, "My husband's a very nice boy, but he babbles, and most of the babbling is nonsense."

"Ah, what difference does it make, Susie?"

"It simply makes for hard feelings, Dad, where none should exist."

"I assure you dear, there are no hard feelings on my part."

And you know, whether she meant it or not, the way she gave me a real smile and a pat on the hand, like a daughter—it was nice!

Friday she and her mother arrived 11:00 A.M. at Sylvie's, because mourning is off Friday noon to Saturday night. On the Sabbath we praise God, not mourn. Gross is being sarcastic? In this world of trickery, hatred, murder, and war, what's there to praise? Then let me tell you. Thank God that if you want, you can put trickery, hatred, murder, and war out of your own heart.

So Friday noon we took off our mourning slippers and put

our shoes on, and Charlotte said, "Shall we have lunch home today Moe?"

So I had to take her aside, into another room, and explain that the way life was—with the hard feelings forgotten and a thing of the past—still she had to admit that we'd drifted apart, and maybe it was better, for her too as well as me, I honestly thought so, if we let matters stand as they were till the seven days' mourning was over. Then we could make formal arrangements.

"Arrangements? There'll be no arrangements!"

She gathered herself up and, believe me, she became bigger and bigger, gigantic, with flashing eyes, until I actually had one leg braced back for the explosion about to blow us to smithereens.

When Susan stepped in, all sweetness, and set a grip like iron on her mother's arm.

"Why don't I drive you home, Mother, if Dad isn't ready?"

It sank in, even on Charlotte, what only should sink in on our Great Men. Once you let loose your Bomb, what's left to do business with? She went back to normal size, and she said, "Then I'll see you later, Moe." Coward Moe, I gave her a nod.

Better never than later, but better later than now.

Oy, when a child of yours is unhappy! Yeh, I mean this letter from Liz.

So I cry to myself some nights when I go to bed . . .

Was it my fault? Did I pick her her George, so she'd have to run away and know running was right, and feel bad just the same?

> What I like are the big cold palaces with pictures and statues inside them, and what I don't like are the little cold taxi-drivers and other assorted cheats. The former though are what count and the latter though they are always counting don't count. Nevertheless, the nastier little episodes have their way of popping back into your mind when you least expect them, causing shivers and public grimaces. So you shrug and you say, he knows that he's poor and he's sure that you're rich, so what can he do? The only thing is, you can shrug off a cabdriver or a gondolier, but a husband isn't so easy, Pop. So I cry to myself some nights when I go to bed, but don't worry, without sound effects, so your daughter hasn't become a disgrace for the neighbors yet.

Some husband to cry for, that bastard, that heartless mechanical man!

> The most immediate of whom is Selma, my new friend, my guide and my mentor, all smiles and red hair, and my age to the

year. She swears she'll teach me Italian and to take life easy. So far I'm a slow learner, but I enjoy her light touch and that's a good sign. She's here as a graduation gift to herself, just having finished college, where she worked her way through. As she packed her bags back in Brooklyn to leave home and for good, her poor widowed mother said, "Then I'm killing myself." And what do you think Selma said? She said, "Here's ten dollars Ma, go to the beauty parlor instead." And what do you think Ma did? She went! Ha ha, I was amazed!

Or here in Florence at a bar up on a hill, we were enjoying the view, and the steam heat, and those little cups of black coffee, when along two young gentlemen came. One sat right down behind our ear and the other stood semidetachedly gazing into the distance. Who doesn't want to be charmed—but by a weasel with hair oil on top? Casanova kept muttering his sweet unilateral nothings, "Are you Americans? Are you English? Are you Germans?" But the friend looked so gloomy, between us and the rest of the wintry prospect—the bare trees on the hillside, and the river, and the town—that I caught myself thinking that if I knew Italian I would have said something reassuring just to cheer that boy up. Now here's the terrible thing, Pop. On top of that thought I had this one: that that gloom could just be that fellow's act! Finally Selma answered in Italian, "We're Chinese," and we left the bar. Then I told Selma how I used to be trustful, and now I'm not any more, and she laughed at me. "Soul-searching over that pair? You know what il signor Hair Lotion said to his pal when we were walking away? He said, 'She said that they're Chinese. They aren't Chinese. They're French.'" And it's true, they were like a vaudeville team, the clown and the straight man.

But, even though I do listen to Selma and try to learn, or rather unlearn what I have learned, I just don't feel trustful. But don't mind my crying, Pop, there's not that much to cry about, probably only my guilt and confusion, so bear with

Your loving Liz

Ruth said fine, she's getting over it. But me, I felt lousy to read black and white of such damage, that a child should begin

with too generous and end up a cripple. Not that I said that
when I took pen in hand and wrote.

Mind? I answered her. Where should she cry, if not on
these shoulders? Not, God forbid, that she should have cause
for tears. And actually, did she? The conclusion she reached,
that sent her flying, an outsider could have reached sooner.
What did that mean? That a mistake occurred, the mistake
was seen, and the mistake stood rectified. Tell me guilt comes
from that, and I believe it. What won't I believe if Liz does the
telling? But understand it I can't. This I can say though: don't
give in to such guilt. Trust, Lizzie, one lemon don't make a
barrel. Accept expert testimony, that tried running life by the
double-entry system and nearly went bankrupt if not for some
recent good luck. Of course without luck it's all losers, but if
luck knocks on the door, don't answer nobody home. Monsieur Weasel and friend? A slight whiff of bad gas: No
importance, as she herself said. A bum is a bum in any
language, and two bums are two bums. But in general, I said,
when you're young, and intelligent, and attractive to people,
like to this funny girl Selma, why shouldn't you trust? Within
reason—but trust!

That's what I wrote. I could have written more, but was this
the moment in the girl's life to bring up my troubles with her
mother? Still to Ruth I could say that the fact that I ever laid
eyes on that letter showed how life could surprise you with the
message trust even where the trusting seems bad. Would you
have ever imagined that Charlotte would take this letter out of
my mailbox and make a special trip to hand it over to me all
sealed and proper?

The truth was, after God's day of rest and my day of rest, I
didn't go back to the last two days of mourning at Sylvie's
either rested or with trust in my future.

The Saturday off it poured when I went to shul, a good icy
rain with a wind just like life: No matter which way you

turned you got it straight in the kisser. Back home while Ruth was making us lunch the day was still wet and gray, and I still had to go out again, to the hospital to see Bella. Who'd visit her otherwise, her brother Sidney from Jersey?

All of a sudden there was a thunderclap, and Ruth stood there in deadly fear, staring out of the window for the mushroom cloud to lift over the city, the end of the world. Then she glanced at me with those terrified eyes.

I said, "January showers bring February flowers."

So she gave a hysterical laugh and she kissed me on the hands. She said, "Do you know what I dreamed last night, Moe? You kept telling jokes and I couldn't stop laughing."

"Which ones did I tell?—it just slipped my mind."

So off she went with her laughing again and her thanks Moe. Thanks for what? When I feel such pride when I make a dumbcrack and Ruth laughs!

But oy what a world to laugh in. Then the ward around Bella, my first time there in a month, with the carbolic and groans, and poor blind Bella herself with her mind all confused and those raw sores on her elbows and back when Ruth bathed her, and powdered her, and turned her to her side—what the nurses should do.

Bella kept saying, "Thanks Charlotte, thanks Charlotte."

"Ruth," Ruth said.

But in one respect Bella's still normal: When did she ever listen? She said, "That's a great wife you got there Moe Gross, you can thank your lucky stars. If it wasn't for her— Hey Moe," she let out a sob, "I'm a goner, and I only was twenty-two years old."

"What happened, Bella, when you were twenty-two years old?"

But what could have happened? She was young, that's what happened.

"Yez'll get me a good coffin, huh Moe, so's the worms won't

get at me? I hate worms. Solid mahogany, not one of them skinny pine boxes for Jews, okay Moe? I always liked solid mahogany, but Lou'd never let me buy any. Then none of my family'll laugh, 'Ha ha, look at dumb Bella there in that plain cheap pine box.' It's a dying wish, Moe."

"Sure Bella, but who's dying? I'll be driving you home soon."

"Nah, I'm down to my last ride Moe." She crooked up her finger, and she felt at my face to make sure I'd come closer. "I don't need none of them listening, and then they tell me I'm nuts. I could see when I woke up this morning, Moe. He was standing right there, where you are right now, looking down at me. He said, 'Hello, Bella. You know me?' Sure I knew him. He was the Angel of Death. 'That's right,' he said, 'I never could fool you, Bella.' 'The only thing is,' I said, 'I never been too religious though.' 'So what?' he said. 'Whatever you done wrong, you'd never a done it if you'd of known any better. You tell 'em that when you get there.' So I played him cagy, and I said, 'Get where? Where do you mean?' And he said, 'Heaven, where do you think?' You think he was kidding me Moe?"

"Kidding you? He took the words right out of my mouth!"

"Gee thanks, Moe, I hoped so . . . Moe, would yez do me a favor? Would you go take a look at my apartment? It must be getting all dusty."

"Maybe the stuff would be better in storage till you get back?"

"Oh no, don't let him do that, Charlotte. Once they move out your stuff, then you're surely a goner . . . Gee I'm sleepy, it must be that injection they gave me. Hold my hand, Ma—"

So Ruth sat and held her hand, and then I did, and then Ruth did again, and Bella slept and she panted. Then Doc Ginzburg stepped in on his rounds.

He said, "This looks like the coma, Ruth."

Poor Bella, such was the Sabbath.

So wouldn't you say live while you're living, and let the chips fall where they may?

But that ain't how Gross lives. At home, I mean Ruth's, it ate me since that run-in Charlotte and me almost had Friday that Charlotte would never let me have a divorce, never. Or even suppose Charlotte said okay divorce, could I pay for divorce?

Of course Ruth said, "So?"

"So? What about us," I said, "neither here nor there."

"You hundred percent American," Ruth said, "you always have to be either here or there. Did I propose to you yet?"

"In this family Gross does the proposing."

"Then propose."

"How can I, without a divorce?"

"So?" Ruth said.

There were smiles, you can imagine, and kisses and love. But afterwards—

"So forget divorce," I said. "When I'm bled for support—and bleeding by the gallon I surely can count on—what then?"

So Ruth lying on my shoulder sang in my ear, "You'll support Charlotte, I'll support you."

Only, blind love may be, but at age fifty-seven not too blind to see what stretched ahead day-in day-out—fights, bitterness, God knows what—with the you support Charlotte, I support you. And where did that leave me? Neither here nor there, with my worry.

What season is bad for good cheer? And what season is good for gloom? But if you like your depression heavy, like the white sky pressing down, go a few blocks through ten degrees Fahrenheit with winds tearing like claws, then into your sister's hothouse where she avoids drafts by windows shut tight. Right away the temples begin throbbing, the nerves are stretched out like a rubber band. And last week there, what did we have to do but talk over the old days together, when we were children, and it was sweet, and it hurt, how those kids used to be us, and now gone forever. So then you feel close, and that entitles Sylvia, right away, as soon as you have on your slippers and sit down on the mourning stool, to draw her stool over and start her tattoo on your brain.

". . . and she's your wife, after all. So it hasn't been smooth sailing every minute together, the way it was with me and my Phil," a pause for the wipe of the eye, "but how many wives are perfect? Charlotte admits her mistakes. But even if she didn't, who ever heard of a Gross walking out on his wife—"

"Well there was Grampa Aaron for one, then there's Brother Moe for another."

"—the mother of his children? No one. And if I can speak frankly like a sister, and make a comparison, just the use of your judgment, not even your judgment: your eyes—"

Through the window the houses across the way dance in the heat waves over the radiator, you yawn, you pick up the paper and leaf through the morning's bad news—Sylvie goes on and on. I began to have daydreams: Charlotte makes a dash for the bus, like Weak Heart Sadie two years ago, and bang!—like a cockroach, under a limousine black as a hearse.

So what good's a cold war with all the prosperity, if it takes murder or riches to unload a wife?

When in walked Charlotte, merry as springtime, bright from the cold, with a cheerful hello she was only staying a minute, and handed me that letter from Liz.

She said, "Call me, Moe, let me know what Elizabeth says, how she is. We had words, unfortunately, the last time we spoke."

I held out the letter. "Here, open it. See for yourself."

And she gave me a nice smile!

"No thanks, Moe, I must run, I'm meeting Sue to shop for maternity things. But call me—remember."

And such tact! Shame on you Gross, always thinking the worst. She was really a different woman.

AFTER THE BLINTZES AND SOUR CREAM—homemade and good as Delancey Street—Charlotte began clearing the table, and she took time out to press her hand on my shoulder and her thigh on my arm, all of a sudden a Jewish cook, and now, all of a sudden, a real sexy lady. So I could smile inside, that the way to a man's heart the new Charlotte figured was through his stomach, or else through his prick. She really was changed. Only Gross—the Wild Bull of the Pampas that whenever he sniffed pelt used to begin on the house and finish off on the housewife—I was changed too. First I'd thought oy, the volcano is going extinct? But then I realized: With Ruth who needed others, even to look at?

Tonight me and Ruth'd shivered out into this cold down to zero and sat in the hospital with Bella, the third week of her coma poor thing, with that constitution of iron. Ginzie should only be right that there's no pain any more. Then I dropped Ruth off home, and I came over to Grandview Place here to try to tie up in person what my string of phone calls to Charlotte hadn't tied up. And pleasant as the new Charlotte was, all smiles, insisting I eat, so far she only said what she wanted: me back. That apart, how much support would she want? Not a hint. So I sat, still neither here nor there.

But now she smiled down at me, "Then your mind is absolutely made up?"

"Ah, that's an unfair question after those blintzes, Charlotte, but it is."

Still she leaned, still she smiled. "Sue says that we should go to a marriage counselor."

I gave 'er a pat on the backside so she shouldn't be insulted when I backed up my chair for some breathing space.

I said, "Charlotte, years ago, when things weren't so good between us two, I once asked you for a divorce. Then I said that for a good-looking woman like you the easiest thing in the world would be finding better than Gross. To tell the truth, that was just talk. True, false—I never gave it a thought. I think back now of what I was then, and believe me, I don't feel too proud—a wise guy, trying to twist people around. But now, without twisting, I can honestly say what I said then. Do you know, you look twenty years younger since you started to smile more? Who are you? Have we met? Ain't you Susan Gross Davis's sister? You look just like her. What do you say, Charlotte, let's be friends, and forget those long years when we weren't such friends."

"Couldn't we be friends together?"

"I don't know, Charlotte, other questions aside even. Together, in the day-to-day life, I don't think so."

Still I waited to hear the word cash, and still only a shrug from Charlotte. So I hemmed and I hawed and I said I'd better start packing. Charlotte chirped, "You go right ahead," and there she was straightening up in the kitchen again.

What a relief! Discuss, don't discuss, she won't lose by her pride. Who dreamed it would turn out so nice, like humans, not animals? Sure, sure I'll give her, whatever she wants within reason, you don't just walk out. And hey, if people can learn, can be better like this, maybe we can still stick with the planet awhile.

And look, ain't it eerie, how insane a person could be in his life? I tossed the socks and the underwear into my suitcase, and remember those shirts, yeh, the ones ripped to rags on the floor here when I squinted in through the fire escape window last month? Here they were, nice and neat in my drawer. Yet Moe the Loon, last month you saw them, and Charlotte stood accused tried and guilty in your eyes. Then ain't that a sickness, when the eye invents sights, and the mind is made up that they're out to get you?

Thank God, that let me come out of it!

Charlotte must have put up with plenty I never gave half a thought to, it takes two to make a bad marriage. So she came in while I was packing and I brought up the money subject myself, I asked how was sixty a week.

Charlotte smiled. "Susan said squeeze you dry if you won't come back."

"Youth and high hopes. What's there to squeeze in an old lemon like Gross? I wish I had more to give."

And this Charlotte, still with that smile, she didn't mind one bit!

"How do you feel, Moe?"

The truth was, I felt slightly sick.

"It's funny you ask. Not so good, right this minute. I must have had one blintz too many."

"Ha ha, I'll say you did!"

Then the nausea set in.

I began gulping, I ran to the john, but when I leaned over to vomit I couldn't. Then, with cramps doubling me up and cold sweat on my face, was when I had panic. My pal Cohen that I worked with, he doubled up one day after lunch and we thought it was food. It was cancer. Two weeks later I saw him stretched in his coffin. Again I tried vomiting and only could retch. Oy, my insides. Don't ask me, folded over, weak, like a cripple, how I got back to Charlotte.

"Call the doctor," I sat down on the bed, "I'm deathly sick—"

"Then it's working."

"What? Please, quick, call up Ginzburg."

"There's no need of that." And the smile was cheerful, insane. "Susan says get flies with sugar, but I say get rats with poison!"

"Charlotte, is this time for jokes? My feet, I can hardly stand up—"

"Then sit down." And she gave me a push. "What did you think, you'd pay a small indemnity for stealing my life? Mister Crafty, with his arsenic Danish—for *my* dear people. Do you remember that little suggestion of yours, for poisoning my life? Well murderer, how do you like it on you? Does it taste slightly bitter? Ha ha ha! And I did it with poison, and your doctor can't help you, and your whore can't either—ha ha ha!"

"Charlotte, I'm sick, don't you understand?"

"You aren't sick, ha ha ha, you're dead!"

Completely insane, so maybe it was poison? For poison there are cures. But oy, who gives poison? She opened my bag and she began emptying it back in the drawers.

"You weren't here tonight. You were too busy dying on account of something you ate. Somewhere else, ha ha! Is your whore a good cook? Maybe she fed you poison for the sixty a week, you generous man, who killed my nephew Howard and murdered my whole life. Oh, you vermin!"

I took the phone in my pain and I began dialing Ginzburg. Charlotte caught hold of my arm, "Let go of my telephone," but Gross the ox, oy Gross in a box, I gave her an arm and she flew. All doubled up I finished the number, and I heard the girl's voice. I moaned, "Help, this is Gross up at Grandview Place," and then I had to fight Charlotte again.

But I was all out of fight. I flopped down on the couch and I sat jackknifed there, with my hands over my poor insides. And even then, insane woman, she grabbed hold of my wrists, she jammed them into my coat.

"Please Charlotte, it could be cancer—"

"Get off my couch." She stuck my hat on my head. "All right, now up, out of here, the gutter for rats—"

She dragged me, she pushed, she gave me a kick. I tried to quit on the stairs but she wouldn't let me. She manhandled me the whole three flights down, and she kicked me, with her shoe, into the street.

She wanted me in the gutter, that's where I wound up, in the dark, in the freezing cold. Oy, my feet were like knives, my mouth was like ink, and my head, my throat— I just couldn't, but I leaned along the parked cars in the gutter, I hoped maybe a prowl car, or a cab could come by. Then a cab came, and it stopped, and I could only lean on the fender, in front of the headlights.

Oh, and she got ahold of me again—

"I beg of you Charlotte—"

"It's Ruth, Moe, you called me not the doctor—"

"Oy Ruth it's cancer, or poison, she said that she poisoned me—"

She hustled me into that cab, she told him the hospital.

LIMP RAG GROSS, they must have wheeled me back from the table and shifted me onto this bed—dead, alive? My throat was plastered together, I was that terrified. My fellow inmates, they snored, and when I opened my eyes, there was Ruth in the night light. And oy, looking so serious!

She said, "That bitch really did feed you poison—thank God!"

"Yeh, that's all it was?" But Gross, think it over. "Then how come they let you in here all hours, like to a case at the last gasp?"

"That was cheap. It only cost me two dollars to the nurse."

"If I could believe you—"

"Would I lie?"

And look, she tried smiling, and there were tears in her eyes. Sure she'd lie, for my sake. I tried smiling too, but I doubt if I made it.

"Sleep, dear," she said. "They gave you something."

Who wanted to sleep, and maybe never wake up? But it pressed on me, oy, my head swam, hard as I fought it—

I woke up in the light though, and a nurse was there busy already. I asked her what my chart said, and she said, "Just something you ate." But who knows what they tell you, and who lays there half-dead with arms heavy as plaster, just from something you ate? Two of my roomies drifted over to swap diseases with me, but should I say poison? Who poisons people, insane as she is? I told them just here for testing, and Gross saw too bad for a dead one on those faces.

Then Ruth showed up early again.

"You paid the day shift off too?"

"No, they don't care. The visitors can do the hospital work." She stroked back my hair, like Mrs. Schultz with Papa when he lay in this same hospital dying. "Still feel weak, huh?"

Now why would she say that?

But later Ginzburg blew in like the morning breeze. "Gross the ox, what are you looking so scared for?" He grinned in my face. "It'll take more than a little rat poison to finish you off."

"It was actually rat poison?"

"So they say in the lab."

"Rat poison . . . Sure, that's my Charlotte all right. Then they'll really blow up the world yet."

"Could be," Ginzie said. "Meanwhile you can thank your lucky star that she brought you in here in time." He listened to my chest, then he gave me a slap on it. "Got to go visit sick people now." And he went.

All of a sudden I did feel a lot better, I sat up in bed.

"Ruth I swear, I'm getting hold of that monster with her

arsenic blintzes and I'm thrashing her till she honestly believes
that death would be sweeter!"

"You are like fun. Between the hospital report and all your
eyewitnesses you've got her just where you want her, without
making a move."

"What eyewitnesses?"

"Me, the cab driver."

"You got the cab driver? Hey, you're practical!"

She gave me a wink, Ruth. "You're in good hands."

Which meant she was in full charge of Gross? . . . But I
liked it, I liked it!

WHAT A COFFIN!—solid mahogany, carved, with a soft rich
glowing finish. Bella would have loved it, it was a shame to put
in the ground. How much it cost me, don't ask. This much I'll
tell you. Between the flu, and the mourning for Papa he should
rest in peace, and being fed poison last week by my ex-wife
that I'm still married to, and now poor Bella gone, here's a man
short of cash, and also of patience.

Because who put me on the carpet after the rabbi dropped in
dirt on that box? The deceased's bereaved brother. Yeh, my
cousin Sid from New Jersey, the man of distinction with the
Homburg and the Florida tan. We'd hardly taken one step
back toward our transportation, me and Ruth to the jalopy and
him to his Cadillac, when he had the gall to give me his
headshake.

"That elaborate casket wasn't at all appropriate for a Jewish
woman, Moe."

Raw as the day was, with the wind whipping downhill into
poor Bella's bargain basement, that stopped me in my tracks.

"Did anyone call you up on the telephone yesterday? Did
anyone say the words Brother, come in make arrangements
with the funeral people?"

"But Moe, I explained that my wrapping machine broke down. The way it turned out I was at the factory until late last night and it still isn't fixed."

"Your sister Bella is fixed though, for good. Yeh, if it was up to you, she would have taken the subway to the cemetery here, like the old man in the joke, and crawled into the hole by herself. Well, she was inconsiderate. She died in the hospital."

"But that casket must have been awfully expensive."

"Gross pays the bills and you're crying?"

"Didn't Bella leave anything at all? How about the Social Security benefits?"

"So that's what it is, you figure you been done out of the cost of poor Bella's coffin that she begged me to buy her, you bastard you, you cheap prick!"

"Moe—" Ruth said.

"Yeh you're right," I said, "it's a disgrace for the dead: Bella, Lou, all these poor stones. Not that Sid gives a damn. Here Sidney, take these keys, they open Bella's apartment. I ain't been to her house the three months she laid in the hospital dying while you never once paid her a visit, but untold wealth is stashed away in her mattress, she herself told me. So Brother, you go, you sort out her stuff, you call the Salvation Army and what they refuse you can carry downstairs on your back to the garbage, or else tip the porter and maybe he'll give you a hand. And it's your mattress."

"Moe, I only was asking. You know I don't have time for Bella's apartment. I just saw that fancy casket, and look, I have children whose interests I'm obliged to consider, and I thought maybe— Well, never mind. But why not just leave the apartment? The super'll clear it out."

"What did the super do to you that you should do that to the super?"

"Yes, you're right, you're right. Here"—he held out a tenner—"do me a favor, take this for the tip to the porter."

"Do me a favor Sport, give that to your favorite charity."

"Whatever you say, Moe," his currency went back down south fast, "only please, no hard feelings. I assure you there are none on my part."

"How could you have any? For hard feelings you need feelings."

You think that fazed Sidney? He laughed. "Moe, you're incorrigible." Then, on our way to the cars again, he laughed to Ruth, "You keep looking at me, is my tie knotted wrong?"

"No, I've heard so much about you," Ruth said.

"And do I match what you've heard?"

"Not altogether. You're a good-looking man, and you sound very nice."

"Then," my cousin still laughed, "that proves you can't believe everything you hear."

"Or that you see?" Ruth gave a grin.

Sidney just went on laughing, but Gross laughed even louder.

And to tell you the truth, I've taken on harder jobs in my day than closing Bella's apartment, and without a Ruth for a helper. A look after all these months at that bare livingroom, and I had to say, "She's been robbed."

"But of what?" Ruth asked me.

And true enough, the card table stood thick with dust but still there, the three bridge chairs, the TV. And inside was her pride and joy the bedroom set, even if Lou only let her have walnut veneer not mahogany. I remember his saying, Lou the optimist, "Who needs gloomy black furniture?"

Ruth sorted out the few dresses and the handful of underwear, and we had to look at each other, the way a life could rush by and leave nothing. Then there were snapshots— thank God none of me—and in a family group on some roof with women and children first and the men in back of them with the TV antennas, you saw Lou Berenson bald-headed and pared to the bone, with gloom and to spare, and in the front Bella smiled.

Ruth said, "Thanks, Moe."

"For what?"

"For existing."

"Why it's the only way to live," the wisecrack jumped out. "But you're right, we're two lucky ones."

Linen, dishes, bedding: it fit in one carton. A few cans and a rotten banana out of the icebox, that wrapped it up.

"Except," Ruth said, "for the mattress."

I had to laugh.

"God took Bella, but her ghost still walks."

Ruth twisted her shoulder up, it was cute, like a girl.

"Go ahead, Moe, have a look."

So I went ahead had a look.

How Bella had ever managed to sleep on that mattress don't ask me. Wherever I stuck my hand, all lumps and spine.

Then I struck gold.

Conscience money her relatives sent her, still in the envelopes, odd welfare checks she never bothered to cash. Treasure Island, it covered the card table. The prize was Lou's blood money from the last place he worked for: $2,000, Death Benefit to Spouse. Tough Luck Lou, he took Bella's dowry and blew it on the horses, and here he got it back for her mattress.

"Ain't it funny, how I used to dream of a find like this, and now, when it comes, considering Bella, and Lou, and one thing and another, it's not such a pleasure. Well, there's my divorce on the table."

Ruth said, "Never mind your divorce. That's the house in the country that your friend Barney wants to get rid of."

"Not get married?"

"So it's funny, I used to dream too, Mrs. Ruth Gross, showing you off to the family and friends. But now, what for?

I know what I've got, and who needs their blue ribbon, even if they gave one. Three dollars for a marriage license, all right. But to pay for a divorce, and probably a settlement with all of her arsenic—it's not worth the money."

"Yeh? I don't know. What's so great about a man and wife being single?"

She gave me a kiss. "You'll get used to it."

SQUIRE GROSS, after supper I picked up the paper and I sat down on the back porch. Some squire. Since spring when we bought the place, Gross rebuilt that porch all alone, every plank, every nail. Inside the house too, I rip up, I hammer, I panel—with the end nowhere in sight.

In the country at last Gross, and tears? Ha ha, the house is my pleasure!

The meadow stretches out on one side, then it drops down to the valley, and when the air dances like this, this clear blue, gold, and green, you can see the town curled way down there in the distance. We liked Barney's summer cottage, even his insects, but instead—Ruth said, "You want to live in the country, let's live in the country"—we came here. How did we find the place? We did research, what do you think, like my former son-in-law Georgie Young, only our Foundation was named Amin and Gross. We read maps and we studied brochures. Next we searched country papers for house painter wanted. Then we were ready for the Field I mean the fields, the streams, the meadows, and the mountains. We looked for an old house we could afford, and if broken-down equals old, we found it in spades. But not bad, eh, for only five months' work weekends, holidays, evenings, and, the time the boiler broke, dawn? And how about Ruth's flower garden there, and those four rows of corn almost ripe for the picking?

There she was now, with her clippers. God sent her Jill, but He sent her hollyhocks too like big red medals hung up on stalks, so she could attend to them at a distance from her visiting daughter-in-law.

And down the back lawn—some lawn, but to Gross grass is grass—Lizzie and Bobby sat under the oaks, near the edge of the meadow, in the long shadows, talking.

Ah America, you beautiful land!—if you don't go and blow yourself up with these Great Men of ours. Today our Leader states he'll protect us from Cuba! Who'll protect us from the protection the paper doesn't say. I held out the news of the day and I let it plop gently on the porch.

". . . to poison your father?"

So my ears perked up. That was Bobby.

"Yes," Lizzie said, "but at least with real honest poison."

Bobby gave her a grin. "Is there dishonest poison?"

"Come on Bob, you know what I mean. Lies, personal venom, all that sort of thing."

He knew what she meant all right. Lizzie came up to us as soon as summer school ended, so she was on the reception committee when the Amin contingent arrived hours late yesterday, with Jonathan Mark whining in Bobby's arms, and Jill sharking at Bobby all the way into the house.

"Losing his way not once but twice. How stupid can you get?"

Bobby said, "Yes dear," but that dear is immune to sarcasm. All evening long she kept at him, until it became too much for Ruth and she ran into the kitchen.

At that point the hypocrite Gross had rubbed together his hands and told Jill, "The main thing is you're here!"

Now, I could hear Bobby standing up for his fate. "Okay, but where does that leave your mother?"

"Certainly not where she belongs. She's with my sister, being bad for the baby, not to mention for my brother-in-law. Her main trick is to keep baby needing her, so she takes the bottle from baby as soon as baby pauses for breath."

"She sounds nuts to me."

"Well as I said, balance of mind has never been one of her outstanding qualities. I'd left two suitcases in the old apartment, and it seems she tore up all my underwear. She said, 'They were filthy rags and they're still rags—so?' and she tore up all that good clothing . . . When Charlie's home, he's on baby's side. But how can they win? She's the nursemaid, that's why Sue wanted her."

"But doesn't your sister mind?"

"She gets in a lot of reading."

"Well there you are," Bobby said. "What can your brother-in-law do?"

"Nothing, if he insists on being infatuated with his wife."

"Ha ha, that's a good one. But even if he wasn't—"

"But," Lizzie smiled straight at him, "people should be fair to themselves too, shouldn't they?"

Bobby said, "What?" Who knows, maybe his hearing aid suddenly went on the fritz. But for the overhead blast that came next, a hearing aid was not needed.

"Bobby get up here and help with this baby!"

"I'll go," Lizzie said.

"Oh no," Bobby said.

"Sit down," Lizzie told him, "relax. I love babies, that was the grounds for my marriage annulment."

"I said Bobby!"

Lizzie waved up at the window. "I'm coming, Jill—" But Bobby said, "I'd better, Liz," and he went. So Lizzie's eye fell on the downstairs eavesdropper Gross, and she gave me a smile. Then she stretched out again with her book on the lawn chair.

Say, what's this?—Ruth was dragging that little park bench I hammered together for her. So I walked down to give her a hand.

"Find a new view?" I asked her.

Ruth said, "Did you hear her, from the window? She's like the Nazis, appeasement is no use."

"So we won't have her up here any more."

"Then what about Bobby? He likes the country so much, poor kid . . . Right here is good, for the bench. Mr. L'Hommedieu is coming over with his gun when it gets dark, to chase away the raccoon."

Seems last night the raccoon tumbled through Ruth's tinfoil into the trench she'd dug around the corn patch and he saw it was nothing, so he was back chewing the corn again.

I said, "Suppose he should hit him?"

"Mr. L'Hommedieu? He couldn't hit the side of a barn, let alone a raccoon." Then she went back to the party of the first part. "I could poison Jill, we could have blintzes for supper. Only it's no joke."

"Or else you could cook 'er tough as she is, we could have her for supper."

That got a laugh out of Ruth, and we sat down together and she leaned her head on my shoulder.

And look—a flock of tan-bellied smallbirds zigzagged out in the meadow, and one fella 'lit on a tall blade of grass so thin that it was a wonder it held him. But he sat, and he popped that bright head around, interested, at the grass, the green bushes, the trees.

And the air was sweet, it was sweet!